A Divided State

A Civil War Novel

A Divided State

A Civil War Novel

Joe Poindexter

Dedication

This book is dedicated to my lovely wife, Rosalie. A strong Christian lady, Rosalie has changed my entire life. She shares every aspect of my life including golfing, church work, and writing. She is responsible for much of the work in preparing the book.

Acknowledgment

There is one other person that I have to mention. That person is Di Freeze. There can be no other publisher that is so knowledgeable and helpful, yet so friendly and so nice. Thanks, Di.

Contents

Introduction

ALMOST 60,000 ARKANSAS MEN served in the Confederate forces. Records, though incomplete, indicate that 3,080 died from battle-related causes and 3,782 died from disease.

However, a smaller proportion of Arkansans, mainly from the northwestern part of the state, joined the Federal service. In all, 8,829 Arkansas whites enlisted and 1,713 lost their lives while defending the Union cause.

On September 10, 1863, Confederate forces under General Sterling Price marched out of Little Rock, leaving the capital city undefended. Union General Frederick Steele took control of the city, and a Unionist government would control the northern half of the state until the end of the war. The original Arkansas government, affiliated with the Confederacy after secession, was forced to leave Little Rock. Using wagons to carry the state archives and important papers, the Confederate government moved to Washington, Arkansas, where they would govern the southern half of the state until the end of the war in 1865.

Unfortunately, with two state governments, Arkansas now faced a problem of law and order. Armed bands of bushwhackers, jayhawkers, deserters, guerillas, and even regular soldiers stole from citizens over much of the state. Arkansas was divided.

Chapter 1

Up On The Hill

January 1861

THE NORTH WIND WAS blowing harder now. If only he had put on more clothing. Eva was usually right when it came to the weather. But deer season was always cold in Arkansas. He would have to be careful if he made contact with the old, gray buck. No doubt, the old gray was at least five years old. Willis knew that the old buck had several close calls. Stay downwind, he heard himself say. The teenager slowly moved down the hill with the wind in his face. The biggest problem was the ever-present rocks. It would be easy to stumble over the moist rocks.

The sudden movement of a rabbit darting into the nearby thicket caused Willis to quickly look to his left. He had now reached the thicket where the old cedar stump was located. He slowly sat down on the rotten tree stump. Daylight was approaching. Willis, partially hidden by a small cedar tree, moved his feet into a comfortable position and placed the old musket across his extended legs. Several dry leaves floated down from the large stand of white oak trees to his right. He was sure that deer had been feeding under the old tree on acorns. A few crows had begun to leave their roosts and call out for fellowship.

His mind began to wander. He thought about the recent

news involving the nation. His pa, Amos, had told him about the new developments in South Carolina. According to Amos, South Carolina had passed some kind of law that said they were leaving the United States. The people in South Carolina were opposed to the new feller, Lincoln, and his ideas, so they made their move before Lincoln became president. Amos also heard that some other states, including Mississippi, voted to leave the Union. Willis knew that Mississippi was just across the Mississippi River from Arkansas. Amos had also learned something about a new Southern government being put together somewhere in Alabama. How would all of this affect the state of Arkansas? There would be two countries. Would Arkansas continue in the Union or would they look at joining the new government? Amos was obviously concerned about the situation—Willis had noticed that. Willis would have to ask more about what was going on.

Suddenly, his thoughts were interrupted. A couple of crows were excited. This sometimes meant that a large animal was moving. The wind had picked up some and the cedar tree limbs in front of him began to move. The sun was just peeking over the east ridge only a couple of miles east of his home. It was colder than earlier. A snap—the gray was getting close. Willis pulled back the hammer of the musket and slowly moved the gun up against the side of the tree. There was movement just behind and to the left of the huge, white, oak tree. He was probably feeding on the huge acorns under the big tree. The gun was ready. The trigger was cold to his right-hand forefinger. Steady now. Remember—squeeze softly.

"Eslie." The young man jumped when he heard his name. "Eslie, I almost shot you. I thought you were the old gray," said the shaking Willis.

"I was after him too," Eslie said, looking at his good friend.

"He slipped around both of us." The boys lowered their muskets.

Eslie Southard was about an inch taller than Willis. He always said six feet. Except for that, the boys were about the same size. Being a little shorter, Willis had a stockier look, with wider shoulders and narrow hips. The more slender Eslie had dark hair, brown eyes, and a darker complexion. He would have been quite handsome except for a dark birthmark just over his right eye. This mark always bothered Eslie.

"Well, we got plenty of time to get him," Willis said.

"Hope I didn't mess you up, Willis. This is your property," replied his good friend.

"Hey, forget it. Besides, Ma will have breakfast ready—come on."

Willis noticed that his friend didn't object, although he had always been noticeably shy. Eslie's mother had died during his own childbirth. He was the only child of Ralph Southard. Since Ralph always had some kind of alcohol at any meal, Eslie seldom ate breakfast. He had eaten a few times with Willis though.

Willis was blond-haired with a lighter complexion. One could not help noticing his green eyes. They were set in a rather square face with a dark mole off to the right side near his right sideburn. When Willis smiled, you could not help but notice the slight dimple in his cheeks. His ma, Eva, thought he was even better looking than Amos, her cherished, hard-working husband.

The boys started up the hill to the south. After passing through the persimmon grove and across the creek, they could see the rough-hewed, cut-pine home at the top of the hill. The house, built more than 30 years ago by Theodore Lofland, Willis's great-grandfather, was of the typical dogtrot design. The western half of the house included the master bedroom, the living room, and the kitchen. The roof extended across the standard breezeway to the eastern portion of the house. This part of the structure consisted of two bedrooms. On each end of the house was a native rock fireplace for heating purposes. Across the front of the house was a long, covered porch. On the north side of the house, or the back of the house, was a long porch corresponding to the one on the front of the house.

The breezeway between the two sections was twelve feet across. It frequently served as a sleeping area during the hot, summer months of Arkansas. The house had been built on eight different, carefully selected flat rock piles, with one of the rock stacks at each corner of the house and another stack in between the corner stacks on each side of the house. The rock pilings were about two feet high, causing the house to be about two feet off the ground. In the wintertime, Ahab, the old black and tan coonhound, usually slept under the floor near the fireplace. Willis's grandfather had placed two windows on each side of the house when he built it. Later construction created two additional windows.

Smoke was coming out of the rock chimney. Amos was already coming from the barn with a full pail of milk.

"Where's the deer?" he hollered at the two friends. Willis gave him the thumbs-down sign. By now, they could smell bacon frying.

"Hope your ma don't mind me coming."

"Don't worry, she won't mind." Willis thought, I love this place. And to think it goes back four generations. Both his grandparents and great-grandparents were buried up the road at the Young Gravelly Cemetery.

"Eslie, glad you could come for breakfast," he heard Eva say as he opened the squeaky, kitchen door.

"Thank you, ma'am," Eslie said, shyly ducking his head.

As usual, breakfast was delicious, especially the homemade biscuits and gravy. Even Eslie had a second biscuit. Talk was mostly on the morning deer hunt. Eva almost dropped the grits when she learned that Willis had almost taken Eslie for the old gray deer. "Ya'll, be careful. Hope that will be a lesson to be careful while huntin'."

Willis remembered his thinking about the likelihood of war that morning. "Pa, tell Eslie about we could have war."

Willis saw Eva frown as Amos finished chewing a strip of bacon. Before he spoke, Amos glanced at both boys; anyone would have known what he was thinking.

"Well, nobody anywhars knows what's going to take place. All's I know is what I heared at Danville last week. Course the ones that tell me are telling what they heared at Dardanelle."

Eva had stopped doing dishes as Hayes and Georgia Ann came in to eat. "Mornin' and sit down. Bet ya'll are hungry."

Hayes said nothing. Georgia Ann looked at Eslie and said, "Hi." Hayes, a smaller version of Willis, was eleven years old. His idol was his older brother. Everyone noticed that he walked in Willis's footsteps. He may have even been somewhat jealous of Eslie and his relationship with Willis. The blonde-haired Georgia Ann was eight years old and the apple of Amos's eye. Both began to eat while carefully watching the visitor. Amos, even more reluctant to talk now with the younger kids at the table, continued to try to answer Willis's question about the possibility of war.

"Here we are still in the Union and seven to ten other states like Mississippi next door are talking about pulling out like Carolina. Mississippi and Arkansaw both share the big river. Will we be able to get along with Mississippi if we have war? What about Missouri or Texas? Don't know whar this is going to end up. Course nobody in Arkansaw voted for Lincoln cause he wasn't on the ballot. We thought that Breckenridge feller would win."

Willis and Eslie carefully listened as Amos talked. Both knew that Amos was as knowledgeable as anyone in the county. Then Amos abruptly pushed back from the table. "I've got to go slop the hogs."

Willis was disappointed that his pa chose to say no more about the events. It was probably because the younger kids came in at the time. Eva was pleased that the conversation had ended.

"Well, Eslie, what's on your schedule for today?" she asked, wanting to make more conversation with the visitor. "You're not going deer huntin agin today, are you?"

Eslie looked back toward Eva. "No, I won't go agin today. I will probably hunt in the morning agin. I may go down on the Fourche River. Several deer down not far from Rhodes Landing. I think Lyle's huntin' down there near the old log barn."

"I gotta go see if Pa ever got in last night," Eslie said, slowly pushing back his chair from the table. "I didn't see him before I left to hunt this morning. Thanks for breakfast, Mrs. Lofland. It was really good."

"You're welcome anytime, Eslie," Eva replied as she began stacking up the dishes.

Willis got up and went out on the front porch with Eslie. "Looks like snow," he said as Eslie stepped down from the porch.

"Probably so, and we are still short on firewood. Know what I will be doing today; see you Willis."

"Watch for the big buck," Eslie said as he started off for the timber and the shortcut to his house about a mile or so east.

Willis went back inside to finish his coffee. Eva was washing the dishes, humming while she worked. Even in her homemade cotton dress and no makeup, Willis thought his ma was still an attractive woman for thirty-eight. She was always so neat. But Willis really noticed how cheerful she was everyday. She was always in a good mood, regardless of how others were. Willis thought, when I get married, I hope it's someone like Ma. As he took a seat at the table again, she spoke.

"Willis, I worry so much about Eslie. He has no home life with no ma, no brothers or sisters, and his pa is really a drunkard. That poor boy seldom has any good in his life. And yet, he is so courteous and nice."

Willis picked up his breakfast plate and empty coffee cup and carried them to his mother. "Ma, you're right. He is one of the nicest people I know and probably my best friend. I don't really know how to help him 'cept for inviting him over a lot and just showing him I really like him."

"We need to pray for him and his pa as well," Eva said, dipping the soapy dishes into a fresh pan of water.

"Snow flurries," Amos announced as he opened the back door. "Willis, will you come out and help me carry the firewood up on the back porch? Looks as if we gonna need it. Hayes, put your coat on and come help us carry up firewood."

Hayes made no reply, but he came from the bedroom with his old, heavy coat. Willis picked up several pieces of firewood and started toward the back porch. He noticed that his pa was carrying almost twice as much wood as he was carrying. Willis had seen his pa lift an unbelievable amount of weight. Amos could easily throw a heavy sack of field cotton up on a wagon, several times in one day. Yet, he was not a big man.

Amos was a couple of inches shy of six feet tall. However, forty years of hard work had caused him to develop a stocky, stout frame. He had a rather square face with a slight Roman nose, larger ears, and a dimple in his chin. His curly, brown hair was already receding, causing him to have a higher forehead. His eyes were bluish-green. Under his left ear was a scar approximately four inches long, which extended down his chin. The scar was the result of a sawmill accident when Amos was only fifteen years old.

Pa is really strong and active, but he is also a good-looking man, Willis thought as they passed each other with armfuls of firewood. Willis also appreciated his pa's calm disposition. It was understandable why he had been elected a church deacon.

Chapter 2

A Sermon

THE LOFLANDS SAW FEW people over the next two weeks due to the heavy snow. Amos measured it at ten inches, certainly unusual for central Arkansas. The farm chores were more difficult due to the heavy snow and freezing temperatures. Milking and feeding the animals was uncomfortable now. The animal watering troughs had ice that had to be broken. Most of the firewood had been stacked beside the barn. The wood had to be carried from the barn to the back porch, about a hundred yards. Bringing the firewood to the back porch had now become Hayes's chore. As they had done with Willis, Amos and Eva were determined to teach the two younger children how to work. Georgia Ann was learning about cooking, canning and she had even cooked pies.

Sunday was usually a big day for most of the people who lived in the Gravelly area. Most of the people in and around the town of Gravelly either attended the larger Methodist church in town or the small Rock Creek Baptist Church at Young Gravelly. However, the Baptist church was about ten miles east of Gravelly. The people in the central part of Yell County would frequently attend either church. Denominationally, there were few differences in the views of the churches. Some Baptists did oppose the drinking of alcoholic beverages. But, both groups were comfortable in each other's church. Frequently, each church's members would attend the revivals held in the other church in the summer. Since the Loflands lived about twelve miles east of Gravelly, they were only two miles from Rock Creek Baptist Church. They were active members in the church where Amos served as a deacon. Eva was also a member of the six-member choir.

Pastor Hiram Dugan, a sixty-two-year-old itinerant preacher with only one good eye, was the pastor at the small Baptist church. The preacher, also a local farmer, had little education. However, he was quite intelligent and a dynamic speaker. Reverend Dugan, around six feet tall and with a heavier build, had a long head with very little hair at all on the top of his head. The pastor had heavy, blackish-grey sideburns that came down below his large ears. Above his dark eyes were dark, bushy eyebrows. Dugan's very serious look was intimidating to the younger kids like Georgia Ann and Hayes, especially when the pastor got loud and occasionally hit the podium with his hand.

Today, there were twenty-six people in church, a good crowd for February. The reverend took the podium, literally, in his hands and looked over the congregation. Everyone was waiting for the pastor's deep voice. "Friends and neighbors, we live in critical times today. Overhead, there are the threatening clouds of war. Let's turn to I Samuel 17 in your Bible—and I hope you have been using your Bible this week. Please read with me."

The preacher began with verse one and read through verse ten. "The Israelites under King Saul had been invaded by the massive Philistine army. The Philistines were noted for their aggressive warfare and their daring on the battlefield. Their weapons were probably better than those of Israel. But, as we know, the Philistines had a secret weapon—a huge giant over nine feet tall. He had a 200-pound coat of mail or iron. He had a spear with a tip that alone weighted twenty-five pounds. No one had stood against this giant and lived. He would bring quick death to a normal sized man, and worst yet, the Israelites knew he was a champion. They were terrified. Who would think of going against this giant?"

Eva glanced at Hayes. His eyes were big as biscuits. He was impressed. The preacher cleared his throat and continued.

"But, the Israelites have forgotten about their own champion—Lord God Almighty." There were several amens, the loudest by old man Rader. The pastor, pleased with the "amens," spoke a little louder. "Friends, we must not forget our champion if the Philistines ever move toward our state."

"Amen," Willis heard Amos say.

"And let's remember, the Lord works in mysterious ways. He didn't use a man or a general when he drowned Pharaoh's army in the Red Sea. There was another "amen." "But in our Scripture today, God has a leader in mind. The shepherd boy, David, was no ordinary shepherd. Now I don't know about Ben Lavich—who raises sheep up towards Bluffton—are you an ordinary shepherd, Ben?"

Ben and several others laughed. The pastor took a sip of water from a glass and then continued. "Neighbors, we have a choice here in the South. We have a choice—a choice between religion and atheism. The North prefers a new Constitution, a new Bible, and a new God. It is possible that Mr. Lincoln will ignore the sovereignty of the states and run his armies roughshod over the seceded states—our sister states—our relatives and neighbors. Innocent people could die—people who have done nothing to be treated in such a manner. And people, it could involve our state. It could be your homes, your firesides and, God forbid, your wives and children. They could steal our land—the land that the Lord has given us for a heritage. If we are forced—and I say forced—to fight, it will be a war for the maintenance of the broadest principles for which a free people can contend—the right of self-government, and, I will ask you another question. How many slaves in our community? Are you hiding some, Amos? You got any up on the hill?"

Everyone laughed when Amos responded to the question. "Not less Willis thinks he is a slave."

The laughter occurred again when Willis shook his head in agreement that he was a slave. The pastor stopped the laughter when he loudly announced, "The answer is none—not one. Yet, the Philistines are preparing for war. If war comes, we pray that our Lord will send us a leader—a leader for our armies."

There were several "amens" and some applause. The speaker again raised his deep voice. "We need a champion like David, a God-fearing man who will stand up to Goliath and help us save our homes, our communities, and our churches. Friends, remember, Samuel interviewed all of Jesse's older boys and rejected them before he found the young shepherd boy. Why? This was God's choice."

The pastor stopped, reached over, and took a drink of water from a glass, wetting his lips, and then resumed. "We must pray for God's man—the man God will bless and lead. Above all, people, pray that we will not have a war and that Americans will not have to kill their American brothers."

Willis looked around at the congregation. They were all listening carefully to what their pastor was saying. No doubt, the sermon would be discussed often during the coming week. Most of the church responded with loud "amens." The pastor wiped his mouth with a handkerchief. "Let's turn to page 101 in our hymnal, Lord, Spare Your People."

After three verses, Amos gave the benediction prayer and the congregation began visiting and moving toward the front door where Pastor Dugan was greeting and taking compliments for his sermon. As Willis filed out of the church, he noticed that most of the people's comments were very complimentary.

Once seated in the wagon for the trip home, Eva asked Amos what he thought about the pastor's sermon. Her husband was already thinking about the pastor's comments.

"He said some good things," he replied without looking at his attractive wife. "It won't be our war. If we want to pull out of the government and even join another one that has views closer to ours, why not? We are supposed to be free. But, it seems that the Washington folks want to put a gun to our head and say, you will do as we say. You know, I don't see much difference in the South's move to independence being any different than our forefathers who had to fight England for their independence. We wanted freedom then and in came the troops. We may demand a new freedom now, and if so, the troops might show up."

Eva listened and then replied, "I also agree, and I don't want our place to become a battleground. Yet I think about Willis, Eslie, Bartis, and many other young men who will almost surely have to fight if we have to defend our homes and our state. Amos, you may have to go fight. You are only forty years old. What would we do if we lost Willis or you or maybe both of you?"

Eva decided to change the subject when she saw that the young kids were listening to the conversation. "Hayes, what was your and Georgia Ann's Sunday school lesson on today?"

"We talked about the good Samaritan," said Hayes.

"And his donkey," added Georgia Ann.

Hayes laughed and then said, "You know, Ma, after hearing the teacher today, I think the first two men that passed the hurt man without helping him were Yankees and the Samaritan was from Gravelly." This time both Willis and Amos laughed.

"Hayes, remember there are many good Northern people and some bad Southern folks," Eva quickly said. "So Jesus' parable or story could have taken place almost anywhere.

Chapter 3

Chores

A WARMER APRIL BROUGHT an increased need to have all the farming equipment ready for early planting. Amos owned forty acres around the house — mainly pastureland. He also owned thirty-five acres down on the Fourche River bottom. He had leased another ten acres near his own river bottomland. The land along the river had proven to be excellent cotton land. The year before, this land had yielded more than 110 bales of cotton. At fifty dollars per bale, Amos had made a comfortable living for his family.

But Amos had not forgotten the cotton crop of three years ago. In the spring of 1858, there had been heavy rain. Both Rock Creek and the Fourche River had overflowed into the adjacent fields. There was more than two feet of water on much of the land for more than a month. Even after the water went down, the fields were too wet for plowing. The year 1858 turned out to be a disappointing one for the Loflands. Amos was even forced to borrow money from Chambers Bank in Danville. It did not help when one of his mules broke a leg and had to be destroyed. But last year was a better year, and Amos had paid back most of his loan.

Willis replaced a couple of bolts on the old plow and sharpened it with a file while Amos replaced some brads on the mules' harness. Amos earlier had the mules shod. Both mules — Murt, a dark brown male, and Kate, a white female — had survived the winter in good shape. Even a damaged wagon wheel was replaced. "Hitch up the team, Willis. I'm going down to look the field over and make shor it's dry enough to plow."

Amos went in to get a jug of water and tell Eva where he was going. "I'll be back by lunch."

"Well, be careful," said Eva, as always.

"Willis is going up to the west pasture to fix the fence," Amos said, looking back.

Eva was baking a pie for Miss Clandell, an eighty-six-year-old single lady that lived down the hill and across the road. She and the kids would walk down the hill and take the pie to her and check on her. Hayes usually brought firewood in for her, and Georgia Ann picked flowers for the old lady.

After Amos reached the main road in the wagon, he directed the mule team to the east toward Rock Creek crossing. The pasture gate that Amos used to reach his river bottomland was just before one crossed Rock Creek. Murt and Kate seemed eager to be out on the road today. The sun was well up now and the morning chill was gone. Birds were off the roost and moving.

Amos, looking down the rocky road, saw another wagon come around the bend about half a mile down the road. As the two wagons drew closer, both drivers looked carefully to see who was approaching. Soon, Amos recognized Homer Parker as the driver of the approaching wagon. Homer was Lyle's father and the owner of the feed store in Gravelly. Both drivers pulled on the reins of their respective mule teams and stopped the wagons, side by side.

"Homer, what are you doing out this way so early in the morning?"

"Hey, Amos. I went to Danville yesterday and came back by Rover and spent the night with my wife's sister's family. Don't guess you know about the cotton gin in Danville burning down?"

"No, what happened?" Amos inquired.

His mules had moved and Homer pulled back on the reins. "Don't think anyone knows what the cause was. Some say it was caused by one of Beller's hired hands smokin'. One of Beller's men said it might have been a Negro, which was probably just an excuse."

"I doubt that, Homer. We haven't known of any crimes caused by blacks—we don't have very many in the whole county."

Homer looked back down the road and answered Amos. "You know how some are now about the blacks—they cause everything that happens. By the way, Amos, I do have some more important news you haven't heard."

"What's that?"

Homer was eager to share the story with his friend. After taking a drink of water from a large fruit jar, he continued. "Well, the South Carolina militia fired on a Federal fort near Charleston. The fort fired back and the armies continued to shoot at each other for hours. According to most, the militia got the best of it. The Federals finally gave up and surrendered the fort. Then the militia released the Federals and allowed them to go back north. The question all's asking is—is this the start of war? No doubt, the new Lincoln government is not likely to allow their fort to be captured by a state."

Amos, listening carefully, said, "Homer, that's bad—real bad. How many killed?"

Homer looked down the road as a young doe darted across the road. "Said nary a one killed."

Amos slapped at a big horsefly on his neck. "You know, Homer, we don't know if war will come or not. Even if it does come, we don't know which side Arkansas would be on—probably the federal side, but still, our sons, and maybe even you and I, would have to go."

The store owner shook his head in agreement. "Hope Lincoln uses good judgment. Know what I mean—hey, come by the store this weekend if you are in town. Guess I'd better be going. Is Eva and the family okay?"

"Yes they are, Homer. Thanks for asking and thanks for the information." As Amos proceeded east on down the road, he now had a lot more on his mind. While he really did not need to go to town on Saturday, Amos was sure that he would go now. There would be some talk of a war—he hoped there would be some good news by then. Surely, cooler heads would prevail in Washington.

The thing that worried Amos the most was how the other Southern states would react. Amos wondered if they would stand behind the federal government or if they would support their sister state, South Carolina. Amos could remember the Mexican War, though he never understood the causes of the conflict. One thing that he did remember, though, was that a brave Arkansan by the name of Archibald Yell was killed in the Mexican War. Yell, the state's second governor and later a senator from Arkansas, died in leading a charge in a battle. The county, Yell County, was named after this war hero.

In thinking about the possibility of war, Amos forgot to turn the mules into the lane leading down to his Fourche River fields. Amos pulled on the reins and the mules stopped and slowly backed up to the gate leading down to the fields. Guess Murt and Kate were also thinking about a war, Amos thought.

It would be easier, Willis thought, if the old shovel had a good handle. The handle had been replaced more than once with a bodark limb handle. But digging postholes were difficult almost anywhere in Arkansas, especially in the Ouachita area. Willis's friend, Bartis, owned a posthole digger, but then Bartis's father had a little money. Willis wondered if Bartis would even try to use a shovel for digging holes.

Willis had to admit that he did take a little pride in being able to put up a fence in the rocky hillsides of Yell County. As his right foot applied force on the shovel, the poorly fitting shovel handle came loose from the shovel. Willis had already repaired the handle once since starting his job around 7:00 a.m. Again, he started back up toward the toolshed, located behind the smokehouse. He would be delayed again.

By now, Amos would be halfway to the fields along the river. Willis had helped Amos load the plow on the wagon before he left to fix the fence. After finishing with the fence repair, Willis was supposed to walk over to the river bottom, take Amos his lunch, and take over the spring plowing. Amos had made it very clear that Willis was to be there by lunch. Harley Hunt and Amos were going to butcher hogs in the afternoon. Willis was glad he would be plowing rather than butchering hogs. He sure loved to kill deer, but that was different than killing a tamed animal that someone had raised.

Willis entered the toolshed and picked up the hammer that he had used earlier as his ma walked into the old lean-to shed. Eva had two biscuits and sausage left over from breakfast. Always concerned about his health, she offered Willis the leftovers. It was either Willis or Ahab. While Eva always saw after her family, she also took good care of Ahab. She had even let him come into the house last winter when the temperature must have been below zero.

Eva, though only thirty-eight years old, looked a little older. She was a short woman of medium build. Her auburn hair was already showing some gray. She usually pulled her hair back over her forehead and down her neck. Since the hair was thin, Eva's head seemed smaller than it really was. The lines in her face, mostly the result of working in the fields in the sun, were also the result of a variety of health problems. Consequently, Eva had a rather sad look. Sparkling blue eyes offset that look. She smiled often and she had an excellent sense of humor.

Willis truly loved his mother. He thought that Eva was the hardest-working woman that he knew. She could cook anything, even any kind of game that he or Amos brought home. If fish were caught, Eva cleaned them. She was also quick to skin a rabbit or squirrel. Sometimes, especially at night, Willis wondered how Eva kept going. She was up at 5:30 a.m. or so, with a big breakfast of eggs, pork, grits, biscuits and gravy, or something as good. Willis liked to say that Eva's red-eye gravy was the best gravy in Yell County.

Eva never hugged Willis or showed much affection. He really couldn't remember the last time she had—maybe at the baptism down on Rhodes Landing when the pastor had baptized Willis. Eva or Amos very seldom told Willis, Hayes, or Georgia Ann that they loved them. However, Willis knew his parents loved them a lot.

Brother Dugan had preached several times that a parent shows a child that they really love them by properly punishing them. If that was the case, Willis knew he was loved. Amos had whipped him several times with his belt. The last time must have been about four years ago when that little mouthy Stella Ann Stuart talked to him at the Sunday meeting at church. He had made the mistake of also talking to her during the sermon.

Eva had also whipped the children several times, usually

with a peach tree limb. However, Eva never got angry when she whipped the children. You could even get her laughing, if you begged not to be whipped. Willis remembered one time that he had done something wrong and Eva had said, "Go out and cut me a switch." Willis went out to the orchard and cut a limb not much bigger around than a toothpick. When he brought it into Eva, begging and pleading, she broke down laughing and just warned him.

Willis took the sausage and biscuits and laid them down on the workbench. Eva immediately reminded him that the bench was dirty and that he needed to give Ahab his second breakfast. Then Eva asked if he would have the fence repaired by lunch.

"If I can get this ole handle to stay in." Willis turned the handle and nailed the second nail into the old tree limb handle. As Willis tested the shovel, Eva slipped Ahab the soiled leftovers and started back to the old, gray house. Again, Willis put his right foot on the shovel, pushed it into the soil, and pulled out a large piece of soil and rock. He looked over at Ahab as the hound finished chewing. "You pig; you were waiting on that sausage."

Willis followed his mother back to the house in order to get a drink of water. He walked over to the hand-dug well under the porch on the north side of the house. A three-foot encirclement of native rock held together by cement, part of which had crumbled away, surrounded the well. Above, attached to the porch roof, was an old, squeaky pulley. Around the pulley was a rope attached to a water bucket. Nearby was the family water pail and dipper. Eva usually left the water bucket outside during the daytime in the summer. Rather than drink from the pail, Willis lowered the old well bucket down into the water, allowed it to partially fill, and then slowly pulled it back up. He reached for the dipper and filled it with fresh cool water. It was good.

Eva had moved down to the west end of the porch where she had a large, wooden tub of water. Inside were the family's clothing, assorted items, and the old washboard. At the top of the old washboard was a large piece of the lye soap that Eva had made last year. Two sheets and pillowcases were already hanging over the old, wire clothesline.

Willis went back to the toolshed, picked up the repaired shovel, and turned to go back up the fence line. Bartis Edwards had just come up the hill, riding bareback on his gray mule. "Hey, let's go fishing."

"You gonna break that old mule's back," Willis said, glancing back. The short, chubby teenager jumped to the ground and threw the makeshift rope bridle on the ground. Bartis had a chubby face, usually red, and an already receding hairline. His red hair matched the hundreds of freckles that dotted his pale face. His wide mouth, usually open for speaking or for food, had a scar across the upper lip, just above a partially broken front tooth.

The mule, named Stupid by Bartis, had kicked him in the mouth years ago when Bartis had tried to slide off its back. Stupid bore a corresponding scar over his left eye where Bartis had responded to the mule's kick, with the use of a well-placed, two-by-four board. Willis, remembering the story about the mule kicking Bartis, said, "Your mule still blind in that left eye?"

Bartis, who frequently responded in jest, said, "Stupid, would be no better off if he had four eyes, but he is more gentle with one eye."

Willis looked at Bartis and answered his earlier question. "Bart, I would like to go fishing. Crappy are probably really biting now, but I'm fixing the fence now and I'm supposed to plow for Pa down in the bottoms after lunch. Wish I could. Pa's plowing this morning and I gotta spell him by lunch so he and Harley can butcher."

Bartis, who never seemed busy anytime, looked at the old shovel. "Should have brought the posthole digger. You'd get through faster."

"Now you tell me, Bartis," Willis smiled. "I reckon we're going to Bluffton on Saturday. They're gonna have a revival meeting at Bluffton Community Church next week. Pa and Ma want to go. You wanna go with us?"

Bartis picked up the mule's rope reins and looked at Willis. "Might go; probably be girls at the meetin'."

"Well, we will go early and stay over for the revival."

Bartis leaped on the mule and looked back at Willis. "Ya'll pick me up at the house and I'll go, but don't 'spect me to join the church or nothing like that. Them preachers give me the willies."

Chapter 4

Gone Fishing

SATURDAY WAS MORE LIKE a typical Arkansas summer day—warm, clear, and humid. The Loflands and several other Young Gravelly families traveled over the back road across Rock Creek and on to the town of Bluffton. Amos's family covered about nine miles before arriving there around noon. Many of the wagons had been pulled up under the shade of several large trees on the south side of Main Street. Several families were already eating packed lunches. Most of the younger children had already moved up to the churchyard where an active game of Red Rover was in progress.

Willis and Bartis left the wagon and walked back to the east side of town where there was considerable activity. The town, though not bigger than Gravelly, had a bank, blacksmith shop, feed store, post office, and two impressive cotton gins. The gins, owned by the Hunnicutt family, processed most of the cotton for the western half of Yell County. Almost every family in Bluffton and Gravelly raised some cotton as a cash crop. While cotton was not produced in large quantities like the Delta area of Arkansas, the river bottom areas of the Fourche River had surprised many with the number of cotton bales produced.

The two young men stopped briefly to watch the Red Rover game and then moved on to the post office where a new, beautiful, black carriage was parked. "Man, that is an expensive buggy," Bartis exclaimed.

"Must be three hundred dollars or so," Willis agreed, closely examining the wheels. "And that matched set of black horses is not shabby either."

"When I get my plantation, I will carry my wife around in a buggy like that," Bartis told Willis.

"Then you'd better take care of Stupid, your old, gray mule, so he can pull it for you."

Since there were always men visiting down at the Hunnicutt gin on Main Street, Willis and Bartis started across the street toward the huge gin building. Charter members of the "spit and whittle club" were already meeting. Several Gravelly men were already in attendance including Amos; Ray Hatfield, the postmaster from Gravelly; and Orb Jones, the Loflands' next door neighbor. Eslie and Lyle Parker were squatting down near the group.

With much tobacco evident, Bartis reached in his back pocket and pulled out a twist of chewing tobacco. He bit off a piece of the twist, stuck it into his mouth, and offered the rest of the twist to Willis. Willis, who had tried chewing tobacco before, declined to take the tobacco. After all, Amos was here. Willis was really glad that Amos was here, since it gave him an excuse not to accept the chew.

Willis and Bartis moved over by Eslie and Lyle. Eslie, resting on one knee, was alternating tossing his pocketknife into the dirt and spitting tobacco juice ten to twenty feet out in the street. Lyle was listening to a gentleman who was dominating the conversation. The speaker was a short man with a rather large stomach extending over a belt that in turn was being held in place by brown suspenders. They matched his light brown suit and hat. The man looked quite serious and spoke very well.

Willis quickly saw that the seated group was listening as if the man knew what he was talking about.

With humidity and temperature quite high now, the speaker realized that he didn't need the coat. He took it off and motioned toward someone behind him. A tall, slender, black man in old, tattered clothes moved up to take the man's coat. The black man turned to take the coat back toward a wagon parked nearby. Sitting on the wagon tailgate were three more black males, all between the ages of fifteen and thirty. These men were also shabbily dressed. The two younger black males had no shoes. As Willis looked to the wagon and the Negroes and back to the man in the brown suit, he noticed that most of the Bluffton crowd was looking at the blacks. As Willis looked back again to the wagon, he now noticed that the Negroes were all looking down at the street as if avoiding the people's stares. Willis had some difficulty in not studying the four men. He was sure that the men were slaves owned by the well-dressed man. What was their life really like? Willis would like to know the answers to that question.

The well-dressed man—Walker, someone said—was speaking about the topic of the day, the possibility of war. "Gentlemen, it appears that Lincoln might use force against our neighboring states that have seceded. If our state secedes, we will be subject to force as well. And we hear some talk of doing away with slavery, an institution that is not only constitutional, but also one that is approved of in the Bible. Men, just look over there. See four of my slaves. They are ignorant and lazy. They could not survive if it wasn't for me. They eat well. They have a comfortable home. They are taught Christianity, and contrary to what the Northerners say, slaves are not mistreated."

Walker raised his voice, and directed his attention toward the slaves. "Hogree, do you want to be free?"

"No, sur, Massa, we loves our home in Camden."

"See, what did I tell you. The Yankees have taken our lack of representation in Congress and turned it around into a slavery issue."

Lyle's father, Homer, a deacon in the Gravelly Methodist Church, spoke up. "But Lincoln said that he would not interfere with slavery."

Walker raised his voice while pointing his finger at Homer. "Do you know any politician that won't lie? Even Governor Rector is guilty. Politicians are very honest while running for office. After they get in, they forget most of their promises."

Bartis stood up, looked at Homer, then at Walker, and said in a threatening tone, "Don't make no difference if Lincoln is for or agin slavery. We would whup his army. A Southerner can lick three or four Northern sissies."

A low hum of voices together followed as several men spoke in favor or against Bartis's comments. Willis had been listening carefully. He believed that the planter knew what he was talking about. He was obviously educated and successful. He owned a lot of land, along with slaves to farm it. He also was good to his Negroes.

Willis glanced over at the slaves. One was picking at his toes. Another was talking low to a third slave. The fourth black was looking across the street at a group of children playing. They didn't look happy, but they didn't look sad either. Willis wondered what it would be like to be a slave. He would like to talk to one of the Negroes, but he had never talked to a Negro. They seemed all right.

Willis remembered once asking Amos how much a slave cost. Amos had laughed and said that they could not afford a slave at five hundred to eight hundred dollars.

"That's more money than we make in a year," Amos had

said. "Besides, you also have to feed um, house um, and give um clothes. Plus, you can't trust um. They could run off, or worse, rise up and kill you like that Negro, Turner, in Virginia. No, you leave the slaves to the big plantation owners like Harvell over at Dardanelle."

Strangely, the conversation came up the next week during Sunday dinner. After church, the Loflands had sit down to one of Eva's Sunday dinners: fried chicken, mashed potatoes, green beans, rolls, and peach cobbler. As usual, during the dinner meal, Amos and Eva talked about Preacher Dugan's sermon. Since Amos was one of the men who usually expressed several "amens" during the church service, he usually agreed with the preacher. On this Sunday, Preacher Dugan had preached from the book of Ephesians. The reading included verses from chapter six. The writer, Paul, was discussing the relationship of the master to slave. The preacher referred to verse five, where Paul told the Ephesians in Asia Minor, "Slaves, obey your earthly masters with respect and fear and with sincerity of heart, just as you would obey Christ. Obey them not only to win their favor when their eye is on you, but like slaves of Christ, doing the will of God from your heart." He also quoted verse eight: "Everyone will be rewarded by the Lord for whatever good he does, whether he is slave or free."

Putting down a piece of fried chicken, Amos reached for the gravy. "Preacher really tied the sermon to the slavery issue. It's hard to say if slavery is Christian. That Garrison feller up north surely puts it down."

"Pass this to your pa," Eva said, picking up the bread and handing it to Hayes. "If God is opposed to slavery, we must oppose slavery."

Willis intently listened to the conversation. "If Paul, certainly a man of God, was led by God in writing to the other

Christians, then they must have approved of slavery back in those times. That one verse said that a slave should obey and that the Lord would reward him. Does the Lord approve of slavery?"

"That's true," Eva spoke up, "but the other verse said that a master must be good to his slaves."

"But Eva, that's basic in Christianity. A man can sin by mistreating a white man as easy as mistreating a slave."

"But Amos, there's all kinds of stories about how plantation owners mistreat their slaves. Some even father children by negro women." Eva glanced at the three children, realizing she had said too much.

"I'm sure a lot of that is true, but a lot of that is stories made up by abolitionists like Douglas," Amos replied.

"I doubt that I will ever own a Negro, probably never be able to afford one, but it still seems funny that Northerners say it's evil and wrong, and yet the Bible seems to support slavery," said Willis, who usually had little to say during Sunday dinner.

"Pa, we gonna buy us a Negro?" Hayes spoke up for the first time.

"No, Hayes, we will do our own work."

"Ma, why are the Negroes usually so dirty and shabby?" asked Georgia Ann, who had also been listening.

"Honey, they don't have enough money to afford clothes," Eva replied. "Lands, you all wear patched clothes yourself."

Willis was still interested in the subject. "Pa, you reckon we're gonna have to fight here in Arkansas? Lyle thinks we are."

Amos was sopping out his plate with a piece of bread. "Doubt it; someone like Clay will come up with another compromise."

"What's a compromise?" asked Georgia Ann.

Amos looked at his daughter. "Sissy, it's when people on different sides of an issue gives some afore trouble starts."

Eva had gone back into the kitchen to bring out an apple pie. She set it on the corner of the table and cut five pieces, with two larger pieces for the two men. She wiped her hands on her apron and sat down. Georgia Ann reached for the pie, hit her milk glass, and knocked it over, spilling milk over the table and onto the floor.

"Honey, be careful," replied Eva, reaching for a dish towel to wipe up the mess.

Georgia Ann was embarrassed. Hayes thought it was funny and reminded his sister that this was the third time this week that she had turned over her milk. Willis had placed a piece of apple pie on his plate and started to cut off a forkful of pie. "If war occurs, if necessary, I'll probably go fight. Bartis and Eslie say they will fight."

This conversation made Eva uncomfortable, especially when her oldest son expressed an interest in war.

"Pa, would Arkansas fight against the states that left the Union?" asked Willis.

"Hard to say. The governor is against a war. Really, no one is for war. Remember what grandpa said about the Mexican War: Old men decide to go to war, but young men have to fight the wars. Our state convention voted to stay in the Union, but most everyone I know is against fighting our own neighbors. Some say another convention will be called to again consider secession. Another problem bothering some, mostly slave owners, is that Lincoln is against slavery in the territory."

Eva had begun to stack up the dishes. "What's wrong with that, Amos?"

"It's really quite important since the non-slave states tend to stick together and vote together on things that they are for. We already have twice as many Northern states in this category than in the South. We in the South can hardly be heard in Congress anymore. Issues like the tariff are always decided by the Northern bloc." Willis listened closely to his Pa. It was amazing that he knew so much about the country's affairs, yet he had only gone to school for eight years. Willis agreed with his mother. Though no serious book learning, Amos was a smart man.

A knock on the screen door interrupted the conversation. It was Eslie. "Come in Eslie," said Georgia Ann. She seemed to like Eslie better than Bartis, probably because Bartis teased her so much.

Eslie, in his characteristically shy manner, opened the door and looked directly at Willis. "Thought I'd go down on the Fourche and try to catch some fish. You wanna go, Willis?"

He was still in the old clothes that he had worn to Sunday school. Eslie seldom stayed for church service. He had been embarrassed one Sunday when Preacher Dugan called on him to pray. Eslie could pray in Sunday school, but he was embarrassed to pray in church because he couldn't think of anything to say. After that Sunday, Bartis told Eslie, "Just pray to own lots of Negroes and land." Bartis could even clown about prayer.

Willis pushed away from the table and looked toward his mother. She knew he was too old to ask permission to go anywhere but she loved him for being so thoughtful to ask. "Go on, but watch for snakes." She always cautioned him about snakes, even though they did not see many snakes.

"Mother, can I go?" asked Hayes in a hopeful tone.

"I believe you better stay here and feed the scraps to Ahab. Besides, I think you are supposed to dry dishes on Sunday."

Hayes made a frown but said no more. Amos did not permit

the kids to argue or backtalk any adult. The boys went out on the back porch, where Eslie helped himself to a dipperful of water. Willis went out to the toolshed where a couple of old cane poles had been thrown up on the roof. He checked for hooks and then turned to Eslie and asked if he had any bait. Eslie said that he brought an old tow sack that they could use to net some crawdads and minnows from Rock Creek.

"You guys be careful," ordered Amos, who had started up to the barn.

The boys started east across the pine-covered hills and occasional fields. It was only about two miles to Rock Creek. It was a beautiful day, with only a slight breeze in the air. As the two friends walked through the Lofland pasture, Eslie described his fishing trip only two days ago.

"I caught four catfish, all over a pound, and hung an old carp. I cooked 'em that evening and Pa really liked 'em. He's the one who suggested I go today, so I thought you might want to go."

Willis wondered why Ralph didn't go fishing, because he did very little around their farm. Not far away a hound was on the trail of a rabbit or deer. It sounded like the dog was moving toward them as the excited bark grew louder. Then it drifted away. Willis also noted that the Lofland east fence line was in need of repair.

"Preacher Dugan came by the house today after church and talked to Pa. He's been trying to get Pa to go to church. I wish he would go." Willis could only add that he hoped Ralph would also get in church.

Rock Creek was relatively still now. It was mostly a series of holes of water among the rocks. However, this made it easier to use the feed sack to net minnows and crawdads. In ten minutes the boys had enough crawdads, along with a few minnows. They followed the creek down to where it emptied into the Fourche River. The river at this point was about fifty feet across. Except for some occasional deep holes of water, the river was usually not over six or eight feet deep.

The Fourche water, like Rock Creek, was not moving east very fast. The boys sat down on an old log, which was about four feet from the river's edge. Eslie placed the old tow sack in about six inches of water in order to keep the bait alive. The fishing lines were baited and tossed out into the river.

"This is right where I was sitting the other day." Eslie and Willis had been sitting on the old log for at least half an hour. Eslie had caught two small lionsides and Willis had caught a couple of perch. Except for a couple of large fluffy clouds, there was almost blue sky and the temperature was around eighty degrees.

Willis had said little while the two friends fished. The only thing that Eslie had said at all was when he pointed out a wild hog that came down to drink out of the river. Willis pulled slightly on the cane pole, causing the cork bobber to move closer to the bank. He then allowed the cork to stop moving.

"Eslie, you ever had a girlfriend?" The question was rather surprising to Eslie.

"No." The quick answer reflected Eslie's feelings on the subject.

"Me neither, really." Both men were quiet for several minutes. Again Willis broke the silence.

"I got a letter from Rosalie yesterday." Eslie glanced over at Willis, as if to question him about the letter.

"She and her pa are going to be in Gravelly next Saturday. Guess her father needs some nails and stuff. You reckon she told me this so's I would be in Gravelly on Saturday?"

Eslie did not reply immediately. "You going to Gravelly?"

"Probably. She's a nice Christian lady and she's quite pretty."

Willis had wanted to talk to someone about the letter. Of course, talking to Eslie about the opposite sex was like talking to a rock. The subject was dropped when Willis hung a good fish.

"He'll probably weighed two pounds."

Eslie could discuss this subject. Eslie reached for the fish. As he stepped toward Willis, he felt something nick his leg. He looked down to see a copperhead, rapidly move back among the rocks.

"Willis, that copperhead got me above the ankle."

"You sure? Check it out."

Eslie pulled up his trouser leg. There was a small puncture and a scrape where one fang had failed to penetrate the skin. Eslie pinched the flesh together, trying to get blood flow.

"Eslie, we better go; you gonna be sick."

The poles were pulled in, the lines wrapped around the poles, and the two began retracting their route over the pastures.

"You feeling okay?"

"I guess—maybe he didn't get any poison in my leg."

"We can't take no chance, Eslie. We need to get you home and off your feet. May have to get Doc Rhodes to look at you."

Willis was worried, and he could tell that Eslie was more than worried. Both remembered Lyle being bitten by a water moccasin while wading in water not over six inches deep. Some said that a snake couldn't bite in the water, but Lyle almost died as the result of his snakebite. They were now in sight of the house. Eva was sitting on the back porch churning milk into butter. Georgia Ann was near her mother playing with her doll.

"Ma, Eslie got snake bit by a copperhead!" Willis hollered.

Eva quickly stood up and told Georgia Ann to take the

churn in the house. She got well water and took it in the house for the teakettle. She threw a couple pieces of wood in the wood stove and hurried back to examine the snakebite.

"I have a headache now," Eslie said. "I may be feeling sick."

Eva examined the bite area. "You're going to have fever 'fore long. Let's get you to bed."

"You mean here?" Eslie asked.

"Sure, I mean here. Time we get horses harnessed and get you home, it would be another hour. You got to be off your feet."

Eslie was embarrassed over receiving her attention. Without a mother, he never received this kind of care. Eva told Eslie to get into Willis's bed. Then, she brought a dishpan with hot water and soap and carefully washed off the wound.

"Some say you should cut the area near the fang marks and force it to bleed, to get out poison. Doc Rhodes said that really didn't help unless you do it within seconds of the bite. He says the poison is already pumped with the blood through the body."

Eva took some ointment and rubbed it over and into the wound. Eslie was developing chills, and Eva knew his temperature was going up. She placed extra blankets on him and sent Georgia Ann for a pan of cool water. Once she had the water, she began using a wet rag to wipe Eslie's forehead. After bathing his face with the water, she placed the cool washrag on his forehead.

Eslie had gone to sleep. It was growing late in the evening, and Eva told Willis to go up to the barn and milk. She said that she and Georgia Ann would continue to change the cool washrag until Eslie's temperature went down.

Amos found out what happened when he came back from cutting sprouts. Eslie lived about three miles away, by the road, and he decided to saddle one of the mules and go over to tell

Eslie's father. A long night followed. A time or two, Eva even considered sending Amos for Doc Rhodes. By morning, Eslie's temperature had dropped some and Eva knew that he was out of danger.

That afternoon, Eslie was loaded on the wagon for the trip home. Amos drove the wagon team over to Eslie's house on Carroll Mountain. Willis had been to Eslie's house four or five times, but he had never been inside the one-room cabin with the lean-to back room. One of the reasons that Willis had seldom gone to Eslie's house was because Eslie's father, Ralph, had a serious drinking problem. Every time that Willis had gone to Eslie's home, Ralph had been drunk, to some degree. This embarrassed Eslie.

Willis also knew that Ralph would often hit Eslie when he was drunk. He remembered Eslie coming to school a couple of times with a black eye and once with a busted lip. Eslie never admitted that his father abused him, but everyone was sure that he did.

Murt and Kate, the old brown mule and the white mule that Amos owned, could hardly pull the wagon over the old, washed-out lane that ran back up on Carroll Mountain. Willis had to get out of the wagon and move a large limb that was partially blocking the lane.

"I can walk from here," proclaimed Eslie, obviously embarrassed about his home life.

Amos told him that he would take him all the way up to the house. The washed-out lane turned back to the right, up over a heavy outcropping of rock. The home came into view. It was a one-room structure with a small porch on the front of the house. The house had only four windows, two of which were covered with boards. The roof had a large hole on the end opposite the fireplace. This hole had also been patched with old boards.

A chimney was located at the east end of the house. At the rear or north side of the house, a small lean-to type room had been built on to the main structure. The house set on several flat rocks that had been stacked at each corner of the house. Chickens wandered from under the house. Off to the east was a well surrounded by native rock masonry. A rather shaky, rounded four-by-four board had been positioned to act as a windlass for the well bucket. The smokehouse, a small chicken house, and an old barn with no door were out back. The old barn was leaning sharply to the right. Not far away was the outhouse, and a garden plot was further east from the house.

Amos stopped the team of mules in front of the porch. Willis noticed that one of the steps up to the porch was gone. The door was open, and as Amos and Willis helped Eslie down from the wagon, Ralph came to the door. Even the quickest glance would reveal that he had been drinking.

"Wondered when he was going to get home. Been doing mine and hisin's chores. Weren't no cause to bring him home. He could've walked."

Ralph had a beard that needed trimming and his hair was also quite long. He was shirtless, and Willis thought he had as much hair on his chest and back as on his head and face.

With help from Willis, Eslie stepped up on the porch. "Sure beholding to you'uns for caring for me, Mr. Lofland. Maybe I kin help you with cotton at pickin' time."

Amos had gotten down from the wagon to walk over and shake hands with Ralph. "No worry," he said as he glanced back to Eslie. "We's glad to help. I'd stay off my feet until tomorrow. Fever may come up agin."

Willis watched his friend go into the house. Through the open door, he could see an old table and two chairs, a bed, a wood box, and above the box, a faded picture of a pretty woman on the wall. He guessed that the lady in the picture must be Eslie's deceased mother. The only other thing Willis noticed was a whiskey bottle on the table.

Amos was talking to Ralph. "I may need some help with the cotton later on, if you'd be free?"

"Doubt if I'll have time," Ralph said, glancing back at the wagon. "Eslie might help though." Willis knew that Ralph took any money Eslie made.

Amos shook hands with Ralph and told him to come over and visit, and then the Loflands got back in the wagon and started back down the mountain. There was silence for several minutes.

"I feel sorry for Eslie," Willis eventually said. "He really has a poor life with his pa. Sure hope that he didn't hit Eslie for coming in late."

Amos was thinking about the same thing. "Eslie's a good boy," he finally spoke. "Maybe best for him to leave home soon as possible."

After another quiet spell, Amos spoke again. "Willis, our country's in a real mess — about broke up. While we are still in with the Lincoln government, it may not be for long. The new Southern government is calling Arkansaw to take her place with the other states that's already backed out. Don't mention it to your ma, but it looks right serious. Reason I mentioned it to you is you're soldier age. You may or you may not choose to join the militia, but you will probably have a choice right soon."

Willis respected his father's views. He also knew that Amos usually thought things out real good before he spoke. Willis finally responded. "If it was necessary, I'd go and so would Bartis and Eslie. Lyle probably would. Don't know about Hoss and Mule Calvert."

Amos listened to his son and finally spoke. "War is no place for anyone, but Eslie may even be better off there than at home with Ralph."

Chapter 5

A Cavalry Unit

WILLIS HAD LOOKED FORWARD to Saturday and the trip to Gravelly. The town of Gravelly was not as large as Bluffton, probably because Bluffton had the two cotton gins, but usually there were more people at Gravelly on Saturdays. The smaller communities to the west and north, Nola and Dutch Creek, were even smaller than Gravelly. Therefore, the people from those communities came to Gravelly for shopping on Saturday.

Gravelly was on the same road as Bluffton, approximately ten miles west. Unlike Bluffton, Gravelly had only one main street. However, Main Street was usually busy. Two general stores, the post office, a feed store, and a blacksmith/harness shop, along with a real estate office, made up most of Main Street. Recently, a new lawyer had opened an office in town. Parker and Son owned one of the general stores and the feed store. The son was Lyle Parker, one of Willis's best friends. Lyle spent much of his time helping with the feed/grain store.

Willis and Hayes hitched up the mules to the wagon while Eva and Georgia Ann got into the appropriate clothes. Amos would not be going with the family since he and several other men were going to work on the church at Young Gravelly. Rufus Haskins, one of the other deacons, had picked up Amos earlier. They were to meet Preacher Dugan at the church.

As usual, Hayes wanted to drive the mule team. Willis had no problem with this since Murt and Kate needed no direction. Eva and Georgia Ann came out with their Sunday best on, partially holding up the long dresses with their hands. Willis helped the females board the wagon and they took a seat by Hayes. Willis then went to the rear of the wagon, where he sat down on the wagon floor facing the opposite direction with his legs hanging off the wagon.

"Let's go, Hayes," Willis demanded.

The forty-five minute trip passed in a hurry. It was almost 10:00 a.m. when the Loflands arrived in town. Several people had parked wagons at the school, which was three blocks east of Main Street. The town was already active, as people moved up and down the street, doing more visiting than shopping. Like most Southern towns, Gravelly had a favorite meeting place for the men. In the case of Gravelly, the place was Parkers Feed Store.

The store, like most of the businesses, had an elevated, board walkway built up about a foot higher than the street itself. This elevated walkway also served as a convenient dock for loading feed and grain onto the wagons. It was also a good place to sit and watch the town people move about town.

Homer Parker had also put a long, ten-foot bench out in front of the store for people to sit on. Consequently, the feed store was the principal meeting place for male shoppers in Gravelly. Since Eva's uncle, Baxter, lived in Gravelly not far from Main Street, Willis had Hayes take the wagon to Baxter's home. The family then walked on back to Main Street. Willis and Hayes stopped by the feed store where Willis went in to find Lyle.

After visiting with his friend, Willis came back outside the store to visit with the eight or ten men that had already gathered there. The major topic was the price of cotton. Since many of the people in Yell County had some cotton, cotton prices were always a serious topic of discussion.

"Look! Here come soldiers," Hayes interrupted as Homer was leading the discussion.

Everyone turned to look east down the street. A cavalry unit was marching up the street toward the gathered group of men. There were about thirty men in two neat rows, all smartly dressed in equally neat, blue uniforms. Several people hollered and waved as the soldiers moved into town. The troops reached the area in front of the feed store.

"Halt," commanded the officer in charge, a flashy young colonel with gold braid and shining sword. He then moved over to the group of men sitting in front of the store.

"Gentlemen, may I ask if the owner of this business is available?" he addressed the group. Someone pointed to Lyle.

"Guess I can help you. Lyle replied, after glancing around and not seeing his father."

"Sir, I am Colonel William Martin, 33rd Illinois Cavalry," said the colonel, rather surprised at such a youthful store owner. "We left Plainview early this morning. We're on our way to Fort Smith. Would you have a place where we might water our horses?"

"Sure," Lyle quickly replied. "Follow me around to the side of the building. We got a water trough there."

Lyle, followed by Willis, Hayes, and other younger members of the group, went around to the water trough. The officer returned to his men, gave orders, and the group proceeded to move around to the water trough. The officer gave the reins of his horse to a young aide and came back to speak with Lyle.

"Bout how far to Fort Smith?"

"Probably three to four days," Lyle guessed, looking at Willis.

"Ya'll getting ready for war?" a boy of about sixteen asked the officer.

"No," responded the officer, surprised at the question. 'They just needed another cavalry unit in the Fort Smith area."

Willis and Lyle exchanged looks.

"By the way, what's the next town?"

"It's Nola," responded the sixteen-year-old. "I live there. Four miles, but not much town."

The officer shook hands with Lyle, offered his thanks, and mounted his horse. No other soldier had touched the ground.

"Forward," commanded the officer, and the group marched out of town west toward Nola and Fort Smith.

The moving cavalry unit replaced the subject of cotton. Speculation was offered as to why the cavalry was moving to Fort Smith.

"They're getting ready in case war breaks out," said a visitor.

"Probably be war regardless of which side we are on," spoke up Bill Hansen, the new lawyer in town. "Lincoln wants us to help bully our neighbors like Mississippi and Tennessee. Hey, they are cotton farmers and country folk just like us. They are good people. I am definitely not for destroying the homes and farms of these good, Southern people. They haven't done anything to us. And furthermore, I don't think that they would want to war on us.

"Stop and think about it. Most of us either came from our sister Southern states or we have relatives living there now. As for me, my sympathies are with the states seeking the freedom to determine their own kind of government. Some of you know that there is serious talk in the state assembly about voting again on secession for our state. And, if there is a second vote, I believe that we will also leave the Union and probably go with the new Montgomery government in Alabama. But, if we unite with the new government, then we may be invaded by the old Lincoln government troops. Either way, we may be forced to go to war. If we have such a choice, I believe we should stick to the basic rights that our founders gave us. And that is that a powerful, central government in Washington should not run roughshod over the sovereign states that voluntarily agreed to be a part of it. Friends, there is a strong resemblance between the coming Lincoln government and the government of George III of England."

"Exactly what is this secession that we hear talked about?" asked a farmer from Dutch Creek.

"Secession is where a state or states would choose to back out of the Union and become independent states, or maybe even an independent country," said Hansen, enjoying the attention of the group. He hitched up his pants, let a stream of tobacco fly into the street, and continued. "They would sever all ties with the United States and go it alone."

"Bill, can a state legally dropout of the federal government?" asked Lyle, who was now quite interested in the direction of the discussion.

"Most people that are familiar with the Constitution believe that secession is legal," the lawyer responded. "They know that each state entered the Union voluntarily and therefore they may leave it if the state prefers."

"What could they do anyway if a state decided to leave?" Willis asked.

"Don't forget, the federal government owns a lot of property in each state," said Hansen, spitting the tobacco plug into his hand and then tossing it toward the center of the street. After spitting small bits of tobacco out, he continued. "They have agencies like the Postal Service. They have forts, guns, and military supplies. They also extract a good amount of money from each state in terms of land sales and so forth. They are not going to give all of that to a state."

"Let them have all their movable property and leave us be," responded Lyle.

"Most people back south think that Lincoln will never permit secession to occur," the lawyer answered. "In other words, he will use force to keep the present Union."

A wagon going by with Rosalie and her father interrupted Willis's thoughts. They stopped in front of Laurel's Store. Willis watched as her father helped Rosalie down from the wagon. She wore a white dress trimmed in blue. Her waist must have been no more than eighteen inches. Her long, blonde hair was arranged in long curls, and a touch of rouge caused her cheekbones to stand out perfectly. She is beautiful, Willis thought. Turning back to look toward the feed store, she saw the group of men staring at her. She smiled slightly, daintily lifted her dress, and moved into the store behind her father.

"You reckon there's a prettier woman in the county?" the teenager from Nola asked.

"Probably not," said the talkative lawyer. "Who is she?"

"You talking bout Willis's woman," Lyle grinned as he looked at Willis. "She's from Chula. Father's the preacher there."

Willis had gotten up and started down the street toward the store. The conversation returned again to the nation's problems.

"One thing's for sure. We gonna know something in a couple weeks." The lawyer turned around and started west to his office.

Willis walked in the store as if unaware that Rosalie was there. He walked over to look at the new muskets that had recently been brought into the store. However, out of the corner of his eye, he could see Rosalie at a counter looking at some thread. He turned to watch the attractive woman.

"Willis, haven't seen you for a while," said Reverend Gotham, Rosalie's father. When the preacher mentioned Willis's name, Rosalie turned, looked toward Willis, and smiled. "Come over and say hello to my daughter."

Willis did not really need an invitation, although the reverend's invitation made it easier for him. He reached out his hand and grasped Rosalie's small hand.

"It's good to see you again."

"We always enjoy coming to Gravelly," responded Rosalie.

Willis would have preferred a less formal welcome; however, he knew that Rosalie usually knew the proper way to handle such occasions. "Father's preaching at the Methodist church tomorrow. Why don't you all come up and visit tomorrow?"

Willis could not help noting the perfect, white teeth, the high cheekbones, and the light green eyes.

"Ma and Pa will probably have to attend our church tomorrow; you know Pa's a deacon and everything. They're working on our church today, but I may be able to come up though."

"I'll make sure you're out of preaching by two o'clock," joked the preacher.

"Where ya'll staying tonight?" Willis certainly wanted to see more of Rosalie than just on this occasion.

"We'll be staying with Odis Hunnicutt. He's my cousin on my father's side."

Willis glanced back at Rosalie. He thought she wanted to say more. Willis turned to leave.

"I'll try to get up in the morning. It's sure good to see you all again."

"Come if you can," Rosalie smiled, slightly embarrassed.

Willis turned and almost knocked over an empty keg of nails.

"Willis, it would probably be all right for you to see Rosalie later on today," the pastor said. "We'll be through with our buying fore long."

"Thanks," said Willis, glancing again at the attractive girl. He left the store and started back toward the group sitting at the feed store, thinking that he would have to watch for her to leave. As he walked down the street, he noticed several men across from the feed store, including Lyle. He could hear raised voices as he moved toward the group.

"None of your business," exclaimed an angry stranger. The man was looking toward Lyle, speaking to him. Behind the stranger was an old, black man in tattered clothes. His head was bowed and his hands were in his pockets. Lyle spoke with a raised voice, but not in anger.

"He's your Negro and your property, but hey, man, I wouldn't treat a mule the way you're treating him. Correcting him is one thing, but knocking his head off is something else. Besides, he's an old man."

The stranger looked around the group that had gathered. "I bought this Negro last month at Warren. Paid three hundred dollars for him. He's got to learn I'm his new boss. Now get out of my way."

The man looked back at the black man. "Come on," he demanded and proceeded on down the street. The group began to break up, most going back to the feed store.

"What happened, Lyle?" asked Willis, continuing to watch the man and his slave walk away.

"Awe, his Negro was loading some stuff he'd bought at Hurley's. The old man dropped a sack of flour. That son of a gun backhanded him right across the face. Looked to me like he was going to hit him again. Should've minded my business, as he said, I guess."

They had reached the feed store. Willis admired his friend for defending the old man. But as Willis knew, that was the way Lyle was. The lawyer had observed the entire incident. He spit another stream of tobacco juice into the street, looked the opposite direction, and said, "Lyle, you've not been around many Negroes. I don't believe in mistreating them myself neither, but they are like children. Gotta raise em to respect you. Sometimes necessary to rap one occasionally."

"Yeah, he's right," said Lyle's father, who had now gotten back to the store. "Son, you probably shouldn't have interfered."

Lyle was now embarrassed. "Probably right, but it looked to me like he had just bought him a Negro and was showing off for everyone. That old man is probably near seventy years old. Had to be if he only paid three hundred dollars for him."

The conversation ended, and it was back to discussing the price of cotton. Willis was still thinking about how much he admired his friend.

Willis finished loading the groceries that his mother had bought, and then he helped his mother and sister board the wagon. Hayes had taken the seat on the back of the wagon.

"Git up," said Willis, popping the reins.

"Willis, I saw Reverend Gotham and Rosalie," Eva said. "Did you see them?"

"Yeah, saw 'em at the store," said Willis, who had been thinking on how he might see Rosalie.

"Guess the preacher's preaching at the Methodist church tomorrow," Eva said, and then there was quiet for a while.

"How long you gonna stay at Baxter's today?" Willis asked as they approached the house.

"We need to leave by four o'clock," she answered, combing out Georgia Ann's hair.

"Ma, think I'll go over and see Odis a while," Willis said as they were pulling into the driveway of Baxter's big two-story house. "Haven't seen him for a spell."

After a brief time of visiting with Odis and Reverend Gotham, Willis went out on the front porch where Odis's wife, Sharon, and Rosalie were sitting. In a few minutes, Sharon excused herself with the pretense of preparing supper. The two young people were left alone on the big porch. The afternoon was still warm, with only an occasional south breeze. Rosalie had a fan in her hand, which she used occasionally.

"Father fears a coming war," she finally said, breaking the uneasy silence. "It seems to be the only thing that people talk about anymore. Willis, what do you think?"

Willis had been looking at Rosalie as she spoke. He looked back up the street. "All I know is what others say. Pa has mentioned it several times, so I know he is worried. The new lawyer here in Gravelly was talking about the situation earlier today."

Willis looked back at Rosalie and noticed her studying him with a worried look. "Why, Willis, why? Christian people are supposed to be able to settle differences without resorting to violence. Can't we sit down and talk about the differences that divide us?"

Two small boys passed the house with cane poles over their shoulders. They waved toward the house.

"Rosalie, do you remember much of the history that you had in school?" Willis asked, but didn't give her time to reply. "I remember Mr. Lackly talking about Henry Clay, who was from Kentucky. He suggested several compromises that sorted things out and prevented war between the North and the South. Mr. Lackly said Clay was praised for his ability to create compromise that at least halfway satisfied both the North and the South."

Rosalie was listening carefully.

"Mr. Lackly said that, really, all Clay did was delay the end result. We may be out of compromises."

Rosalie took a breath, moved the fan back and forth in front of her face, and looked again at Willis. "Is it slavery? Will we fight a war over slavery?"

Willis wiped some sweat off his forehead. "Rosalie, except for a stranger in town today that owned a slave, I don't think a man in Gravelly or even Yell County will fight in a war to defend slavery. Now, if for some reason—and I can't imagine one—another state militia marched us on, I'm sure that most men here would fight. Even Governor Rector seems to want to avoid war. Lyle, Bartis, and Eslie would all probably fight if forced too. I would too."

The reply disturbed Rosalie. Willis had dreaded this moment, but at the same time, he knew he must say what he had thought about many times. "Rosalie, if there is a war, and if I join up, I will be back and I would…I would…want to see you a lot."

"If you do go, would it be proper to write you?" Rosalie quickly replied.

"It would be proper," Willis replied, his face blushing. "I hope you would write me. I would write you back."

Sharon stepped out of the house with fresh-baked cookies. Willis hoped that she did not hear his reply to Rosalie.

Sunday was another warm day, although the possibility of rain was in the air. Some worried about severe weather or tornadoes in May or June. Brother Gotham brought a message from John in the New Testament. The preacher talked about forgiveness. He discussed Jesus' forgiveness of the apostle Peter, even after Peter had denied him three times. It was an impressive sermon. As Willis listened, he wondered if the preacher was suggesting that the divided country should be as forgiving as Jesus was toward Peter.

Sharon had prepared an impressive meal of pork chops, corn, beans, and mashed potatoes and gravy. After dinner, Rosalie brought out a three-layer chocolate cake with heavy chocolate icing. She had prepared the cake on Saturday evening after Willis had left. Everyone including Willis complimented Sharon and Rosalie on the excellent meal.

The men retired to the back porch while the women retired to the living room. Otis lit up his pipe and puffed a couple of times. " Rosalie is some young lady. She is pretty. She is a good cook. She can milk and feed hogs. Gonna make someone a good wife."

He stole a glance at Willis, who was picking at the sole of his shoe. Willis said nothing.

"She is that all right, and pretty as her mother," the preacher replied. "She is a good Christian, and she runs our place. Without a mother for so long, Rosalie has become an adult quicker than most. Gets up at five o'clock, works hard all day, and goes to bed at ten or eleven o'clock."

Willis was glad when the conversation changed to state politics. The ladies were out in the yard, now looking at the flowers. Sharon had raised a variety of beautiful flowers. One rosebush in particular, bearing a large red rose, had several other perfectly shaped roses. Sharon cut off a couple of the roses for the kitchen. Willis got up and ambled across the yard toward the ladies. On reaching the women, he bent down to smell one of the large red roses.

"Want to take a walk?" he asked, looking at Rosalie.

"That would be nice," she said, looking at Sharon, who nodded and turned away.

The two started down through the pasture toward the creek,

which flowed easterly in the direction of the Fourche River. The banks of the fast-flowing creek consisted of rocks, boulders, and willow trees. There were also several large pine trees on the banks of the creek. The creek had begun to threaten some of the trees by carrying away the soil from their shallow roots.

The crystal clear water rushing over the rocks created a swirling sound, and they could see minnows in one of the pools. The two young people sat down on a large rock near the stream. Willis began to describe what happened to Eslie on the day the copperhead bit him.

Rosalie listened intently as Willis explained how Eva had cared for Eslie. He looked over to see her looking up into his eyes. Willis could not go on. He lowered his face close to Rosalie's face and noticed that it was even more beautiful close up. She did not move, but gazed into his eyes.

Willis moved his face closer. He could really smell the sweet aroma of Rosalie's perfume. He touched his lips to her slightly open mouth. When she did not move away, he compressed his lips slightly on her red lips. Even though the touch was only a few seconds, Willis could feel Rosalie slightly tremble before she pulled her head back slightly, parting their lips.

"I really feel sorry for Eslie," she said, looking down at the flowing creek and then back to Willis. "I guess he's had a tough life with his father."

"Yeah, you really don't know how bad he has it," replied Willis, who was slightly embarrassed but also enthralled. "Please don't ever say anything, but I know that Eslie's pa has abused him a lot. Yet, he still shows the greatest respect for him."

Rosalie listened until Willis finished. Then she looked at him and said, "We'd probably better go."

Willis quickly stood up and reached out his hand to Rosalie.

She took his hand and stood up.

"Willis, don't take this wrong, but...I...I..." Rosalie was trying to be discreet as to how she would finish her comment. "If you join the army, please be careful."

Willis thought he felt her hand tighten somewhat before she released it. The two started back toward Odis's house.

Willis joined the men on the back porch. The friends were discussing the status of Arkansas as a state as Willis took a seat in an old rocking chair.

"By now, most of the state is aware that our Unionist Governor Rector has changed directions," Odis said. "He has called another meeting of the convention to again consider secession. Most now believe they will vote for secession this time."

"If that happens, we must join the new Southern government at Montgomery," Odis said, spitting tobacco juice into an old spittoon.

"And what then?" Willis spoke up.

"I fear war," the pastor, looking over at Willis. "It seems that the president will not allow the Southern states to leave the Union peacefully. I see a parallel with Israel in the Old Testament. Remember, after Solomon's reign, Israel broke apart. There was a brief civil war. The two parts, Israel and Judah, had their own kings and their own capitals. Israel's capital was Samaria. Judah continued to have Jerusalem as their capital. The two countries continued to drift further apart. They also forgot God and continued their idol worship.

"Once separated, the two countries eventually fell to different foes. Israel was defeated and deported to Assyria. They will disappear from history. Judah lasted another 140 years, before they were defeated and deported to Babylonia, where they would live in exile for seventy years. The people who survived were allowed to return to their homeland eventually. We now call them Jews. Peddler Openhiemer is a Jew. But, the point is, if we become separate countries, will we be strong, or could we easily be defeated by some European power like England or France? As Americans, we must continue to worship God, and we must use common sense now about our future."

Chapter 6

The Slavery Issue

MAY OF 1861 WAS cooler than past early springs. Willis and Amos hitched up the mule team and started to Gravelly. Amos was supposed to pick up a new John Deere plow. The rest of the family would not be going since the wagon would be pretty well loaded with spring planting seeds and supplies. About two miles down the road, the Loflands came upon Eslie walking.

"Whoo," Willis pulled up the mules. "Hop in Eslie. Where you going?"

"Thought I'd go to town and see what's going on," Eslie said, jumping on the back of the wagon. Then he moved up behind the wagon seat, where he knelt down on his knees facing the front.

"Why didn't you ride your mule?" Willis asked his friend.

"Aw, Pa took the mule last night and he didn't come in this morning," he said, looking off to the side of the road. "Thought I might find him at Gravelly."

Willis wished he had never asked the question. As usual, on Saturday Gravelly had several people in town for various reasons. Being a little on the chilly side, the townsmen had moved the Saturday gathering down to Calvert's Blacksmith Shop. Cob Calvert had a livery stable with a large wood-burning stove inside. Bales of hay had been moved about the store to serve as seating for the group. Cob, a big, husky Scandinavian, was near sixty years of age and consequently did little heavy work in his business.

However, he had two sons, a year apart in age. Nineteen and twenty, both were well over six feet tall, with broad shoulders and huge, hairy forearms. The boys, Horace, usually called Hoss, and Homer, nicknamed Mule, were thought to be the strongest men in the county. Someone had told Willis that they had been named after ancient poets. He wasn't sure about that, since Cob could barely read.

Amos led Willis and Eslie into the livery barn and closed the door. Several men were seated about the huge, black stove, which was now slightly red in places from the heat. Noticing the three men entering the barn, Cob yelled at Amos and came over to extend his huge hand.

"How's it goin', Amos? Where'd you pick up these two ole hounds?" he asked, referring to the two younger men. He also shook the hands of Eslie and Willis. "Come by to pick up my new plow; has it come in?"

"Sure has. Come in and sit down, and I'll have one of the boys load it on your wagon."

"Hoss, pull Amos's wagon round back and load up that new John Deere plow," Cob hollered at the eldest son.

Hoss left the group of visitors and moved toward the front of the barn. When he reached Willis and Eslie, he suddenly reached out, grabbed each with a big arm and produced head locks around the boy's heads.

"You guys been killing any deer out of season?" he said as he released them. Everyone knew that the two Calvert boys ignored all hunting and fishing regulations. Laughing, Hoss left through the barn door to get Amos's wagon.

"Let's get wiser," Willis said, straightening up his hair.

The boys took a seat on the back of an old buggy that had been brought in for repairs. The usual Saturday group was seated around the fire. Most of them spoke to the three newcomers. Odis had his pipe going full blast, emitting a sweet smell of aromatic tobacco. Several men had chews in their mouth.

"Parched peanuts," said Lyle, reaching out a pan towards Willis. "Grab some."

Willis took a handful and passed them on to Eslie. Amos was still off to the side talking with Cob. As in many of the recent gatherings, Bill Hansen was directing most of the conversation. Willis looked around the circle and then ducked as Bartis playfully threw a peanut at him and missed.

"That's the way you'll shoot Yankees," Willis joked. After the newcomers were recognized and welcomed, the conversation returned to the former subject—the coming elections and the meeting of the state convention to again decide the fate of Arkansas.

"I have talked to several assemblymen in Little Rock including Gil Harvell at Dardanelle," the lawyer was saying. "With Lincoln's recent threatening speeches, there is overwhelming sentiment that the new convention will now vote for secession. One assembly member even thinks that sixty to sixty-five convention members will now vote for secession."

The lawyer put his hand over his mouth and coughed a couple of times. One man, a strong Unionist, got up shaking his head and left the group.

"The next step is joining the new Confederacy at Montgomery, Alabama. Incidentally, they now have a provisional president. Feller from the Vicksburg area by the name of Davis. Now, it's possible that the log splitter will try to attract the seceded states back into the Union. But I doubt it."

"Men, I'm in favor of sticking with the Union," said Mule,

holding up his hand. "We haven't done bad here with our store. Besides, Lincoln can't do much lessen the Congress allows."

Someone agreed vocally. Others openly voiced their opposition to Mule's comments. Hoss had gotten back from loading the new plow on Amos's wagon. He picked up the last part of the conversation. "I think we gotta give the new president a chance. He even said that he would not mess with slavery in the South."

"Slavery to most of us is not the issue, although Lincoln is against extending slavery into any new states," Amos commented. "That means that the territory west of Indian Territory is going to be made into free states. That in itself is not so bad. However, again, remember, it's really a problem of representation. We will eventually have a handful of congressmen from the South and a huge majority from the non-slave holding states. Will we be able to get anything through Congress?"

This brought a mixture of comments, almost all in agreement with Amos. The lawyer got up off a bale of hay, put his thumbs in his belt, and looked around the barn as if ready to make an important statement.

"I differ from my good friend Hoss. Our culture, our lifestyle, our economy, almost exclusively agricultural, is most like our Southern neighbors. We raise more cotton than three of the states that have already seceded. Our fortunes lie with trusted Southern people from Mississippi, Louisiana, and Texas, not with the manufacturing interests of Illinois, Massachusetts, or Ohio. Mark my word, you will see Maryland, Virginia, Tennessee, Kentucky, Missouri, and maybe even Kansas become a part of the new Confederacy."

This reasoning made a lot of sense to the majority of the men. Most of the families that had settled in Yell County had not only come from the Southern states, but many also still had relatives in those states. Bartis, for once, had been very quiet. Unlike some of the younger men, he never minded giving his opinion.

"There's still another question to be answered that we haven't brought up." Raising his voice slightly, he said, "What we gonna do if Lincoln decides to use force against the South in order to keep it from breaking up?"

He looked back towards Hoss and Mule. Neither one responded. Lyle felt the question was a good one.

"Men, you heard me say before that I ainst gonna go fight for slavery. I wouldn't do that if I owned slaves. But, the day that out-of-state troops cross the state line to attack us and our homes and property, I'll fight. I think any man that wouldn't might be a coward."

Willis thought Lyle had put it pretty clear. He looked over to see Hoss drop his head and shake it slowly, as if he could not believe what Lyle had said. Most of the younger men, including Willis and Eslie, agreed with Lyle. A couple of the older men, including Amos, said nothing. After all, their sons' lives could be on the line. Doctor Rhodes, well respected by all, had been sitting and listening to the conversation. Now, he slowly stood up and looked over at the lawyer, as if to point out that he had another view of the situation.

"No doubt, slavery is questionable," he began in his low, bass voice, "even if used in the Old Testament times of the Bible. But we in this country have gotten ourselves into a serious situation. We allowed slavery in all states. Before long, we had thousands of slaves, some say three or four million slaves. Most were located in the South where they were utilized to produce cotton. In some of our Southern states, like Mississippi, we have almost as many blacks as whites. And, many plantation owners have abused their slaves, causing the blacks in many places to hate Southern whites. With mistreatment, some blacks have risen up to challenge and even kill whites. We had the Nate Turner rebellion, where Turner and about thirty of his followers rose up and murdered several plantation owners and their families in Virginia.

"So now, we have a new fear. Could there be a serious slave uprising? In '57 or so, John Brown, a white man, with several white followers, attempted to capture the federal arsenal at Harpers Ferry and seize weapons to use in rebellion. He was caught and hanged, but who could be next? Abolitionists say free the slaves. But, what would happen if we had three million freed slaves on the roads—especially if led by abused, aggressive slave leaders.

"What's the answer? Lincoln at one time suggested that the blacks could be sent back to their homeland, Africa. Plantation owners want their slaves to cultivate cotton and make them money, but yet many of them are terrified about a black rebellion. We have brought this problem on ourselves and now we must come up with a solution to the problem. Northern folks don't always understand the problem, although they may understand if three or four million freed blacks move to Northern states to live. They may then fear rebellion. Lincoln believes that war may be the solution—but what after that? So, gentlemen, we must consider the entire picture."

The doctor turned and moved toward the door. Cob changed the subject to the spring plowing, and gradually the group broke up as men moved on about town to take care of business.

~~~

HAYES WAS NOW OLD enough to handle most of the chores around the farm. Except for a serious bout with the measles,

Georgia Ann was providing more help to her mother. Eva and the two younger children prepared and planted the family garden, approximately one half acre. Financially, the Loflands were doing as well as any farmer in the Fourche River valley.

As usual, May arrived with the heavy, spring rain. The rains kept the Loflands out of the fields and even washed away some of the choice bottomland near the Fourche River.

Willis had written Rosalie a letter in late April. He received a reply from her the second week of May. In the letter, Rosalie agreed with him that she too had really enjoyed the time they got to spend together earlier. She asked about Bartis and especially Eslie. She reminded him that she had been praying for Eslie and his father.

Rosalie mentioned that her father had been quite ill again. Willis hated to here this because he knew that when the preacher was sick, there was no one but Rosalie to do all the farm work. And Willis knew that this included feeding cows, slopping the hogs, taking care of the chickens, and working in the garden. But Willis worried even more about what would happen if Rosalie's father passed away. Rosalie had no other relatives west of Memphis. But Willis realized that the reverend had made it through several such illnesses and he would probably survive several more such illnesses.

Rosalie ended the letter with an invitation, through her father, to come to Chula and visit them. Eva, suspecting that the two young people were in love, encouraged Willis to make the trip to Chula. As Willis carefully folded the letter and prepared to put it back into the envelope, he heard someone shouting. Hayes had completed his daily chore of watering the chickens and gathering the eggs and was in the breezeway, excitingly talking to Eva.

"He did it again. I told you! The red fox killed and took another chicken, except this time it was the rooster."

"Oh no," responded his mother. "I'm going to get that Yankee fox."

"Maybe he was starving or needed food for his pups," said Georgia Ann, who usually defended the fox or any other chicken vandal.

"Georgia Ann, you're so dumb!" Hayes said angrily, turning toward his sister. "You'd defend that fox if he killed one of the mules."

"Young man, you will apologize to your sister for calling her dumb. That's no way for a Christian to talk," Eva said.

Hayes delayed several seconds before he issued his apology. "I'm sorry, and I hope the fox is sorry."

Eva never saw Georgia Ann quickly stick out her tongue at Hayes and leave through the breezeway.

Willis had heard most of the conversation. Now he addressed Hayes.

"This evening, we will go out and practice on your shooting," he said. "We don't want you to miss the fox when he shows up again."

"Can we, Willis?" Once again, his idol would come to his aid.

Chapter 7

A Good Trip

WITH IMPROVED WEATHER, AMOS and Willis spent most of the month of May plowing river bottomland along the Fourche River. Cotton prices were up now, with cotton selling for almost twelve cents per pound. Amos knew that in a good year an acre of river bottomland could produce several hundred pounds of cotton. Weather permitting, Amos hoped to put in twenty to thirty acres of cotton.

With last year's recovery, a second team of mules was leased and Willis became a full-fledged partner in the family operation. Amos leased another ten acres north of Rhodes Landing to help Willis get started. Except for the possibility of heavy rain or war, the Loflands were hopeful of a good cotton crop and financial rewards. As Eva said, "The Lord is blessing us richly."

Two weeks passed before Willis could get away to Chula. Amos, noticing that the water level in the well was getting very low, decided that the well should be cleaned out. The well, hand dug as most wells, was about three feet across and about twelve feet deep. The only way to clean it was to send someone down into the well to begin removing rock, mud, and soil. This also required the water to be dipped out every so often. Willis, who had seen the well cleaned before, volunteered to go down into the well.

Amos would draw out the rocks and soil with buckets using the well pulley. After Willis reached the bottom of the well, he found that the water was only about a foot deep. As Amos sent buckets down, Willis would fill them with water and Amos would pull the buckets to the top and empty the buckets. After eight or ten buckets of water had been removed, the water level in the well was only about a couple of inches deep. Willis then began digging out the sediment at the bottom. After a period of time, Willis, now standing in about six inches of water, reported that he was scraping on rock. He also said that the water from the water table was coming in now, much faster.

"Get all the loose rock and soil in this last bucket and we will call it a day," Amos said.

Willis filled the last bucket. "Okay, Pa, that's it."

Amos drew up the bucket and then helped Willis get out of the well with a rope.

"Good job, son," Amos said, slapping him on the shoulders. "Ought to last for a year or two."

"Pa, you had the worst of it, pulling out those heavy buckets."

Eva had watched much of the work from the kitchen window. Now she stepped out on the porch. "I believe ya'll could handle some cherry pie. Wash up. Willis, wash off your feet and I will bring pie out here on the porch."

As Willis sat in the porch swing and ate the pie, he thought, yes, we have a good life. We may work hard and we may get dirty, but we have a good life. Would a war change things? Would the Loflands lose everything? What about Rosalie? Who would clean her well? Thinking about it, he once again thought of how much he wanted to see her.

~~~

THREE DAYS LATER, WILLIS took the leased mules and wagon and left for Chula. He reached Bluffton before 10 a.m. Since it was a Tuesday, there was little activity in Bluffton. Just before reaching the town of Rover, Willis came up on a man walking. When he stopped the mule team to see if he could give the man a ride, he noticed the man was black. This was quite unusual, since blacks were very seldom seen out alone. It was also unusual for a black to be seen anywhere in Yell County.

The young black male, who appeared to be about seventeen or eighteen years of age, had stopped walking to see what Willis wanted. The Negro was about six feet tall and had a light skin color, almost like an Indian. An old straw hat with holes in several places covered his closely cropped hair. The stranger wore old overalls, with large holes at the knees, no shirt, and well-worn shoes.

"You want a ride?" Willis asked the Negro, now standing with his hands in his pockets.

"Reckon so," said the man, who looked surprised that a white man would offer him a ride.

"Go ahead and get on board," Willis said, looking down at the man's old shoes and then back at his face. "I'm going about five or six miles before I turn south for Chula."

"If'en you don't care," said the Negro, putting a foot on the wagon well to climb up. Once he was in the wagon, he sat down toward the rear.

"You can sit with me in the wagon seat," Willis said, carefully watching the man.

The man got up, moved up to the wagon seat, and sat down beside Willis. Willis strapped the reins and the mules moved on up the road. After a while, Willis looked over at the man.

He couldn't help but notice how muscled up he was.

"Live around here?" Willis asked.

"Naw," the man answered, never taking his eyes off the road.

"Where you going?" Willis asked after some silence.

"Darenell." Once again, no eye contact.

"Do you live there?" Willis asked, assuming he meant Dardanelle.

"Yes'uh, I does," the man said, stealing a quick look at Willis.

Willis was now curious and certainly did not want to break any of the state's black codes. "You know Mr. Harvell? He owns a big plantation there along the Arkansas River."

"I's one of Massa Harvell's niggers," the man said, looking at Willis.

Willis now knew that he could be breaking the state law by illegally transporting a slave. Looking down the road, he could see his turnoff at Rover, about half a mile to the east. There was no more conversation until Willis got to the road leading south to Chula.

"I'm going south here," he said, pulling on the reins and stopping the mule team. Then he reached in his pocket, pulled out a dollar, and reached out to hand the coin to the man.

Willis could tell that the man wanted to say something, and he finally spoke. "Sur, I thanks you much fo' the ride and I not 'lowed to take money. Massa might believe I stoled the money." He paused before continuing. "Sur, I was runnin' way until I gots to believing about my mammy, whose a house nigger at Massa's house. Plum change my idea and am going back to Massa." He stood up to prepare to climb down out of the wagon.

"What's your name?" Willis asked.

The man seemed to wonder if he should give his name, but finally answered. "Name's George."

Willis took out Rosalie's last letter and a carpenter's pencil. He turned the letter over and wrote a note to Harvell. The note read, "Mr. Harvell, I helped George get back to Rover. He will be back there by tomorrow. I hope you won't punish him severely." He signed the note, Willis Lofland of Gravelly. Willis, who knew the man could not read, gave him the note and told him what it said. Willis told George that he should give the note to Harvell.

"Thank yo, sur," the man said as he turned to go.

As Willis proceeded on south to Chula, he could not stop thinking about George. He only hoped George would get back to the plantation safely. He could not stop wondering how slavery ever got started.

~~~

IT WAS A BEAUTIFUL day, probably around eighty-five degrees, with little wind blowing and only an occasional cloud. As Willis passed the occasional farms, he always noticed the condition of the farms. Usually the farmer or his wife would be out either plowing or working in the garden. They always waved as Willis passed by.

Willis almost felt guilty for being away from home and not working. In the distance, he could see the Gotham farm. Considering the fact that Rosalie's father was a widower and also a preacher, Willis thought he did a good job of taking care of his farm. However, Willis also knew that Rosalie did a big part of the work around the farm, even helping with the hay.

Willis directed the mule team to the left, down the long lane running to the house. There was a cow, two calves, and four or five goats in the pasture to the left side of the lane. The preacher's two mules and a donkey were in the pasture to the right side of the lane. Nearing the small, two-bedroom home, Willis saw Rosalie out drawing water from the well. She saw him, put down the wooden bucket, and quickly started toward the wagon, while touching her hair with her hands. Her dress was homemade from a cotton feed sack, and covered by an apron. Her head was bare of a sunbonnet. The long, blonde hair, carefully brushed, hung down below her chin. Willis could not help noticing the tiny waist and the ample bosom. A big smile was on her face, and Willis could see her perfect, white teeth. She is truly beautiful in any attire, he thought.

He stepped down from the wagon just in time to meet Rosalie's outreached arms. Willis pulled her to him, wrapping his arms around her body and liking the feel of her arms on his shoulders. Pulling back, he looked quickly at Rosalie's beautiful green eyes, and then moved his lips down to her slightly colored lips. She responded in kind. The kiss was soft and brief, but meaningful.

"Willis, you surprised me. I wasn't expecting you or I would have dressed better."

"You could not look better, Rosalie," he said, examining her pretty face.

"Let's go sit down in the swing," she said, taking his hand. "Do you want something to drink? I have some lemonade."

Willis noticed the well-groomed garden, and he knew that Rosalie had done much of the work there. He allowed her to take a seat and then took a seat beside her.

"Where's your pa?"

"He went over to the Olivers," she said, waving a fly away. "Mrs. Oliver is very sick. We are afraid she may not make it. Father has been over there since yesterday. The Olivers are not members of the church, but they have been good friends. They only had one child, and she passed away at about eight years of age, so they need help."

"Will your pa mind me being here while he is gone?" Willis said, a little worried now.

"Oh, no, Willis, he trusts both of us. He thinks a lot of you and your family. Speaking of your family, how are they?"

"They are all well and good," he replied, hardly taking his eyes off of Rosalie. "Working hard as usual. Pa and I had to clean the well last week. It wasn't too bad. How 'bout you and your pa?"

"We're doing fine. Father is about over his illness, but I do worry about him. He is almost sixty now, and yet he works as hard as ever."

She looked at Willis and then quickly stood up. "You must be starving to death. Let's go pick some fresh tomatoes, and I will make us a ham sandwich."

"Sounds good to me," replied Willis, getting up from the swing. They went into the garden, which was just north of the house. Willis looked up and down the rows of the garden and then at Rosalie. "This is a beautiful garden. Everything is so neat. There are no weeds and the plants have been hoed around so well. Do you take care of it yourself?"

Rosalie reached down and picked a large, orange tomato. "Father helps some, and the Lord provides the rain and sunshine. I get plenty of help." She picked three more ripe tomatoes. "Come over and look at the corn. It's really growing well. If I can keep the deer and coon out of the garden, I think I will be able to can a lot of vegetables this summer."

Willis was looking at a ripe cantaloupe. "Is it okay to pick it? I love cantaloupe?"

"Sure. We will have sandwiches and cantaloupe for lunch."

The two friends started back to the house, stopping once to look at the green beans. While closing the garden gate, Rosalie invited Willis to come into the kitchen while she fixed lunch. When he entered the kitchen, he again noticed how neat and clean everything was. Rosalie asked if he would draw fresh water, and Willis took the dipper out of the bucket, laid it on the cabinet, and went back outside to the well.

The well was about twenty feet from the house. A roof extended out over the well opening. Willis released the well rope and allowed the bucket to descend down into the well. Two crows flew over toward the vegetable garden. In the distance, Willis could hear a dog barking, as if on the trail of an animal. As he slowly pulled the filled water bucket up to the top of the well, he thought about Rosalie. She was really something. How could he be so lucky? No doubt, she liked him as much as he liked her—or was it, as much as he *loved* her? Yes, he knew it. He loved her. She would make a wonderful wife. Should he bring this up to Rosalie?

Willis opened the back screen door and entered the kitchen, where he set the water bucket down and put the dipper back into the pail. She had picked up the flyswatter and was trying to kill a fly. Willis walked up behind her, put his hands on her shoulders, and slowly turned her around. He slowly pulled her close as he looked into her beautiful, green eyes.

Rosalie dropped the flyswatter and reached for his shoulders. His arms tightened around her, as her arms tightened around him. He lowered his lips onto Rosalie's slightly open lips. Their lips met and compressed. The kiss was warm and longer this time. Finally, Rosalie slightly pulled back and their lips parted.

"Rosalie, I want you to know…I love you very much." Their faces were still close together.

"And, Willis, I love you as well," she said and then turned. "I had better finish our lunch."

"What can I do?" asked Willis.

"Why don't you peel the cantaloupe? There's a knife in that second drawer there."

Willis found the knife and began to cut away the heavy outer coating of the cantaloupe. The interior was very orange. He cut it into two halves and began to remove the seed portion of the interior part of the cantaloupe. "It's just right," he announced.

Rosalie had cut two pieces of ham from a large salted piece of ham. She placed the ham on buttered pieces of homemade yeast bread that she had earlier baked and put two slices of tomato on each sandwich. After placing the sandwiches on plates, she put the plates on the table. Then she reached in the icebox, brought out a pitcher of lemonade, and produced a jar of sweet pickles.

"Sit down, Willis," Rosalie said, wiping her hands on her apron. They both sat down together at the table.

"Willis, will you ask the Lord to bless our meal?"

"Lord, we thank you for this beautiful day," Willis began his prayer. "We thank you for this wonderful food that you have helped us have. We pray for Mrs. Oliver, the sick neighbor. We thank you for Pastor Gotham and his concern for the sick." Willis paused, maybe a little unsure. "And Lord, take care of Rosalie. She is a wonderful Christian lady. In Jesus' name. Amen."

Rosalie raised her head, looked over at Willis, and then placed her hand on Willis's forearm. "Thank you, Willis."

The beginning conversation was mainly about the strong thunderstorm that had gone through three days ago. The heavy wind had blown three large pine trees over, down around the Gotham's hog pen. It had also lifted a couple of boards off the roof of the smokehouse. After hearing about a skunk that carried off a chicken the week before, Willis changed the subject.

"Rosalie, a war may break out soon. Arkansas will be getting ready right soon. Many men will sign up to fight for our state. Eslie, Lyle, Bartis, and I will probably sign up, if necessary. We don't know yet, but if that happens, I will miss you so much. I will worry about you. When the war is over, I will come back and see you — often. Oh, Rosalie, I want to marry you! We will both be old enough."

Rosalie had not missed a word, although a slight frown had occurred on her face when Willis mentioned the war. She looked down at the table and then back at Willis.

"Willis, I will pray for you daily and prepare for the day that I can become Mrs. Lofland."

"Thank you Rosalie. I will be back to take care of you."

The afternoon flew by as the two young people sat on the porch swing and talked of their early lives. Rosalie almost choked up while talking about her mother. Her stories clearly showed that Rosalie had been very close to her. As Willis glanced at a picture of Minnie, Rosalie's ma, he realized how much Rosalie looked like her. Minnie, like her daughter, was a very attractive woman. Willis was surprised when he learned that Minnie had been a school teacher at Plainview before she married Brother Gotham.

"What did she teach?"

"Mother taught arithmetic. She was very good with numbers. Father said that she always wanted me to someday be a teacher. I suppose I would have liked to teach — I do help in our Sunday school. Willis, I forgot to tell you, we now have a Negro child in the Sunday school class. Her parents are freed slaves from back East. They have three children, and Bessie is the oldest. I just love her."

Willis was interested. "What does Bessie's pa do?" "He is a blacksmith at Rover. Father said he is a very good blacksmith.

He's done work for father."

"How did they get in your church?" Willis interrupted. "The Negroes always have their own churches. Usually whites will forbid blacks from coming to their church."

Rosalie explained that the pastor had got to know Weldon when he had repaired some horse harnesses. Reverend Gotham had asked Weldon if they attended church. Weldon told the pastor that his family was Christian, but there was no black church for them to attend. The reverend explained that he was the pastor at the Chula Missionary Church. Reverend Gotham said he would talk to the church deacons about inviting the family to his church. Willis was carefully listening to the story.

"Father and the deacons met and talked about the family. We only have three deacons and they already knew Weldon. One of the deacons was not too crazy about inviting the family to the church, but father eventually won him over. Now this all happened about three months ago. Weldon brought Bessie and dropped her off at church for the first time about five weeks ago. Weldon sits in his wagon under a big tree until Sunday school and church are over. I know he wants to come in, but he's still not sure if he would be accepted. But, Willis, everyone is friendly and many hug Bessie. Father believes we may get the entire family. What do you think about that?"

"Boy, that's surprising," Willis said, looking up to where his left hand was clasped about the porch swing chain. "I mean, I don't have nothing against it, but I'm surprised that your church would go with it. Don't think it would happen at Gravelly, Bluffton, or at our church. I'm going to tell my folks about this. I know ma would approve, but I'm not sure about pa. You know, Weldon is free and all his family is free. That's important."

"Willis, if you were a deacon and had a vote, would you vote to accept the family?" asked Rosalie, who had listened closely as he talked.

"Yes, I know I would accept them," he replied, after thinking carefully about the incident. " I believe it's the Christian thing to do."

"I told father that you would feel just like us," Rosalie said, reaching over and giving his hand a soft squeeze. "I hope you will meet Weldon one of these days."

Willis got up from the swing and looked back to the west. "Rosalie, I've got to get home. It will be nightfall before I get there. Ma will be worried."

"I know, Willis, but we have had a wonderful visit. I hope you will come back soon."

"We did have a great time," Willis said as the two young people walked out to the wagon. "Will you continue to write me?"

"Yes, I will, and you write me back."

They had reached the wagon. Willis turned to see Rosalie looking up at him. He leaned forward and gently kissed her. Both held on to the kiss momentarily.

"I love you," Willis said.

"And I love you, Willis," Rosalie quickly responded.

"Tell your pa hello and to come and see us," Willis said, climbing up on the wagon. He waved, popped the mule's reins, and pulled the mules into a semi-circle to go back up the lane to the main road.

Rosalie also waved. She did not move until the wagon was completely out of sight. Then she quietly said, "Take care of Willis, Lord."

As Willis traveled back over the same road to his home, he thought much about the day's events and the conversation with Rosalie. He had told her that he loved her, and she had said she loved him. He hoped the war would end before he had to go. Gosh, he would miss Rosalie. And he thought again about the free black family that had been invited to a white church. Willis thought, my world is changing, right in front of my eyes.

It was dark when Willis reached the Lofland home. After unhitching the team of mules and removing all the harnesses, he put the mules back into the pasture. In the distance, Willis could hear the yelps of coyotes. It sounded like the pack was up near the cat den. He moved back to the house and then down the breezeway to the living room.

He quietly opened the door. In the living room, the family had begun the evening devotion. Amos was reading the Bible. He stopped reading when he saw his son.

"Glad you're back," he said. "Have a seat and tell us about your trip later."

Willis noticed that all eyes were on him. As he took a seat in one of the caned, dining room chairs, he had a thought. Ma and Pa always put God and worship ahead of everything, even his own return. Willis respected his parents for teaching their children to honor God first.

Amos finished reading in the ninth chapter of Luke and then looked to Georgia Ann. "I believe its Sissy's turn to pray."

Georgia Ann was glad to be old enough to pray somewhere other than in her own room at nightfall. She began her prayer, "Lord, thank you that you have brought Willis back. Thank you that he didn't get lost or kilt on the road." Willis thought he heard Hayes snicker. "And be with us as we can the green beans tomorrow, and be with Ahab; we think he got beat up in a coon fight. And help Hayes and me not to fight so much and get whippings."

No doubt, Hayes did snicker this time. Georgia Ann ended her prayer.

"Good, Sissy," Amos said. Willis noticed that he gave Hayes a stern look.

"Well, tell us about your trip," Eva said, looking over at Willis. "How are Rosalie and the pastor?"

Willis, much like his father, was good at describing an incident. He left out few details in generally describing events in careful, chronological order. Willis began by telling the family about picking up the black slave, George, west of Rover. His family asked several questions about this encounter. Amos cautioned Willis about his actions.

"Willis, if the authorities had stopped you while George was aboard the wagon, and found that George had no papers, you could've been charged with assisting a runaway. I understand why you stopped, and I am glad that you are compassionate toward the darkies, but still, we must obey the law. Course there is another point. You never know whether he might have a knife and do you in and steal the team and wagon."

Even the two younger children were carefully listening to their father. "See, my prayer helped," Georgia Ann said.

"You prayed after Willis met the slave," Hayes said, wanting some input.

"Well, the Lord saw that nothing hurting anybody happened," Eva said in her usual soft voice. "And Willis is home and Georgia Ann's prayer was good and helpful."

Georgia Ann beamed and Hayes frowned. For the next half-hour, Willis described his trip and his visit with Rosalie.

"Well, Rosalie is a fine Christian lady and a hard worker as well," Eva again spoke up. "I am also impressed that she and the pastor have invited the black family to church. Jesus taught us to act this way."

"It was a Christian thing, all right," Amos said, feeling it necessary to agree with his wife. "I just wonder if our church would have accepted this family. Maybe our deacons should talk about this at our next deacon's meeting."

Eva stood up. "It's bedtime, and we have a long trip day after tomorrow, and a lot of canning to do tomorrow if we go to Dardanelle."

Hayes and Georgia Ann had already taken a bath in the large wooden washtub, with Hayes complaining that he had to be second in the water. They went out the door, across the breezeway, and into their bedroom. After some talk about the next day's events, Willis got up and crossed the breezeway to his own bedroom. Amos also went on to bed. Eva took another half hour or so to wash the kitchen floor. This task, almost daily, resulted in her washing the floor by hand while on her knees. The floor was exceptionally clean every morning at breakfast. Most of the family was already asleep by the time Eva came to bed.

Amos was feeding the livestock the next morning when the rain came, and he was soaked by the time he had completed the morning chores. The rain did not slack off until the afternoon, but it did not hamper the vegetable canning. By nightfall, Eva announced that twenty-one quarts of green beans had been canned and set to cool before being placed in the root cellar.

Chapter 8

Dardanelle

May 1861

FRIDAY WAS A BEAUTIFUL day, starting with a magnificent sunrise. The clouds had moved on east and the light, southern breeze brought in warmer air. It would be a good day to travel. Eva got everyone out of bed early to be ready for an early departure. She had breakfast ready, along with a packed lunch. All family members were excited about the trip to the county seat.

Georgia Ann had only been to Dardanelle once, while Hayes had been there twice. Even Willis had only been there four or five times. Eslie arrived at the Lofland home just after breakfast. He declined to eat, reporting that he had eaten at home. The livestock were given extra rations, since the family would be gone for three days. The chickens were shut up in the chicken house so the red fox would not be tempted. Amos had the wagon hitched to the team of mules by 6 a.m. and everyone was in the wagon and ready to go by 6:30.

Saturday was sale day in Dardanelle, the county seat of Yell County. Except for special occasions, the people from the Gravelly area seldom traveled to the county seat since it was almost fifty miles east of Gravelly. However, sale day was good reason to make such a trip, especially if you had relatives in Rover, Danville, or one of the small towns in between that might put you up for the night as you traveled to the county seat.

After the recent, heavy rain, everyone was glad to see the sunshine. The smell of the ever-present pine trees was in the clean air. Amos drove the mule team, leaving Willis, Eslie, and Hayes to visit at the back of the wagon. The road to Dardanelle led east on to Bluffton, east again to Rover, and then north over the mountains and down into the valley where Danville was located. The county seat was about twenty miles northeast of Danville.

Only two eventful things happened to the travelers, but both were related. Nearing the Rock Creek crossing north of Bluffton, Amos found the low-water crossing to be quite deep, due to the recent rains. He finally took the wagon on across the creek, although the moving water was not far below the wagon bed. After going about a quarter of a mile, the left rear wagon wheel began to wobble and squeak. Before long, the wagon was wobbling so badly that the wagon was rocking from side to side. Amos stopped the mule team and the men got out to examine the wheel. Eslie crawled under the wagon to look at the inside of the left rear wheel. After examining the wheel, Eslie crawled out from under the wagon and looked at Amos.

"Mr. Lofland, the wheel hub has a big crack across it."

"I was afraid of that. I brought a spare but we need to replace the wheel before we go any further. Boys, take the ax and see if you can cut an oak about four inches around. We'll use it fer a lever. I'll look for a rock to use as a fulcrum."

Willis found the right sized tree and began to chop it down. Amos found a large rock and called for Eslie's help. Together, they were able to roll the rock out into the road and in position.

After Willis had trimmed the downed tree of branches, he brought it over to the rock fulcrum. Using the tree lever, they slowly raised the wagon. Willis, Eslie, and Hayes held up the wagon while Amos removed the damaged wheel. Eva rolled the spare wheel over to Amos, and he placed the spare wheel over the axle and replaced the pins.

"That high water back there at the creek didn't help none. I hope we won't have no more problems."

Within an hour the travelers made it to Rover. Amos pulled the wagon over under a huge, walnut tree and the men washed up in a nearby stream.

Eva unpacked a delicious lunch of fried chicken, potatoes, rolls, and peach cobbler. Willis noticed that Eslie was extra hungry.

"That was really a fine meal, Mrs. Lofland," he said after the meal. "Sure good chicken."

"Thank you, Eslie," beamed Eva, always proud of her cooking and always appreciative of compliments. "Still got more chicken if you would like some."

"I couldn't eat anymore, but thank you."

That night, the travelers stayed at Eva's sister's home in Danville. After departing for Dardanelle the following morning, the group reached the county seat around 10:30 a.m.

Dardanelle had been built on the south bank of the Arkansas River in the late 1700s. The Arkansas River Valley extended fifteen to twenty miles south of the river and four to five miles north of it. The river itself ran roughly from the west to the east and eventually on to the state capital at Little Rock. A smaller town, Russellville, had sprung up on the north bank of the river just north of Dardanelle. A ferry connected the two towns. Dardanelle was now an important stop-off point for the river steamboats that came up from Little Rock.

Economically, the town was all agriculture. The valley south of the river produced thousands of acres of cotton, which were ultimately shipped down the river toward Little Rock and even on to New Orleans. Several large plantations existed along the river in the Dardanelle area. Sherwood, the huge, 900-acre plantation owned by Gilford Harvell, dwarfed most of them. Sherwood was said to have more than 200 slaves working the fields. The owner, a former planter from Vicksburg, Mississippi, was also the state assembly representative for Yell County and a very influential voice in Little Rock.

County sale day was also a big social day for the residents. Several activities were usually scheduled for the second Saturday of each month, May through September. Outside of the livestock sale, there was a county picnic at the fairgrounds, a play hosted by a group of schoolteachers in the county, a horse race, and on occasion, a turkey shoot. More important was the chance for folks to see and visit with family, relatives, and friends from around the county, since most people were not able to come to Dardanelle more than once or twice each year. The May sale was usually the best-attended sale day, since it was the first county gathering of the year.

Willis could recall coming to the county seat on four or five occasions. Eslie had been there on one other occasion. That was in '58 when his pa was arrested for disorderly conduct. Eslie had walked and hitched rides in order to talk to the county sheriff about Ralph.

Amos pulled the wagon into the space between two large walnut trees near the fairgrounds. After tying the mules, Amos turned back to address the three younger members of the family. "Your ma is planning on us having a picnic lunch at 1:00 p.m. today. Let's meet back here at the wagon at that time. Your ma and I will look around a spell. Georgia Ann will go with us. Willis, you and Eslie watch Hayes. Be careful if you go down on the river to look at the steamboats — and look for a girlfriend for Eslie."

Amos grinned at Eslie and then reached up to the wagon to help Eva. Hayes, tickled to be designated an older male, looked at Willis and said, "Let's go down to the river."

Eva, overhearing the remark, called for Hayes's attention. "Hayes, you are youngest and you will do as the men desire. Do you understand?"

"Yes 'um," he said, slightly embarrassed now that his status had regressed so quickly.

The boys started back toward the main part of town and in the direction of the river. People were moving in every direction. It was almost difficult to walk with such a large number of people standing and visiting with friends. There were a large number of greetings.

"Hello."

"Where you been?"

"How you doing?"

"Good to see you."

Several Gravelly people were there, including Hoss and Mule Calvert. Bartis, who had spent the last week with his cousin at Ola, was there with his cousin, J.R. Hill, and they joined the threesome. Talk varied from such topics as planting, coon hunting, the horse race that afternoon, and politics.

"Have you heard all the talk about the state convention?" Willis turned to the Gravelly group and asked. "Man, everyone's talking about it."

"What's it about, Willis?" asked his little brother.

The boys continue to walk as Willis briefly explained what he knew to Hayes. "They had a state assembly meeting over at Little Rock last week. The assembly voted to secede from the

Union. That means we are no longer going to be in the United States. Sounds like we may be in the Confederacy."

"Don't bother me none," said Bartis, who was usually looking for girls. "May be interesting to be in a new government." By then, the boys had reached the river dock.

"Man, look at that boat there," said Hayes, pointing to a huge paddlewheel and reading the name on the side of the ship. "Andrew Jackson. Isn't he the president?"

"No, our president is, or maybe I should say was Abraham Lincoln."

After looking at a small fishing boat, the group decided to walk back to the sale barn. The boys had been at the barn for a half hour or so when Bartis, the only one of the boys with a pocket watch, announced it was a quarter of one o'clock. Bartis was usually on time for lunch, and Eva had lunch ready for the men by one o'clock. She had prepared most of it the previous evening at her sister's home in Danville. The menu included sliced ham, potato salad, canned tomatoes, corn, and bread. Eva had also brought a keg of cider along with sugar cookies. Bartis and J. R. were happy to be invited to lunch.

Amos had spent much of the last two hours at the sale barn. He had also heard much talk of the secession convention.

"What'd you make of it, Pa?" asked Willis. "What does this mean?"

Amos, always happy at a sale, had a rather worried look on his face. His wife's face matched it to some degree. "I really don't know, but we'll find out this afternoon. Gil Harvell is supposed to give a speech over at the race track. He's at Little Rock now. He ought to tell us something."

Except for Hayes and Georgia Ann's excited comments over the morning's activities, there was little conversation during lunch.

~~~

Gil Harvell, one of the few slave owners in Yell County, had moved to Dardanelle in '52 after serving in the Mexican War with such notable Southerners as Thomas Jackson, Robert Lee, and Jeff Davis. The planter, a natural politician, was handsome, with broad shoulders, dark, curly hair, and dark eyes. Gil could have had his pick of Arkansas women. Rather than picking a beauty, he married Willene Kilmer, the only daughter of Wilbert Kilmer of Kilmer and Sons, the largest store owner in Yell County. The match proved productive when Willene inherited more than 200 acres of land.

Gil managed to add another 300 acres along with several leases. Except for an occasional flood from the nearby Arkansas River, he had made more money every year since building his plantation. Gil first bought three black male at Vicksburg. Each year, part of the plantation's profits went toward the purchase of additional slaves. He owned 192 slaves in 1860, of which 181 were field hands.

His influence in the county increased as fast as his land holdings. In '58, Gil was elected to the Arkansas Assembly from Yell County. A devout Christian and deacon at the First Baptist Church, he was also an excellent speaker. In the first Arkansas Convention to consider secession, Gil, like most of the delegates, voted with Governor Rector to stay in the Union. Everyone was wondering how Gil would vote in the second convention.

In anticipation of Harvell's speech, a podium had been set up facing the grandstand. By two o'clock, it was full, with several people standing. Michael Havens, the mayor of Dardanelle and an avowed secessionist, introduced Gil that afternoon after the county horse races. Gil teased the mayor about losing the day's horse race before getting serious. No one had thought about the afternoon sun, and consequently, Gil would end up talking for almost an hour and a half, with the sun shining in his face. This only emphasized the facial muscles and quick movement of his dark eyes as he described the situation in Little Rock the previous week.

"Ladies and gentlemen, I have just returned from the recent convention in Little Rock," he began. "As you know, we were there to consider the status of our great state. This is the second convention held in Little Rock regarding this serious problem. In the first convention, the delegates made every effort to view the problems confronting our nation from every angle. Many referred to those delegates, including me, as Unionists. I think that we carefully and tactfully explained why Arkansas must remain in our beloved Union."

The planter used a handkerchief to wipe perspiration from his brow. "I spoke to you several times about my reasons for voting Union. Some of you disagreed with my reasons. Many of you have agreed that our future lies with the United States. As you know, I served in the Mexican War in an effort to defend our country. I love it dearly. The country paid for my education at West Point. The freedom that we experience has permitted me to be successful beyond my dreams. Of course, God has also blessed Willene and me. Everyone here knows that seven of our sister states, including three neighbors—Mississippi, Louisiana, and Texas—have voted to withdraw from the national government. The second convention in Little Rock met the last seven days. Everyone was heard from there. All the events that have taken place since Mr. Lincoln was elected were carefully reviewed and discussed. After seven days it was time to vote. The vote was sixty-five to six in favor of secession."

Applause and cheers were loud. After a drink of water,

Harvell continued. "With a motion to make the vote unanimous, a second vote was held. The final tally, seventy to one." The speaker's voice could not be heard over the long, continued applause. "A feller by the name of Murphy was the lone dissenter."

Several boos were heard from around where Bartis was sitting. "We have also heard from the new, provisional government in Montgomery, Alabama. The noted Georgian, Mr. Howell Cobb, is chairing that new government. A representative from Montgomery, Mr. Howard Chambers, lawyer from Shreveport, Louisiana, traveled to Little Rock and met with our delegation last week. The new Southern government is in the organization phase, but it is emphasizing policies that we in Arkansas believe in. Yet, I doubt that over three delegates would have voted to join our sister states of the South if we had taken such a vote.

"However, one development that occurred earlier did influence the convention delegates. President Lincoln issued a call to the governor of each loyal state for men. The purpose..." Gil paused for emphasis, "to handle the rebellion. People of Yell County, I did not vote for Mr. Lincoln. He was not on our ballot in Arkansas, but I believe him to be an honest man of much integrity. He has promised the nation before the election, and after the election, that he has no — I repeat — *no* plans to strike slavery from the southland. He has stated this on several occasions. Even as a slaveholder, I believed the president. I will admit that I question several of those men who surround the president. However, I believe the president to be a God-fearing man who has only the best interest in mind for the country.

"During the first convention at Little Rock, many delegates, including the honorable Governor Rector, supported the new U.S. government. I, myself, urged the convention to give the president a chance to prove himself. I will be honest; I believe that the great state of South Carolina reacted too quickly. However, as you also know, South Carolina has been threatening to withdraw from the Union for thirty years. May God rest Mr. Calhoun's soul."

The speaker paused again, wiped perspiration, and took a drink of water. He licked his lips, glanced around at the huge crowd, and began to speak again. "My Bible tells me that we are to respect those people in government and even pray for them. May God forgive me, but I am having trouble showing love and respect for a government..." Gil paused and raised his voice slightly, "a government that is requesting that the state of Arkansas provide troops that will be used to coerce or force our sister states to remain Union. This undoubtedly means war. War means killing my fellow human beings. I did that in Mexico, believing that the cause was just. I doubt that God would expect me to pray for a government that would kill Mississippi men, nor do I feel that I should support a government that would do harm to our southland."

Applause broke out all over the race track, especially among the younger men of Yell County. After pausing, the assemblyman went on with his speech. "Ladies and gentlemen of Yell County, the Little Rock convention, except for a single dissenting vote, has voted to withdraw from the United States."

Again, loud applause and cheers could be heard all over the fairgrounds. "Let me make something very clear. The question of slavery is on the lips of both North and South. As a participant in the institution, and even though the Bible sanctions the concept, I see the possibility of this part of Southern culture disappearing. We must admit that the United States is one of the few large countries in the world that continues to use this economic idea. We must begin to look at alternative solutions to our labor needs. One possibility is to attract the immigrants that continue to pour into the north in search of employment. Slavery must eventually go the way of other outdated institutions. But, for the present, the institution exists. With mixed feelings about slavery, I would not be inclined to participate in a war to keep the institution, nor do I think most Southerners would fight to maintain slavery. However, friends, believe me, I will most certainly fight, and fight with everything within me, if my state is invaded and homes, property, and lives are endangered. Who could call himself a man that would stand by and ignore armed militia as they invade our state and threaten our families?"

Applause was even louder now.

"We shall be considering the possibility of joining the Southern states, Confederation. If that is the path we must follow, we will pursue it in the most vigorous manner. But, I would ask every person within the sound of my voice to seek the ear of the Almighty God. Pray for your state officials that we might follow His will as we choose the direction of our state. And like Washington and Jefferson and the rest of our founding fathers said, may God always be in our midst. As any independent country would do, we must prepare for the security of our people. Governor Rector has asked county officials to organize and establish militia units. The militia units will have elected officers for organizational purpose. Units will meet on a prepared schedule to train, drill, and instruct men in the use of weapons, troop movement, and procedures of security. May each training session begin with a prayer to the Almighty. I would also like to announce that I am personally contributing five hundred dollars for the organization of a militia unit from Yell County."

He paused as applause again erupted.

"On the fifteenth of next month, a recruiting office will be open on Main Street next to Hampton's Feed Store. I will be there to assist in organizing our militia. I would ask all young men, ages eighteen to thirty-five, to consider joining the Yell County unit. As we do so, let us ever be in prayer that our services will never be needed."

The speaker stopped and wiped his brow again. "Thank you for listening to a long-winded politician, and enjoy the rest of the day in our beautiful county seat."

The applause started slowly, but before long almost everyone was on their feet, applauding, cheering, and whistling. Immediately everyone began talking about the recent changes in Little Rock.

"I got the first three members of the militia right here!" Bartis said, grabbing Willis by the arm and looking over at Eslie. Both Willis and Eslie laughed.

"What do you think, Lyle?" Willis asked. "You interested?"

Lyle, always serious, had obviously listened very carefully to the speech. "I suppose Mr. Lincoln is considering sending troops into the Southern states or he wouldn't have called for troops. I certainly would not answer that call as an American, and I have nothing against the president."

"Past president," retorted Bartis. "We are no longer a part of the American states and, therefore, Lincoln is not our president."

"But, are you going to join the county militia?" asked Willis.

Lyle was still thinking about what was said. "Since the militia is strictly for security, I think I will join."

"Then we're all in," Bartis shouted.

Hoss had been watching and listening to the conversation from a distance. "Seems to me like we are acting a little too quick. I don't feel scared enough to think we need a militia."

Eslie, who seldom offered an opinion in front of the group, considered Hoss his friend. He looked down at the ground as if trying to think of the correct words, before looking at the husky Norwegian.

"Hoss, it won't hurt none of us to learn about militia. I've even thought about joining the army before. You know, you don't put a scarecrow in your garden after the birds have eaten your plantings. Who knows, if the president sees us forming these militia armies, maybe he'll think afore he sends troops to Arkansas."

"You may be right," replied Hoss after being outvoted. "I hope so."

The trip back to Gravelly was extremely lively, with the conversation remaining on the state's political situation. Everyone was impressed with the senator's speech. Even Eva was impressed with the senator's sincerity and especially his strong belief in God. It was hard to justify war, but if one was convinced that God was involved in the matter, then war was a possibility. During the long trip home, Willis asked Amos if he cared if he joined the militia.

"Son, all fathers want their sons to be patriots. Yet, all fathers hate to have their sons go to war. If younger, I would probably want to join the militia. You are old enough to make that decision. I too would ask you to pray about your decision. If you then feel you should join, I will do without your services during the time that you are away. Hayes is old enough that he can begin handling most of your work anyway."

Willis respected his father more than anyone. He also knew that Amos always tried to see his side of a problem. As the wagon rolled on down the road between Bluffton and Gravelly, the three young men, Willis, Bartis, and Eslie, made plans to attend the militia meeting the following month.

Chapter 9

Coon Hunting

SINCE THERE WAS NO reason to go to town the following weekend, there was no more news of the state's political situation. Willis, while helping his father, thought a lot about the kind of training that the young men would undergo. After daydreaming for a while about the militia, Willis asked his pa about training.

"You have any idea what we'll do at Dardanelle?" Judging by his answer, Amos had also spent some time thinking about the subject.

"I expect they'll teach you how to stand at attention, how to march, and how to shoot. Probably most important though is discipline. A soldier must take orders, whether he likes them or not. You can't question the officer."

As his pa talked, Willis was thinking. He knew that Amos had raised him in a very disciplined family. He had never talked back nor even questioned his instructions. He could not see why discipline would be a problem until he happened to think of Bartis. Discipline would be a problem with Bartis. He had grown up arguing and talking back to his parents. He usually got in the last word.

Bartis might have a problem. Eslie would have no problem. He even obeyed his pa when he knew his pa was wrong. Lyle would also be a good soldier. He might even be officer material, he thought.

"Wonder how they pick officers, Pa?"

"Oh, I 'spec they vote, according to Harvell the other day. But remember, you have to obey the officers whether you know 'em or not. They may pick someone from Dutch Creek or Belleville you don't know."

At church on Sunday, the preacher reported that the state had voted to join the Confederacy and send representatives to Montgomery to represent the state of Arkansas. Few people were surprised at the news. The sentiment was largely in favor of joining the Confederacy.

Saturday night was usually coon-hunting night. Amos had taken the younger men coon hunting for years. Now, with the young men in their late teens, Amos decided to allow them to go coon hunting on their own. Over the last couple years, Willis, Eslie, and sometimes Lyle and Bartis hunted together. All four men had at least one coonhound. The hunt was a serious social event, and a considerable amount of preparation went on prior to it.

First, one needed good boots, especially in the warmer months due to poisonous snakes. Each man usually brought his own horn, used to call one's dogs, and usually made from the horn of a cow. Someone usually brought an ax, which they could use in case they needed to fell a tree with a treed coon. Other necessities were a knife, food snacks, fire flint, and plenty of chewing tobacco. Once, Bartis had brought some "white lighting."

The men usually left with the dogs around 10:00 p.m. They did not turn the dogs loose until the group had reached the best hunting area. Once the dogs were loosed, then the men followed, listening to the different dog sounds. It was easy to determine when the dogs were on trail and when they had treed a coon. Usually, the hunt occurred in the mountains north of the Lofland home. But much of the hunt consisted of the hunters sitting around a warm fire listening to the dogs and waiting for a treed raccoon or a possible dog–coon fight.

On a warm evening, Willis, Eslie, Lyle, and Bartis left Willis's home around 9:30 p.m. in the wagon. Willis directed Murt and Kate down through the pasture north of his home and on to the northwest pasture. At the furthest point, the pasture was about a mile from Willis's home. The travel was easy here, as Willis followed an old pasture road near the tree-lined, west edge of the pasture. After arriving at the northwest pasture, the wagon team was tied up, the dogs loosed and the hunters moved back into the mountains, following the dog sounds. Before long, Ahab hit a trail. Shortly after that, Red, Bartis's seven-year-old redbone hound, picked up that or another trail. Soon, the hills were alive with numerous howls and yelps. Occasionally the men could hear Lyle's walker. It was easy to pick up the deep bass sound. After walking for about an hour, the men found a convenient place for a campfire and a place to wait and listen.

Using some flint stone and dried grass, Eslie, always the best at building one, came up with the fire. The others gathered larger pieces of dried oak to put on the fire. Before long, a comfortable fire was going. Each man had found a large rock or log to sit on. No sooner than the four men had got seated, Bartis passed around the chewing tobacco. All took a chew except Willis.

It was a beautiful night. The sky was so clear that the Big Dipper could easily be seen. A three-quarter moon gave out maximum light. Along with the dog sounds, the men could also hear the normal sounds of the timber. They often heard the yelp of the coyote, and the occasional, mournful hoot owl sounds.

"Man, what an evening," exclaimed Bartis. "I could do this every night."

"You got to love it," joined Lyle.

A shooting star streaked across the sky. Shortly after that, they heard a loud scream.

"It's one of the cats, probably up around the cat den." Willis did see the big cats once in a while, but it was usually near sunrise or shortly after sunset.

"Hope he's eaten supper," said Eslie.

Bartis, who always talked the most, began to tease. "Willis, is it true you 'bout to get married? Heard you and Rose are already looking for a house. Won't be long till you're hunting days are over—couple kids."

Lyle and Eslie both chuckled, knowing that the comments probably embarrassed Willis. Willis tossed a small stick on the fire. "Listen, Walker's treeing. We got a fight soon."

"You trying to avoid the war, Willis?" the teasing went on. "You can't go if you have four kids and one in the oven."

"Bartis, you're the first one looking for girls when we go to Gravelly, and especially Dardanelle," Lyle said, deciding to defend his friend. "I didn't think you were coming home from the county sale after seeing the little redhead."

"Boy, was she a looker," responded Bartis, glad Lyle had brought up the little redhead. "She was pretty as Rosalie. Of course, she was really giving me the eye, but that's normal."

Three or four loud, excited yelps interrupted Bartis.

"There're on trail," Eslie said.

"Old Red's even yelling," Lyle said in agreement.

"Let them run a while," Willis said. "Sounds like they are north of Rock Creek, probably on the old Mannard place."

Willis decided to tell the other three men about the slave that he picked up near Rover. They listened, although Bartis did interrupt when Willis told of giving the slave a ride.

"You crazy, Willis?"

Willis continued his story and eventually finished by telling how he dropped off the man when he turned off for Chula. The other three men listened as they looked into the fire, with an occasional glance toward Rock Creek and the sounds of the coonhounds.

"First time I've talked much to a slave but, hey, I did feel sorry for him," Willis said after finishing his story."

"I'd have done the same thing, Willis," Eslie quickly responded. "I got no problem with Negroes."

"It's really not their fault that they are here," Lyle agreed. "I feel sorry for them."

"They're better off here in the states than in Africa where they might be eaten by relatives," Bartis said, almost interrupting both Eslie and Lyle. " Not our fault that they's slaves. But it is legal. Not agin the law. If we were slaves in Africa, we'd just have to make the best of it. Course, Willis, you could have got your throat cut. Don't ya'll remember that Negro, Nat Turner, back in Virginia. He and other runaways murdered 'bout thirty whites afore they caught him and hung him. Willis, you could be dead."

"I know, but it didn't happen," Willis responded. "Why was George going back to the plantation unless he was a good Negro?"

"To avoid being caught and lynched," replied Bartis. "Willis, you in love and can't think clearly. I'm going to have to start going everywhere with you, including to Rosalie's, to keep you out of trouble."

By then, the dogs were all loudly howling, at the same location.

"Treed," said Eslie. "Let's go."

The four men put out the fire with dirt and then started north toward the musical sounds of the excited hounds. Twenty minutes later, they reached the treed raccoon. He was about thirty feet high in a huge gum tree. The hounds were going crazy at the base of the tree. Above the loud barking of the hounds, the men could hear the deep, bass howl from Red.

"Eslie, climb up and knock him out," shouted Bartis.

Eslie, carrying the candle lantern, moved over near the base of the huge gum tree and picked up a dried, fallen limb. He broke off a piece of the limb about eighteen inches long and stuck it in his belt.

"Gimme a boost," he said, turning to Lyle.

"Okay," Lyle said, clasping his two hands together to form a step.

Eslie put his right foot into Lyle's clasped hands and pushed up while grabbing the tree. Standing as tall as possible, Eslie began to grasp the tree with his knees and above with his hands. He moved several feet up the tree before reaching a large limb. After pulling himself up on the limb, it was easy to reach other higher limbs. By now, Eslie was about ten feet below the treed raccoon. The frightened raccoon was now hissing at the threatening Eslie. As Eslie stood completely up on the limb, he pulled out the piece of limb to use as a club, if necessary. The raccoon turned and started out toward the far end of the limb that he was sitting on, and the limb began to bend downward.

The raccoon had to make a decision—either face the threatening human being in the tree, or jump to the ground and face the barking dogs. The odds seemed to be in favor of jumping. The raccoon hit the ground running. Red and Ahab, carefully watching, were in motion before the enemy had reached the rocky soil. The chase was on again. The raccoon headed straight for the water in Rock Creek, and then quickly went into a deep hole of water about five feet deep. The men were close behind. Willis was able to grab Ahab's old collar. Red, as many times in the past, went into the deep pool after the raccoon, while Bartis screamed at him. Safely is his own element now, the raccoon attacked the old redbone hound. As Red retaliated, they heard growling, screaming, and water splashing all around. Then the two fighting animals went under the water again.

There was still swirling water underneath the surface for a time and then all was quiet. The victorious raccoon slipped over to some bushes in the water and then out of the creek on the other side. The men stood watching without moving. Slowly, Bartis waded out into the creek. He reached down into the water, feeling around for the old redbone hound. Finally, he found the drowned dog. The raccoon, though undoubtedly wounded, had won the battle. Red's deep, bass voice would not be heard again.

After another brief fire to warm and dry Bartis, the men moved back to the team and wagon. Another Gravelly coon hunt was history, but this hunt would be talked about for years.

Chapter 10

The Militia

THE TRIP TO DARDANELLE was an exciting and informative one. Everyone was talking about the formation of the new militia unit. Most of the eligible young men in Yell County were planning on joining the new militia unit.

There were more than fifty men waiting in line in front of the building now referred to as Recruiting Office, State Militia. It seemed to Willis that everyone was at Dardanelle that day. The men in line were talkative and cheerful. Bartis had a stick over his shoulder, showing everyone how to march. As usual, he had everyone's attention. Lyle, up near the front of the line, was watching Bartis's antics with an expressionless face. Eslie was grinning at his friend. Willis wondered how many would be laughing in a few months.

Amos and Eva had said little about Willis's decision to join the army. His little sister had cried and Hayes had wanted to go with him. Willis knew that his ma and pa were worried; yet, at the same time, they seemed proud of him.

The line moved forward as some of the men completed induction procedures and left the building, causing others to move up in line. A rather heavy recruit, a man from Ola that Willis had seen before, walked out of the recruiting office. He stopped near the front of the line to talk to an acquaintance.

"Guess whose forming the regiment? It's Harvell. He's going to train everybody."

"That's good news," Willis said to Eslie. "We'll have a real soldier to train us."

The sign up was over at a little past noon. The new, militiamen were supposed to meet at the Methodist Church at 1:30 p.m. for a general meeting before going home. After eating lunch that they had brought, the Gravelly contingent walked over to the church where several other men had already gathered. At almost 1:30, Gil Harvell arrived. There was something different about his demeanor and his walk. He looked very serious. Gil moved up in front of the men to address them. Everyone grew quiet in anticipation of the talk.

"Gentlemen, I have been commissioned a colonel in the state militia by Governor Rector. While I appreciate the confidence that the governor has shown in me, I feel a very heavy responsibility to the state of Arkansas and maybe even more so to the men that I will command. Men, you know me as Gil Harvell, a deacon in the church, the store owner, the planter, or the politician. As the commanding officer of this unit, my personality may change somewhat, again, due to the responsibility that I must assume.

"Let me make one thing clear. We are not here to play soldier. We are here to become soldiers. That will require me to assume an officer's posture. To do that, I cannot simply ask you to follow instructions. I must command you to follow orders. I have obviously been influenced by my experience at West Point and even more so by my time in the Texas–Mexico War. I suppose that I have been most influenced by the commandant at West Point, Colonel Robert Lee. There were other military men that I admired. Winfield Scott, Hardee, and Rosecrans were all impressive men. But, I am Gil Harvell, different from others. I must organize and direct this militia unit my own way. Hopefully, you will learn the important procedures necessary to become soldiers. Any questions so far?"

Bartis held up his hand and the officer nodded toward him. "Sir, what should we call you?"

"Good question," Gil said, smiling. " It would be best if everyone addressed me from now on as colonel. I will not let the title go to my head."

Lyle raised his hand and received permission to speak. "Sir, we know that an army has different branches such as infantry, cavalry, and artillery. Will we have such branches in the militia?"

"Good question. What was your name?"

"Lyle Parker, sir."

"Lyle, you know quite a bit about the army. In answer to your question, Lyle, the regiment will train as infantry. After a period of time, we will review the duty and responsibility of both cavalry and artillery. Another branch is supply, a service that functions through the quartermaster. We are talking about teamsters, or drivers of wagons. This is also an important branch of service."

Willis glanced around at the men. All were between eighteen and thirty-five years old. All were very serious. They also seemed to be impressed with Harvell and his knowledge of the army.

"In order to be effectively organized, we have what we call chain of command," Harvell continued. "We will have several officers that will function under my command. I will appoint the ranking officers. The lower officers, sometimes referred to as non-commissioned officers, will be elected by the regiment. Each company or branch of the regiment will have an officer with elected officers reporting to him. About the third meeting, and after you have had a chance to observe your fellow soldiers, we will have elections to decide who the lower officers will be. In the beginning, the training may be boring, since much of it can be received only through instruction. You will learn how to form rank, how to march, and how to load and fire your musket from formation. Any other questions so far?"

A tall, thin-faced man with a receding hairline held up his hand, and the colonel nodded for him to speak.

"Sir, some of us'ins only have shotguns. Can we use shotguns a while we are training?"

"Good question. You may not only use shotguns in training, but you may also have to use your shotgun if real war comes."

The colonel looked from the thin-faced man back over the entire crowd. "We can't afford to buy muskets and most equipment at this time. However, I have arranged with Governor Rector to get powder and shell from the arsenal at Little Rock. It should be here by next meeting. Since we have already been here for almost four hours filling out paper and listening to me blow and go, we are going to form rank, learn some basics, and then go home. Many of you have a long trip home. Men, let's move outside into the churchyard."

The colonel turned and walked back toward the front door. The group followed the officer to the clearing just west of the church. After everyone had reached the officer, Harvell began to address the men again.

"I want ten men to form a straight line across in front of me with ten men behind the first ten, and so on, until everyone is in one of the ten lines." The colonel drilled the regiment for almost an hour before reforming at "attention" and then being "dismissed."

The trip home was one that the Gravelly boys would remember for a long time. Bartis, always the clown, did a good impersonation of Colonel Harvell.

"General Eslie, do you know which is your right foot?" he imitated, in a tone quite similar to that of the colonel. "I suggest you carry a rock in your right hand so's you'll remember which is your right side."

As the other three men laughed, Bartis continued, this time mocking Eslie, in the manner of a poor black man. "Sur, I ordinarily wipes my butt with my right hand. I will try to think abouts wiping my butt whens I needs to use the right foot."

The other three men, including Eslie, were rolling all over the wagon laughing. That usually caused Bartis to exaggerate even more. Assuming the disposition of the colonel again, Bartis continued. "General, are you talking about the butt of your gun or are you talking about that sack of blubber you sit on?"

Lyle and Willis were almost crying as they listened to Bartis's almost perfect imitation of the officer. Soon the conversation turned serious as the men discussed the obvious capabilities of the Dardanelle politician. Each man was very complimentary of Harvell.

"I believe we're going to be all right," Lyle said, in his very serious manner, as usual. "Colonel Harvell knows his business. If everyone will listen to him, they will become decent soldiers."

Willis was shaking his head in agreement. "You know, we're lucky here in Yell County to have a West Point man to organize our guard."

Such talk continued as the evening turned into nightfall. It was almost 1:00 a.m. when Willis got home. He was tired, both from the training and the long trip, but he had to admit, he had enjoyed the day. After all, he felt that he had learned a lot about becoming a soldier, and he felt good that he had volunteered for the militia. It was good to know that a man was standing for what he believed.

After all, his grandfather had fought Indians with Governor Harrison, later to be President Harrison. Amos had told him stories about the Indian Wars back east. Willis felt a sense of pride in becoming a soldier like Grandfather Elliott.

Chapter 11

Lye Soap

IT WAS DAYLIGHT WHEN Willis awoke. Amos knew that the boys had gotten home at a late hour and decided not to wake him. Willis quickly dressed and went to the kitchen. Eva had left biscuits, sausage, and sausage gravy on the top of the old iron stove top. He picked up a biscuit, broke it open, put a big piece of sausage inside, and closed the halves. He poured coffee from the old gray coffeepot, took a bite of biscuit, and moved to the door to look out back.

Eva already had a wood fire going under the heavy, black iron kettle, filled with water. A wooden bucket and a round cardboard container were nearby. Willis took a sip of the dark, bitter coffee, stepped off the creaking back porch, and started toward his mother. Ahab, with a strong odor of skunk, approached Willis, wagging his tail.

"You've been hunting polecats? Smells like you got the worst end of it."

Eva looked up to see Willis and asked if he had eaten.

"Ma, you starting already on the soap?" Willis asked, nodding.

The wooden bucket contained hog fat. The brown container label said "lye."

"How'ed the soldiering go yesterday?"

Willis began to describe the previous day's events and especially what Colonel Harvell had said.

"Sounds like you like Mr. Harvell," Eva said, checking the temperature of the water in the kettle. She then placed extra wood on the growing flames. Willis took the last bite of sausage biscuit, much to Ahab's disappointment.

"He knows what he's talking about. He's worked with famous army men back east, including Robert Lee, the commander of West Point. I believe he already has the men's respect. We'll meet again in two weeks and spend Saturday night this time in camp. Also, we're going to elect officers next meetin'."

Eva was listening carefully as her son spoke more and more enthusiastic about the newly forming militia.

"You know, Ma, I'm gonna nominate Lyle for officer. Not only does he know a lot about the army, but he probably also has more common sense than anyone in Gravelly 'cept maybe Pa."

Eva poured a measured amount of lye into the bubbling water. "I'm sure Lyle would be a good officer. He's always been such a hard-working young man. He also sets the kind of example that the men need to follow. But, let's continue to pray to God that this war will stop before hundreds die."

Willis knew that Amos and Eva never prayed now without asking the Almighty to interfere before serious war broke out. Willis reached down, picked up the bucket of fat, and slowly poured it into the hot, lye water. Eva immediately began to stir the mixture with an old, worn, wooden paddle. Hayes, carrying a warm pail of milk, opened the old lot gate, closed it, and walked toward the fire and Willis.

"Man, if you going to whip Yankees, you gonna have to get out of bed before daylight."

He had already begun to assume many of Willis's chores

around the place. Milking was the one that he disliked the most.

"Hayes, you didn't kick old Bossy, did you?" Eva said, looking at her young son. She knew that Hayes was quick to punish the old red, white-faced cow if she kicked the milk bucket.

"I got her shaped up," Hayes said, grinning at Willis. "She's afraid to put her big foot in the bucket now."

Chapter 12

Basic Training

THE FIRST FULL DAY of militia training was quite interesting for the Gravelly boys. As Willis expected, Eslie, Bartis, and Lyle were all there with others to train. Missing were the Calvert brothers, Hoss and Mule. Lyle, who lived close to the brothers, said they would probably join later on.

"I hope so," Bartis said. "As big as they are, both of them can form their own company."

Willis had a different thought. Would they fight against the Union? Since there were no guns for the trainees, the men were "armed" with small, trimmed pine saplings.

"One thing about it," Bartis whispered to Willis, when given his musket, "Arkansas will never run out of guns."

Colonel Harvell began explaining the various commands and procedures that the men needed to know. The young men's respect for Harvell was growing stronger all the time.

By then, most of the Rebel trainees realized that they would have to march on a battlefield toward an enemy that was just as disciplined, and one that was also marching toward them.

"Boy, I hope we get to shoot first," said Frank, a young man from Briggsville who had gotten to know the Gravelly boys. "Going to be bad, marching toward the Yanks and all the time they are shooting at you."

Willis looked over at the slightly built young man. He had long black hair that frequently hung down over his eyes. Frank, a rather nervous young man, often jerked his head back to get the hair out of his eyes. Once the hair was off to the side, one noticed a thin face and a small mouth with protruding front teeth. His face was scarred with pits, probably from smallpox. Unknown to Frank, Bartis had nicknamed him "Buck."

Willis was yet to know how he himself would react in battle. However, he was in doubt about Frank's willingness to fight. He seemed to lack confidence at doing anything.

Two weeks passed before the new militia came back for more training. Colonel Harvell was even more businesslike than earlier. The men reviewed the elementary steps that they had learned at the last meeting. They quickly realized that they were not playing a game. Harvell did not request; rather, he commanded. He was also quick to correct and reprimand the men when they made mistakes.

One of the first men to be reprimanded for talking was Bartis. Three or four others were scolded for marching out of step. It was clear to most that this new unit would be disciplined. After an hour or so, the colonel turned the group over to Captain Hunt, who asked the men to sit down on the grass. Once the men were seated, the captain began to address them in a disciplined fashion.

"Men, today we will work mainly on two things. We will form up in a while and march six miles. On reaching the six-mile point, we will reverse our movement and come back here. The total mileage will be roughly twelve miles. I will be timing our hike. Once we get back, we will go over to the hill and review firing procedures. The idea: get used to marching, getting tired, and then accurately concentrating our firepower.

"Earlier, you were told to pick up a canteen and fill it with water. You will need that on our march. You must preserve your water supply. Make it last. Some other things that you should check: your shoes should be sound and your clothing should be loose enough to allow you to move freely without rubbing you raw. Also, you will be carrying your musket or limb, with your haversack on your back, filled with rocks. At all times, notice where the regimental flag is. In battle, you must know where you are. As the Good Book says, we may separate the sheep from the goats. Hopefully, there are few goats." Willis heard Bartis make a low blatting sound of a goat.

"Men, on your feet. Attention."

Willis was up quickly on his feet, as was Eslie. From the corner of his eyes, Willis could not see any goats.

"Columns of twos."

The men quickly formed two lines each in arm's length of each other. After the regimental flag moved forward and the bugle sounded, Hunt gave the command, "Forward. March."

The two long columns began to move west toward the outskirts of Dardanelle. In the distance, the men could see Mount Nebo. Early on, there were several barking dogs and a few curious onlookers, but the march went quite well. The regiment arrived back at Dardanelle in a little more than four hours. Captain Hunt complimented the men and then commanded them to take a short break.

"Well, was it tough for ya'll?" Willis asked, sitting down on the grass near Eslie, Bartis, and Lyle. All gave negative answers.

"We could have gone twenty miles," said Bartis, who spent less time at hard work than the others. "We are tough, country folk. The Feds are mainly city folks. They don't walk half the night out coon hunting or plow all day in the southern heat."

"You plowed much lately?" Eslie asked Bartis.

"Hey, I've done my share." Bartis winked at Willis. "When I plow, I have a haversack filled with rocks on my back."

Lyle, as he often did, listened without saying much. "I know soldiers are asked to march twenty miles in a day. And we will probably do so when we leave for possible battle."

Captain Hunt came back from conferring with Colonel Harvell. "On your feet men," he commanded.

After the men stood up, the captain continued with his instructions. "We will move to the shooting area and review some of the procedures that we talked about two weeks ago. Also, you should empty your haversack of the rocks at the range."

The men were divided into two groups after arriving at the range. Captain Hunt commanded one group while Colonel Harvell instructed the second group. The Gravelly men were part of Harvell's group. Again, the men were allowed to sit down on the grass. Harvell had four different muskets stacked along with a shotgun. There was shot and gunpowder. Harvell picked up one of the muskets and began talking about the guns.

"Men, we may be at a disadvantage in terms of guns. At least for a year or so, we must use the older muskets and even shotguns. Hopefully, we will be building new guns or importing them from Europe at some time in the future. One problem that we may face is a variety of different caliber muskets. This means we will have some problems with musket balls. Again, we hope to have some of these problems solved before we are faced with battle."

The speaker proceeded to go over each musket and point out differences between the guns. "Men, you will get nervous and excited in battle. You may even forget to follow some of the loading procedures. In the Mexican War, excited men sometimes loaded their muskets with three and four balls, with powder, before ever shooting. Men forgot to load. They forgot to seat the ball with the ramrod. Some would load a musket, charge the enemy, and fire, only to realize that they had left their ramrod behind. Others used excessive powder and then ran out of powder. Keep in mind that a musket can explode. You must check your weapon daily. You will cross rivers and streams, and you must keep your gun and your powder dry.

"Finally, eventually we will get bayonets. A bayonet is a knife on the end of your gun. Once in camp, we will review bayonet procedures. You will have to use your bayonet, and the enemy will have to use his bayonet. Gentlemen, the ultimate question that man asks of himself is, 'Can I kill another human being?' Normal. You can, and you must. The enemy will kill you. They will shoot you, bayonet you, cut your throat, or batter your brains out. And, no, the Feds are not poor soldiers. No, one Southerner cannot defeat three or four Federals."

"You haven't seen me yet," Willis heard Bartis whisper. "I can take out three at a time."

Harvell proceeded to give the men several tips on loading a musket quickly. "Men, there are basically ten steps in loading a musket. Listen carefully as I go through those steps." Harvell selected one of the muskets.

"One: Place your gun in your left hand to load. You will use your right hand if you are left-handed. Two: Pick up the paper cartridge with your right hand. Three: Tear the cartridge with your two front teeth."

Willis overheard Bartis whisper that Frank ought to be good at that step.

The officer continued. "Four: Pour the contents of the cartridge into the barrel, including the bullet, which you should push down with your finger."

Harvell moved his hand to his mouth and sneezed twice.

"Five: Draw your ramrod for use. Six: Ram the bullet into the base of the barrel with your ramrod. This should be firm. Seven: Take your ramrod out of the barrel and return it to its place along the gun barrel."

Harvell looked back to Bartis, who had made a comment. "Soldier, you might learn something that will save your life."

He glanced back over the group. "Number Eight: Place the cap into its position. Nine. Shoulder your gun firmly into your shoulder, and finally… Ten: Steady, aim and squeeze the trigger."

After a short question/answer session, the men went over to the range, where each man loaded a musket, repeated the ten steps, and then fired at a target twice. The Gravelly men all handled the guns well. Harvell complimented Lyle for his orderly and businesslike procedure. He was also quite accurate in firing the gun.

Exactly one month later, the 20th Regiment—mostly Yell County and Montgomery County men—was on its way to more serious training. The new destination was a town where few of the young Arkansans had ever been. Van Buren was a town of about 400 and in many ways much like Dardanelle. It was also a river town on the Arkansas River. Just across the river and another seven or eight miles west was Fort Smith, the second largest town in Arkansas. Everyone knew that Fort Smith had an impressive fort that had been used by the army for fifty years or so to control Indian Territory, which was across the Arkansas River west of Fort Smith.

Fort Smith had troops stationed there for years. When the state legislature voted earlier to secede, the loyal Union troops at Fort Smith were called back to Missouri. Most of the munitions and supplies went with them. However, now Van Buren was the Confederate base in western Arkansas. Close to a thousand Confederates were already camped there, and many more were arriving each day.

The 20th Regiment could arrive at the Arkansas River crossing with a twenty-mile march for six days. The ferry would take them across the river to Van Buren. If good weather continued, the regiment would be there in seven or eight days. However, before the group left for Van Buren, election of officers was to take place. The entire regiment was called together for election details. Colonel Harvell addressed the group for the first time since the third week of training.

"Men. No, soldiers—Confederate soldiers. Paper will be passed out for you to use in the elections. You should each take five of the small pieces of paper, since we will vote for five different officers. First, we will have nominations for each officer position. Captain Hunt will explain the procedures. But before we vote, let me make some comments about the people you are to elect. You have had a chance to see how your fellow soldiers react to orders, commands, and army procedures. You want to elect a leader, not a follower. You want to elect someone that you respect—someone who follows orders without complaining or whining. You want someone you can trust—especially while under fire."

The colonel paused, looked over the men, and beckoned to Captain Hunt. It took almost an hour to complete the voting and to tally the votes. Of the Gravelly men, both Willis and Lyle were nominated. Lyle was elected as lieutenant.

The long march began the next morning. There was a lot of talking and even laughter until past noon. By lunch, most of the men were tired. But Bartis still had enough energy to tease Lyle about his new position.

"Hey, officer, I voted for you. I think you might carry me piggyback."

Lyle just smiled. Everyone else was too tired to laugh. By nightfall, the men were almost exhausted. No one took the trouble to make a comfortable sleeping area. After a little of the new army food, hardtack, and water, each man quickly lay down and pulled his bedroll blanket over him. Fortunately, none of the Gravelly boys had to serve as sentries.

Day two was worse since everyone was tired and sore from the previous day's march. The second-day march turned out to be only eighteen miles. Lyle was not around his friends much anymore, due to his new responsibilities as lieutenant, but he was learning a lot about providing for a large group of men.

Since Lyle had not been able to talk to Willis for a while, he decided to go back to Company B and share some news with his friend. Lyle knew that Willis had not heard about the recent battle in southern Missouri.

"Colonel Harvell referred to the battle as Wilson's Creek. He also explained that the battle occurred south of Springfield, Missouri. According to Harvell, the battle occurred about a hundred miles northeast of Van Buren."

"Gosh, that's not that far away," exclaimed Willis after listening to the details Lyle related. "Who won the battle?"

"According to the colonel, we won the battle. Harvell said the two main Rebel generals were Price and McCulloch. Not long after the battle, McCulloch brought his division back across the border into Arkansas. More recently, Price brought his troops back to Arkansas. The two divisions are now camped not far from each other."

"So, we're going to join up with Price or McCulloch?" said Willis, who had been listening carefully.

"I don't know about that, but I would guess that we probably will. Gotta go, see you later."

"Thanks, Lyle. Take care."

As Lyle moved back down the road to the supply wagons, a rider stopped him. "You Lyle Parker?"

"That's right."

"You are to report to the quartermaster's wagon for instructions."

Lyle saluted and turned to go back north toward the quartermaster's wagon.

Lyle spent the next three days working with the sixteen supply wagons. Most important was selecting lunch stopping points, the overnight camping areas, and making preparation for meals and horse accommodations. The teamsters, for the most part, were familiar with mules and horses and how to use them efficiently while pulling the heavy supply wagons. Lyle's background and personality made him a natural for relating to the teamsters. Due to good planning and excellent cooperation between Lyle and the teamsters, the entire trip was shortened by almost a full day.

Chapter 13

Van Buren

VAN BUREN WAS A busy town now that it had become a serious outpost for the growing Confederate forces. The town was a little more diverse than Dardanelle in terms of the population. Bartis, always looking, observed several pretty women as the column moved through the town.

Willis thought that he had never seen so many military men. Although all were Rebs, several were in blue uniforms and several in gray attire. Willis thought it would be nice to have a uniform. Boy, would he like for Rosalie to see him in a new uniform. But, only seven or eight of this group had uniforms. Those were the upper ranking officers like the colonel and Captain Hunt.

"Willis, look, there are Indians," Eslie said as the men continued on their march through the city.

Willis noticed several Indians dressed much like the farmers who were also there to see the new Rebs. Willis also noticed that one or two Indians wore blue shirts, almost like the military shirts that some of the soldiers wore. He wondered if they were allowed to be in the army.

Later in the day, the marching Rebs neared the camp, which

had been established east of Van Buren in the Arkansas River Valley. It was a relatively flat area, probably created by the inconsistent flow of the river. As the group marched over a small incline, they could see the camp slightly below them. Eslie and Willis could not believe what they saw. There looked to be a thousand men. There were several tents, several small buildings, and even a few, rough log huts. Further to the east, maybe a mile or so, were at least fifty or sixty wagons. Off to the south and closer to the river was a huge, fenced corral, probably made from small pine trees. There were over a hundred horses in the corral. Based on the amount of smoke and the number of fires burning, it was suppertime. Men were going in all directions. Most of the Yell County men had stopped marching and were trying to see everything going on in the camp.

"Move over, horses," someone hollered.

As the men moved over to the side of the rough road, they noticed fifteen or twenty mounted soldiers riding toward the camp. Cavalry, thought Willis. Boy, do they look smart. The leader, later discovered to be Captain Cornwell, glanced a couple of times at the men as he rode by on a beautiful, roan-colored horse. However, the other cavalrymen smiled, and some spoke to the new arrivals.

At the end of the cavalry patrol was a team of horses pulling a small cannon. There is no way the Yankees can beat us, Bartis thought standing there looking at the whole picture in front of him. This was impressive. As he turned to look back north, he saw fifteen or sixteen large cannon. This war might be over quicker than some had said. That's what I would like to do—load and shoot cannon, he thought.

"Let's form up," the captain shouted, interrupting his thoughts. "We want to look like real soldiers when we come into camp."

Even though tired, everyone did his best as they moved on down toward the camp. After another quarter of a mile, the troops were stopped again.

"At ease," came the command, and several of the men quickly sat down. But seeing the huge camp and all the activity caused most of the men to forget how tired they were.

The captain had gone on ahead to find out where the new arrivals would camp. It was at least an hour before he got back with instructions. Instructions were given to the lieutenants, who took them to their respective groups.

After spending the last few days working with the supply trains, Lyle finally had the opportunity to again visit with his Gravelly friends. Everyone was glad to see the first officer from Gravelly.

While awaiting orders for a camping site assignment, the friends, including Frank, sprawled out on the ground, took drinks of water, and began conversing. The privates had several questions for their elected companion. However, Lyle knew he could not answer some of their concerns. No, he did not know how long they would be here in camp, nor did he know when they might meet the enemy.

"If a battle happens, will all of us here have to go, or will some of us stay here?" asked Frank, the always nervous and worried newcomer.

"You are the guy from Briggsville, aren't you?" asked Lyle.

"Yes, suh."

"Well, best I can figure is we all will be going. However, once near battle, some may be held back as reserves. But even the reserves will probably reinforce our army at some weak point."

"Hope I'm a reserve," Frank said, looking down.

"Frank, you won't get to kill any Yankees if you are in reserve," said Bartis, always ready to wisecrack.

No one laughed at Bartis's latest joke. Suddenly, the men seated on the ground heard an officer shouting for the men to reform into rank. Although very tired, the men got to their feet and did as commanded. An hour or so later, after several stops and several turns, the Yell County group got to their assigned camping area, approximately one mile east of the entrance area of the camp.

Unfortunately, the men did not get to go to Van Buren for the next three days due to a heavy training schedule. The day after the men arrived, five wagons arrived, after a trip of fifteen days from Little Rock. Governor Rector had ordered 1,500 muskets, along with gunpowder and lead balls, removed from the Little Rock Arsenal and sent west to Van Buren. The entire camp was excited when the arms arrived, only to find that the muskets were of Mexican War stock. They were obsolete, for the most part.

Two full days were wasted as the guns repeatedly misfired for several reasons and had to be worked on. Some guns were missing ramrods, others had jammed triggers, and most had not been cleaned up for years. One man was seriously injured when the powder exploded in his gun without moving the ball over inches in the barrel. However, the men who were more familiar with guns were able to help others like Frank, who was really afraid of them.

Chapter 14

The Girlfriend

THE WEATHER HAD BEEN unbelievably warm for February, and drilling and marching continued on a fast pace for the first two weeks. Willis finally got another chance to talk to Lyle in a one–on–one situation. Lyle trusted Willis more than the other Yell County men. He stopped him as he was returning from the latrine.

"We'll be moving out on Monday, heading north to Fayetteville. They say it's a town of 700 to 800. Looks like the real thing. The colonel says the Federal army in Missouri is moving south towards the Arkansas border. I think I mentioned the other day that we have a camp in northern Arkansas called Camp Stephens. General McCulloch has troops at Stephens. General Price has his division not too far from Camp Stephens. If you remember, Price and McCulloch's men defeated the Federals at Wilson's Creek. The Federals have put another army in the field and have decided to cross the Arkansas border and challenge our waiting armies. Oh. We will also have another new general arriving soon, maybe by Sunday. He will be in charge of all of our troops. The new man is General Earl Van Dorn. Van Dorn has been serving back in the east in Virginia. He should be a good general."

"Willis, don't tell anyone what I have told you," Lyle quickly said as another soldier approached them. Then, he turned and quickly walked back to the captain's tent.

On Wednesday, the artillery batteries were drilling seriously. This involved positioning the guns, providing gun load powder, and simulating the ball placement in the barrel of the cannon. Near evening, the batteries were going to fire live shells out into the Arkansas River. Much later, the ground literally shook as the twelve-pounders fired the live shell. The smaller six-pounders followed this. By nightfall, every soldier had a much better idea of what war was going to be like. The conversation around the campfire that evening reflected the men's concern about the horror of war. Eslie brought up the question that several men had wondered about.

"You reckon anyone will turn coward and run when the fighting starts?"

"If they do, they will be looking at my back," Bartis joked.

"Well, you could understand running if it was bad enough,' Frank said, looking into the fire flames."

"We will all settle down after a while," Willis spoke up.

However, Willis was not sure that he really believed his own comment. Lyle, who had listened carefully while finishing a cup of coffee, felt that he must encourage his friends.

"Look, guys, we have trained, we have marched, we have solved most of our gun problems, and we shoot real well—probably much better than the Yankees. We have seen the cavalry perform and we have seen our artillery work. Men, we are now soldiers and the Yankees are threatening our state. And, we have a good reason to fight—to defend our homes and families. Let's hit the sack."

"After that speech, I'm ready to go fight now," Bartis said as the men got up from around the fire and moved toward their bedrolls."

"I know what you mean," Willis said.

On Saturday, the camp was told about the new general. The announcement had little effect, except for the instructions that the camp was to be cleaned and dressed up for Van Dorn. By 9:00 a.m., most of the enlisted men were working to clean up the camp. By lunchtime, the officers were quite pleased with the camp's appearance. With the improved camp, each officer was instructed to allow their men the afternoon off to visit in the town, since Van Buren was only about a half hour west of the camp.

The Gravelly boys, like others, suddenly regressed in age to about thirteen years. They left for Van Buren on foot, laughing and talking. Even Eslie was excited about the furlough. Bartis began to gallop like a horse and slap his butt with his right hand.

"Hope the girls know we're coming. If they do, they will run out to meet me. After they fight over me awhile, I will introduce them to you peons. Who knows, Frank, they may even have a black mammy for you."

Willis looked over at Frank and told him to ignore the jokester. But Willis did think about Rosalie. He wished she were in Van Buren. As the five men neared the town, Lyle cautioned the other four soldiers, "Guys, let's use good judgment while we are in town. Remember, we represent our country, the Confederacy."

Willis agreed, but he did want to buy some food. They all had grown tired of hardtack—called cracker by the Feds. The townspeople were still curious about the soldiers, although they had gotten used to seeing several new soldiers.

Since Saturday was shopping day, there were many people in town: farmers, shopkeepers, merchants, laborers, and Indians. And women—women of all sizes, shapes, and ages. Many wore beautiful bonnets that matched their attire.

"Man, something smells good—smells like pancakes," Willis suddenly said.

"Forget the food," Bartis responded. "Look at the little lady over there in blue."

The woman, in her early twenties, was dressed in a beautiful blue dress with a matching blue bonnet. Her dark hair hung down from under the bonnet. She had blue eyes that seemed to jump out at a person. Her pretty face had some light makeup with a tinge of rouge on her wide cheekbones. The lady had heard Bartis's comment. She continued to smile as she moved on down the street in the same direction as the soldiers. Occasionally, she would glance back at the Yell County men.

Willis, seeing a grocery store said, "Let's go inside."

"Not me," said Bartis. "I want to meet Lady Blue."

Bartis left the others and started across the street to meet the lady. After the others had ducked into the store, Willis looked out the store window toward Bartis. He had introduced himself to Miss Blue and they continued walking west toward the river.

Lyle bought each of the men an orange. After inspecting the store, the men left to continue sightseeing. Bartis was nowhere in sight. Frank wanted to see if any ships were at the dock, so the group started down to the river. There were no ships, since the river was down several feet. A stranger explained that the paddle wheelers could come from Little Rock only if the river was deep enough. He also said that ships sometimes got grounded for days on sandbars due to shallow water.

The soldiers came across a pool hall, which several soldiers had already found. Other soldiers from Danville were there playing pool. After watching a while, the Gravelly men left for more sightseeing. By then, the sun was getting low in the west.

Lyle and Willis both commented that they hadn't seen Bartis.

"You don't think he got lost, do you?" Eslie asked.

No one answered. Lyle then assumed his officer role.

"Let's spread out, take different streets, and see if we can find him. Let's meet at the east end of town by the blacksmith shop in about forty-five minutes. By then it will be dark. If we don't find him by then, I will have to report him not present. He could be accused of deserting. After all, we have had four men desert since we got to camp."

The four men split up and selected different streets to search in an effort to locate their friend. Almost an hour later, they met at the blacksmith shop. No one had seen Bartis. All were sure that he would not desert.

"You don't think he got to drinking with other soldiers, do you?" asked Eslie, who was used to looking for his pa.

Willis had already thought of that. "I don't think so. I have never seen that, but it's possible."

Lyle told the men that they had better report back to camp. As they started back, he wondered if he should report Bartis. No, he would wait until morning and give him a chance. Once in camp, the men ate a snack and went to bed. Around 2:00 a.m., Bartis crawled into his bedroll. The movement awakened Willis, but he said nothing to Bartis. The next morning, the Gravelly men were relieved to see Bartis in his blanket.

As Willis prepared his and Eslie's breakfast, Bartis sheepishly crawled out of bed. He was somewhat quiet for Bartis. During breakfast, he stared a lot into the fire.

"Bartis, did you get lost last night?" asked Frank, who had come up to check on Bartis.

"None of your business, Buck," said Bartis, spitting into the fire.

The conversation occurred mainly between the other three

men present, and no one else questioned Bartis. After breakfast, Lyle arrived to remind the men that they would have a march around for Van Dorn, who would arrive that day. The general had been delayed on his journey from Pocahontas. Sunday, however, was a rest day for the camp, since the general did not arrive.

That day, Willis got his first letter from home. Eva was worried that he was not eating well and that he might not have enough blankets at night. She also asked about Eslie and "the other boys." His ma related that Amos was going to butcher a hog and that Miss Clandell, the old maid down the hill, had died. She also said Hayes really missed him, as did Georgia Ann. And finally, she mentioned that Ralph, Eslie's pa, had been arrested again for drunken and disorderly conduct. Willis was not to tell Eslie. Eva said they prayed every night for the Yell County boys, and to write.

Oh, for a piece of her pecan pie, thought Willis. Again, he realized how much he loved his family and how much he missed them. As he put the letter away, Willis thought, poor Eslie, he has no family to write him and he certainly does not need to hear anymore about Ralph's embarrassing behavior. About that time, Eslie walked over with a letter in his hand.

"Willis, just finished a letter from your ma. She talked about Amos, Hayes, and Georgia Ann. She didn't mention, but I guess Pa's all right."

Willis told Eslie that he had also gotten a letter from his ma.

"Willis, what's wrong with Bartis? He's talking a little more, but he's not himself."

"I know, but we'll just have to wait and see what's bothering him. He will eventually mention it. We don't want to bug him."

After lunch, a great deal of commotion occurred up near the camp entrance. Several members of the cavalry corps were coming into camp.

"Reckon the general's here, 'cause there's lots of cavalry coming in," announced Frank, who had wandered up to Willis and Eslie's camping area.

"It does look like a cavalry escort, all right," retorted Willis. "We'll get to see General Van Dorn."

By then several men had begun to walk up toward the camp headquarters. The Gravelly men could already make out Colonel Harvell and other officers standing out in front of the headquarters building. Soon, the important guest appeared on horseback as well. A series of salutes were exchanged as the visitor stopped his horse and then dismounted.

The men were now close enough to hear the officers talking. The new arrival was not Van Dorn. He was dressed in a smartly fitting, gray uniform, but when salutes were exchanged, one of the officers referred to the newcomer as Price. Listening to the introduction, Willis was sure that he heard Colonel Harvell call the man General Price. He thought, this is General Price, one of the generals that Lyle told me about.

After the stranger waved at the large group of curious onlookers, he went inside the old farmhouse that served as headquarters. The crowd, still curious and talking among themselves, slowly began to filter back to the men's camping area. Lyle caught up with his friends before they had gotten back to their own camp.

"What's the deal, Lyle? Who is this Price fellow, and where is the general?" asked Bartis.

Lyle looked over at Bartis, surprised, since he had said little that day. He must be becoming himself again, he thought.

As the men waited for Lyle's response, Eslie noticed movement at the far eastern end of the huge camp. The supply wagons were being hitched to mules to form a supply train.

"General Price is one of our generals," Lyle finally spoke.

"He and General McCulloch were the Reb commanding officers at that Missouri battle up near the state line. He is from Missouri. McCulloch is still with our army up near the state border. The army there was the one that defeated the Yankees at Wilson's Creek. They pulled our army back into Arkansas to await reinforcements. That's us."

"Oh, no," Willis overheard Frank say.

"Price has come down to meet Van Dorn before we move north to join our waiting army. Our people believe that more Federals are marching down from St. Louis. So...a battle is expected. That's all I know now. We will be meeting later today at headquarters to talk about our part in the whole thing." Lyle stopped and looked at his friends. "Don't worry. We are ready. I've got to go check on the supply trains."

Lyle hurried off in that direction. After reaching their camping area, Bartis suggested a card game. Everyone was glad for his suggestion.

Chapter 15

Evansville

TWO DAYS LATER, LYLE arrived to give further instructions to the Yell County men. His handsome face looked tired, with dark circles under his brown eyes. There was no doubt; the men had selected the right man for lieutenant when they selected Lyle. To both his friends and those who did not know him well, Lyle was the hardest working officer in camp. Yet, he remained very humble about his new position. At the same time, Lyle recognized that, as an officer, he must exercise military discipline. The men of the 20th Regiment showed their respect as Lyle began to address them.

"Men, we will move out tomorrow morning after breakfast. We'll be heading north towards Fayetteville. We'll be on the march for seven or eight days. There are some things that you must do. First, clean your muskets and carry all the lead and powder you have been given. Don't overload your haversack; put in your blankets, and only one or two changes of clothes. You will need your cooking gear, but only what you really need. Check your shoes, especially the soles and heels. If you want, put in soap and extra socks. Wear your cap or hat. From the general's mouth, no alcohol is to be taken."

"Shoot!" the men heard Bartis say, although they knew he probably had no alcohol.

"Carry some water, although we should find enough water along our route. As you realize, we're going to be marching into the Boston Mountains, and you will be carrying your musket and a full haversack. It won't be easy. At times, you may have to help get the supply train up hills and across creeks and rivers. The same goes for the twelve-pounders. I want to think that the Yell County men will be the best of the camp."

"What about Van Dorn?" Frank asked as Lyle turned to go. "Our general is not here. Are we going to wait on him?"

"The general will meet us on the way," Lyle responded, glancing over at the nervous Briggsville native.

February 23 was another spring-like day, although the early morning temperature was said to be thirty-eight degrees. Due to several unknown reasons, the army was not able to leave the Van Buren camp until almost 9:00 a.m. The cavalry left first, followed by almost 1,100 foot soldiers, and then the supply train, followed by the artillery. Following the artillery was another contingent of cavalry.

After leaving the Van Buren area, the army moved back west toward the Arkansas/Indian Territory line, just north of Fort Smith, and then began the long march north. Day one of the march was not difficult. Most of the territory covered was hilly, but not exceptionally steep. The wagon supply train that was made up of over fifty wagons encountered few problems.

Once up on higher ground, Willis looked back down on the Arkansas River Valley. The supply train and artillery corps stretched back behind them ten or twelve miles to the south. Camp on the first night was established along a meandering creek, probably carrying water all the way south to the Arkansas River.

The Gravelly boys, near the front of the moving army, were able to select a good campsite. The creek water appeared to be clean and acceptable, so Frank put coffee on the fire. Eslie and Willis started back toward the supply wagons to check out food for the evening. Brown beans, hogback, and cornbread were the menu. No hardtack tonight. The men got enough food for Bartis and Frank, along with their own, and started back toward their camp area.

On the way back they ran into the Laudon brothers from Wing. The brothers had lived in Gravelly at one time. The Laudons were already eating when Willis and Eslie came by their camping area. The four young men grabbed each other, greeted each other, and shook hands. Noble, the older Laudon, looked at Eslie with concern.

"Sorry about your pa, Eslie."

"What about, Noble?"

"For getting thrown in jail in Danville. You haven't heard?"

"No, I don't get any letters from him," said an embarrassed Eslie.

Noble now felt worse than all of them for opening his mouth. Trying to make it up to Eslie, he said he didn't think it amounted to much, and Ralph was probably already home.

"We'll probably see ya'll again," Willis said, looking at the two Wing residents. "Be careful."

He and Eslie moved on up to the creek where they were camped. Willis did not know what to say to his friend.

"You hungry?" he finally offered.

Eslie had been silent since hearing about his pa. "Oh, a little," he finally answered.

The army reached a small community called Evansville two days later. It was the first time the soldiers had seen any civilians since the Fort Smith area. The long line of Reb soldiers moved past a small, log home with a roughly built fireplace chimney. Smoke was coming out of the chimney. A young boy with sandy colored hair, most of which was hanging down in his eyes, came out from behind the house. His pants were tattered, worn, and patched on the knees. Even though it was still quite cold, his dirty feet were bare. The boy, maybe six or seven years old, was carrying an old plate stacked with cookies.

"Ya'll want a cookie?" said the boy, smiling shyly.

"You bet," Bartis spoke first. "Did you make them yourself?"

"Naw," the youngster smiled again. "Ma made 'em. We saw ya'll comin' yesterday while down the mountain. She wanted ya'll to have them since Pa was a soldier."

The soldiers that had stopped to listen to the boy noticed that the boy said "was a soldier."

"Something happen to your pa?" Frank asked.

"Yeh, Pa got kilt up at Wilson's Creek," the boy said, looking down at his moving toes. "Whar he's buried."

"Well, we are sorry," said Eslie as he reached for the plate. He took a cookie and passed the plate to Willis. "But I'm sure he's in Heaven."

Willis took a cookie and passed the plate onto Bartis. "What's your name?"

"Name's John, same's Pa," the boy replied, looking at Willis's musket.

"Well, John, tell your ma that we appreciate her for fixing the cookies. We are sorry about your pa."

The boy moved on to give the cookies to other Rebs as Willis and the others marched on north. There was no talking for some time as each man thought about the consequences of war. Finally, Willis broke the silence.

"What you reckon will happen to that boy and his ma?"

"They will do the best they can, but kids need a pa," said Eslie, who had related best with John. Then he realized that he had said too much.

"I will come back and check on them after the war," said Bartis, who had no brothers.

Frank had listened to it all. He knew that he could be killed and never even have a son. He would not forget this family.

The next evening, Bartis and Willis were both assigned guard duty. Guard duty assignments had been made every day since the camp broke and the army had moved north, but this was the first time that the Gravelly boys had served. Lyle was probably responsible for the friends serving together. The assignment at this time was not critical, since there was no known enemy in the state. However, sentry duty would become more serious as the army approached northern Arkansas. With no serious threat, the guards could visit a while in covering their assigned area. About 1:30 a.m., Willis and Bartis had covered their extreme boundaries and were moving back toward each other. When they met, both stopped and began to talk.

"Awful quiet tonight," said Bartis.

"Yeah, thought I scared up a deer or maybe he scared me up," replied Willis. Then he asked his friend a question he had been waiting to ask. "Bartis, what happened to you in Van Buren that night?"

"Remember that gal in the blue dress—Miss Blue?" Bartis said after a pause. "She was a fine-looking woman."

"You in love?" Willis asked in a low, joking manner.

"I thought I was that night. Boy, was she a looker and very friendly. We went down to the river and talked a long time. Then she suggested that we go where she lived. At first, I thought I might get to meet her folks. Well, her home turned out to be a hotel room. I did get excited then—and I was already in love with her. After we got to her room and I could see Miss Blue in a lighted area, I found out she was at least thirty years old—almost twice my age. Willis, that was no innocent woman. I was shocked when she told me that she charged two dollars. I said for what? The gal said, 'What do you think for? But you had better hurry buster, because I have a date with a Reb officer in about ten minutes.' Man, did I feel silly. I had fallen in love with a woman of ill repute—a prostitute. Willis, I had three dollars, but she didn't get it. You know, I'm good at playing jokes on people, but did I feel silly when this gal suckered me. I've heard about men getting some bad diseases from such women, and I didn't want that."

"Well, what happened then?" Willis asked.

"I looked at her and I said, 'I thought we really liked each other.' She gave me a dirty look, opened the door of her hotel room, and said, 'Reb, you wasted two hours of my time. I don't give freebies. Get out.' Willis, I felt so bad that I couldn't come back and have the men ask about my good-looking girlfriend. I just went back down on the river and sat there for a long time. I hoped everyone would be asleep when I got back to camp."

"Bartis, I think you did the right thing in leaving her. Who knows, you might have caught a disease, or she might have robbed you. Just forget it and keep it to yourself."

"But Willis, she was good-looking, wasn't she?"

"Yes, she was, but she may have two kids at home too."

Willis noticed that Bartis's whole attitude changed after he shared the story with him.

Chapter 16

Stilwell Creek

THE ARMY ARRIVED AT Summers a week later. They had one severe problem along the way. Stilwell Creek crossed the state line from Indian Territory and flowed southeast toward the River Valley. Recent rains in Indian Territory had caused much flooding and had also caused many creeks and streams to leave their banks. Stilwell Creek, normally about a foot deep, was about four feet deep and more than thirty feet wide. Logs and other debris were being carried swiftly downstream.

The infantry had been able to go upstream about fifty yards, where the stream had high embankments on both sides. While the water was exceptionally deep here, the creek embankments were only about ten feet apart. Some of the local country people had placed three long poles, cut from nearby trees, across the creek. They had placed rough, cut pine boards over the poles, creating a floored surface for the rough bridge. The makeshift bridge was about four feet wide, and the infantry was able to use it.

Most of the cavalry at the front of the army had been able to use the bridge, although most of the horses had to be led across the bridge. The officers were sure that the teamsters could get the trailing wagons across the swollen creek since most of the wagons were heavily loaded with armaments and supplies. The cannon might present another problem.

The flooded creek had been a topic of discussion earlier among the staff officers. To detour would mean backtracking about three miles, turning east and going at least seven miles, trying to cross at an old bridge and then moving back west. This detour alone would take at least two days, if everything went well. A detour and delay could be serious now, since the enemy had been seen moving south on Telegraph Road from Springfield toward the Arkansas line.

General Price made the decision—cross Stilwell Creek. Wagon number one, pulled by a four-mule team, made the far side, although water was running almost to the wagon bed itself. With success, wagons two and three entered the moving waters. Before they had reached the opposite bank, wagon four entered the stream. Three wagons were now in the fast-moving creek at one time. Wagon two was within ten feet of the bank when the left front wheel of the wagon hit against a huge rock, a couple of feet beneath the surface of the fast-moving stream. The teamster began to lash the mules, not realizing how big the rock was. The left wheel began to move up the rock, causing the wagon to begin to tilt to the right.

As the wagon bed began to tilt the heavy load of munitions, barrels of gunpowder and lead musket balls shifted from left to right. When the teamster jerked back on the mule team's reins, the wagon, now pushed by the water moving swiftly downstream, slowly rolled in the direction of the water movement and fell heavily on its right side. The teamster leaped from the wagon in the same direction, trying to avoid the excited mules that were pulling the wagon. The mules lost their balance and fell on their right side, crushing Max Blue, the teamster and a native of Mount Ida.

The mule team quickly righted itself, but the third wagon's mule team, excited over what they saw in front, moved up on top of the overturned wagon, and this wagon, in an unlevel position itself, rolled over, much like the first. The teamster did not get out and went under the water with the wagon. As the mule team struggled on ahead, trying to pull the second wagon over the first wagon, the poor teamster was caught in-between the two wagons. The second wagon was carrying several boxes of muskets from the Little Rock Arsenal. All went into the swirling waters.

As broken boards came to the surface, the men watching the scene could see that the musket boxes had broken open and the muskets had come out. The cries and cursing of the teamsters and the sounds of the scared mules brought a lot of men to the scene. Captain Hunt, astride a huge, gray horse, watched the unbelievable action with an open mouth.

"Hold wagon four! Hold wagon four! Pull em back!" he shouted. "Get some men up here to help the teamsters."

Two men were already in the water, trying hard to keep their feet in the fast-moving creek. The first man lost his balance, went under the water, came up about twenty feet downstream, and then disappeared for the last time.

"Any good swimmers want to volunteer to help get the men out from under the wagons?" shouted the captain, not sure what to do. "We'll tie you to a rope."

Eslie and Willis had just gotten back to the crossing from the other side of the creek.

"I will, sir. I'm a good swimmer," Eslie shouted, already removing his boots.

"Tie a rope on him and tie the other end to a good horse," the captain shouted.

Two cavalry members were standing by to lead the wagons after they crossed the stream. One of the riders, a heavy, burly man, dismounted and backed his horse up close to the edge of the stream. He took a rope that was part of the crossing equipment, tied it to his horse's saddle horn, and tossed the other end of the rope to Eslie, who was already in the shallow water. Eslie quickly tied the rope around his waist and moved out toward the partially exposed side of the first wagon. Willis shouted for Eslie to be careful. Eslie went under the water, and the rope tightened. In about a minute, he came up.

"Can't see in the muddy water," he shouting, drawing in fresh air," "but I will try to feel around for him."

Immediately, he dipped under the fast-moving water and the rope tightened. A minute passed, then more, and then Eslie's head came up. He drew a deep breath and without saying a word, dipped under the water again. The men watching the scene saw the exposed wagon side move and then move again. Then nothing, and then more movement.

"Move the horse," Eslie came up and shouted.

The horse began to pull on the rope, and more of Eslie's body could be seen. Then the onlookers noticed that Eslie was holding a man, with his arms under the rescued man's armpits. As the horse pulled, Eslie slowly moved toward the creek bank, hanging on to the unconscious man. Willis and others had waded out into the shallow water to help the struggling Eslie. The two men were helped to dry ground. As other men took the teamster, Eslie lay down on the dry ground exhausted.

"Eslie, you all right?" Willis asked.

"Yeah, I'm all right." Eslie whispered.

The rescued teamster was placed on his stomach and volunteers began to press on his back, desperately trying to expel water from his lungs. Eslie finally sat up and looked over at the man they were working on. "Someway, that wagon washed or moved over him. He was under the front wheel. Probably got broken ribs or more."

"Stop," said one of the soldiers working with the injured driver. "Let's see if he's alive."

A second man checked for the man's pulse, first on the wrist of his right arm and then under the man's neck. "No heartbeat. Somebody else check."

Three other men checked for a pulse. All agreed the man was dead. While this was going on, the captain had sent several men down river with a rope, in hopes that one of the other two men could be recovered, whether dead or alive. The dead teamster was taken on ahead. Captain Hunt had also dispatched a courier to General Price, asking if the wagons were to continue to cross Stillwell Creek or if they were to detour east."

In about twenty minutes, as the search continued, General Price arrived. After getting a full report from Hunt, the general surveyed the accident scene and finally turned to the captain.

"Camp where you are on the far side. Have men continue to patrol the creek for either of the lost men. It will be twelve hours before sunup, and the water should be down a lot by then, and we can cross the wagons. We will delay as well on the north side of the creek. Captain, prepare a burial detail and make a complete report of the day's activities."

The general saluted, turned his horse, and moved back up toward the front of the moving army. That evening, around the campfire, Willis, Eslie, and Bartis were discussing the accident when Frank wandered up to listen.

"Gosh, a man can get killed in the army before ever seeing the enemy," he finally said, and then turned and walked away with his hands in his pockets.

Lyle arrived shortly after that, proclaiming, "I came to see the hero."

"Hero I was late," Eslie said. "I should of got there quicker."

"Eslie, we didn't ever know about it. You volunteered as soon as we got to the creek." Lyle put his hand on Eslie's shoulder. "Eslie, you risked your life for someone you didn't even know. You are a hero, regardless."

"You better believe it, Eslie," Bartis agreed.

Willis looked up at Lyle and told him to sit down and have some beans and bacon.

"I will, if you have enough."

Bartis had already reached for a pan and began to dip out a portion of beans. Then he reached over and took a couple of pieces of the slab bacon, put them in the pan, and handed the pan to Lyle. Lyle sat down with crossed legs and took the pan from Bartis. The men always liked for Lyle to visit them. Usually he was able to share some information about their destination.

"What's going on, chief? We doin' all right?" asked Bartis, who never minded asking questions, even of an officer.

"Today was a disaster," Lyle said as he finished a piece of bacon and swallowed. "Cost three lives and Eslie could have drowned. But it also cost us an important day. The Federals are nearing our border now, and we need to be in a good position to meet them. There are other problems. Not only did we lose men, valuable muskets and shell, but we also have lost several other men since we left camp in Van Buren. I believe the count is more than twelve now. They just left—deserted."

"Gosh, we are not even close to battle yet," said Willis. "We may lose several more before we get there."

"The staff has been discussing this problem. General Price may take serious steps to control desertion."

"You mean the firing squad?" asked Bartis, who had been listening carefully.

"That's a possibility, all right."

"Gosh, that's serious," said Eslie.

"You may want to spread this around," Lyle said as he got up from his seat near the fire and looked at his friends. "Might save a life. Thanks for the grub." The lieutenant turned and walked away.

The army was delayed at Summers to allow the supply train and the artillery to catch up. Once again, farmers and other residents showed up to welcome the troops.

Late February was still warm for that time of the year in Arkansas, and on Sunday, the army was invited to an all–church picnic at the local Summers Methodist Church. The other two churches in town, the Lutheran and the Pentecostal churches, also participated. Sixty to seventy residents came with all kinds of food, from beef and pork, to deer and wild turkey. The women brought a variety of pies and cakes. The Rebs ate home cooking for the first time in three months.

But maybe even more important to the soldiers were the ten or twelve girls in attendance, from ages thirteen to eighteen. According to the soldiers, all the girls were very attractive. Except for a serious fight between an artilleryman and a member of the cavalry over an attractive sixteen-year-old girl, everything went well. With so many potential suitors pursuing the limited number of girls, no one established any serious relationships.

Bartis, for once, did not seek female company. He chose to eat and watched the proceedings. Willis felt sorry for a chubby girl of thirteen who was not getting any attention and talked some to her. At the same time, he thought about his little sister, Georgia Ann, and Rosalie. He wished he could see both of them, along with Hayes and his parents.

The country food reminded him of his ma's great cooking. With serious fighting ahead, would he ever see his family again? What about his friends? Would they survive? He thought about the young man's family at Evansville and the boy who had brought the men cookies. That father was buried near the Wilson's Creek battlefield. Willis hoped the family would make it without the husband and father.

Chapter 17

Chula

1862

IT WAS A DARK night, with heavy, dark clouds gathering. All signs indicated rain or worse. The Reverend Gotham and Rosalie were sitting on the front porch. The lightning bugs had long disappeared with the cool weather. The pastor had been telling Rosalie about a visit with Weldon and his black family. At the time, Weldon said that he was ready to come to church. The pastor related to Rosalie that on hearing the good news, he got up and hugged each member of the freed slave family. Just then, three hooded figures stepped out from behind the Gotham house.

"Oh," Rosalie shouted, as the three armed men moved up to the porch to address the homeowners.

"Preacher man, we're tired of your darkie loving," one of the men spoke. "We've already visited that Negro blacksmith. We have finally convinced him that he is not white. Now, my friends are going to see if you are black underneath your clothes. I will see if your girl is black or white."

The three men laughed.

"Wait, do as you want with me but leave my daughter alone," the pastor pleaded.

As two of the men grabbed her father, Rosalie darted inside the house and tried to close the front door. The third man caught the door and kept it from being closed. He pushed it open as Rosalie heard a commotion on the porch. She heard her father groan as if he was in pain.

The man inside the house advanced toward Rosalie as she slowly moved backwards. "Don't worry, honey. It won't take long, and you might like it."

"Please don't. I beg you, please don't," uttered Rosalie.

By then, her back was against the buffet. She reached her hand behind her to find anything to use as a means of defense. Her hand touched the heavy iron that she had been using earlier while ironing a shirt for her father for Sunday church. The man moved closer, and reached out to grab Rosalie as her hand clasped the handle of the iron. She could still feel the warmth from it.

As the man's hand tightened on Rosalie's left arm, she swung the hot iron as hard as she could. The moving iron struck the man across the head just above his left ear. He fell, blood gushing from his head. As the man's hooded gown came open, Rosalie saw a gun in his belt. The man was not moving, and she quickly seized the pistol and moved back toward the closed, front door. When she opened it, she saw her father lying on the ground.

The two men, standing between the door and her father, were facing the beaten pastor. The smaller of the two was warning him.

"There had better be no more darky loving with either you or your raped daughter. Do you understand?"

Holding the pistol in both hands, Rosalie fired it between the two strangers. Both quickly whirled around to see Rosalie pointing the gun at them.

"Men, don't bother her, she knows how to use a gun," said the pastor, slowly moving up on an elbow. The men did not move, and Rosalie's father slowly got to his feet and seized the men's shotguns.

"Gentlemen, you have no right to prey on innocent people, either black or white," Rosalie spoke. "I'm sorry, but I'm going to have to kill you both."

The preacher quickly looked toward Rosalie, as the taller of the two men rapidly spoke. "No, please, I have a family and children. Please, my family would starve. It wasn't my idea; it was Jon's idea."

"It was Jon's idea," the other man quickly agreed. "Neither of us has ever been bushwhackers until tonight. We agreed to come with Jon."

Rosalie cocked the pistol, and the first man began to cry. "No, please."

The pastor's mouth was wide open as he stared at his daughter, unsure of what she planned to do.

"Father, remove their hoods so they can watch each other die."

Still unable to swallow, the preacher stepped behind the men and removed their hoods.

"Father, go in and bring out one of the candles."

Almost as afraid as the captured men, the pastor quickly went inside, got one of the lighted candles, and then noticed the man lying on the floor motionless. He quickly came out the door with the lit candle.

"Rosalie, is that man in there dead?"

At the question, the smaller man of the two fell to his knees and began to plead for his life.

"Rosalie, no more killing," her father pleaded, assuming the worse. His comment only made things worse for the captives, and now the second man began pleading.

"Did Weldon plead?" she asked, looking at the men.

"He is all right," both men blurted out together. "Jon was fooling you. He only wanted to scare you."

"Jon is not dead, but he is our prisoner," Rosalie calmly said, looking at the men. "We know who both of you are and we know who Jon is. I will let you both go, but Jon stays with us as a hostage. You must promise in God's name never to do such a thing again and apologize to father."

"Forgive us," both sobbed, turning to the pastor. "We are sorry."

"I forgive you," the preacher said. "Learn a lesson." Both men got to their feet, pulled off their hooded robes, and dropped them on the ground.

"Go in peace, and may God forgive you," the preacher said, and the two disappeared into the darkness.

The Gothams went back into the house, where Jon was still lying on the floor, a considerable amount of blood near his head. When the reverend checked and found that he was still breathing, Rosalie put extra wood in the cook stove and put a pan of water on to warm.

The reverend helped Rosalie clean the blood from the floor, and then Rosalie went over to the unconscious bushwhacker. After cleaning the wound carefully, she applied some salve and put a bandage on the head wound. The man was making sounds now, and the Gothams carried and dragged the man over to a pallet that Rosalie had made from several quilts. They covered him with a blanket and her father instructed Rosalie to go on to bed. Then he took a seat in a comfortable chair with the loaded pistol, and he prayed for the injured man.

There were no further problems during the night. Jon woke up around 9:00 a.m. the next morning, unsure where he was.

After a brief time, he finally realized what had happened and where he was. "Why are you doing this for me after what I tried to do?" he asked. "Are the others dead?"

"A better question is why were you trying to harm us?" the pastor asked. "We have never hurt you. As Christians, we love you."

The man said nothing. Rosalie had cooked breakfast, and she brought some gravy and biscuits in to Jon. She put pillows under his head and back, allowing him to sit up enough to eat. She fed the man carefully after the food was blessed, but there was little conversation. Jon slept again for several hours and awoke around suppertime to find that Rosalie had again prepared him a good meal.

"Did you contact the sheriff?" Jon asked after finishing the meal.

"Jon, did you harm Weldon?" the preacher asked, without answering the question.

The man looked first at the pastor and then at Rosalie. "No, we never even saw him." He paused then reached up to feel the bandage on his head. "We had been drinking. It was my idea. I did ride one night with a group from Plainview. We just went out to scare some Negroes. I got carried away last night after drinking too much."

"And you were going to molest me?" asked Rosalie.

"I guess so, but I have never done anything like that before," he said with tears in his eyes. "I was drunk. I'm sorry."

The following morning, Reverend Gotham hitched the mules up to his wagon. Then, he and Rosalie began to help Jon to his feet and to the door. Moving down the porch steps was really a problem, since the man weighed more than 200 pounds. It was even more difficult to get Jon in the wagon bed and onto the blankets, which Rosalie had put there for the injured man.

There was little talk while they moved Jon onto the wagon. Soon, Pastor Gotham and Rosalie climbed up into the wagon seat. Though both heard the man ask if they were taking him to the sheriff, neither responded. After an hour or so, the wagon rolled to a stop in front of an impressive looking home in the outskirts of Plainview. No doubt, Jon was a successful farmer in the area. The large home and nearby barn were more impressive than any that the Gothams had passed on the road.

The wheels of the wagon had hardly stopped in front of the home before the front door of the home opened and out came a woman and two twin girls. The girls, probably in their lower teens, rushed ahead of their mother to see if the visitors had news of their missing father. As the girls reached the stationary wagon, Rosalie glanced back to look at the patient. Again, the man had tears in his eyes.

"Dad, oh what happened?" one of the girls cried out when she saw her father lying on the blankets with a bandaged head. "Are you all right?"

By now, Jon's wife had reached the wagon. She reached out and took her husband's hand, and the patient started to speak.

"Jon, don't talk," Rosalie interrupted. "You are still weak." Then she looked at Jon's wife. The woman, fortyish, slender, and neat, had a worried look on her face. "Your husband was hurt, maybe when thrown from his horse or something. No doubt he took a heavy blow to the head. We found him and we have been nursing him for the last day or so. He was unconscious for much of the time and talking as if out of his head. We learned who he was and where you live from his sleep talking. He's much better now, though he needs more rest."

Rosalie suddenly stopped and looked at her father. He slightly shook his head, as if in approval. "I am Rosalie Gotham and this is my father, Reverend Gotham. We live north of Rover.

"Oh, thank God he is all right," Jon's wife said, breathing a sigh of relief.

Again, Rosalie looked at Jon and saw even more tears in his eyes. "Yes, I believe he will be okay. Let's get him into your house and into bed."

It took all five of the people to get Jon into the beautiful home, and Rosalie noted that the inside of the house was even more impressive. Once Jon was comfortably in bed, Rosalie turned to his wife and told her to watch for a temperature. "Keep cool rags on his forehead. Don't allow him to get up, at least until tomorrow."

Both of the girls had hugged Jon and told him that they were so glad he was home and safe.

"Don't worry," one of the girls said. "He won't get up even if we have to sit on him."

"Well, Jon's home, so let me pray for his health before we go," Pastor Gotham said. He reached out and took Jon's trembling hand and prayed for his improved health. Looking up, he glanced over at Rosalie. "We better go, but Jon, our prayers are with you."

As the Gothams turned to leave the bedroom, Jon cried out, sobbing. "Reverend, what time does your church meet this coming Sunday?"

"Jon, Sunday school is at 9:30," the surprised pastor calmly replied. "Church services are at 10:30."

"Pastor and Rosalie, we will be there on Sunday," John responded, his eyes again filling with tears. "If it's all right, I might bring a friend of mine. He's a blacksmith at Rover. Name's Weldon."

"We will welcome all of you," Reverend Gotham said, tears welling in his eyes. Then he reached over and grabbed Jon's shoulder.

Rosalie immediately left the bedroom to hide her tears. As the Gothams made their way home on the wagon, they talked about Jon and the two men who had posed as bushwhackers.

"Father, I lied to Jon's family about what happened. I was protecting him with hopes that he learned an important lesson. I have already asked forgiveness for my total untruth. While I know God always forgives, did I do the right thing?"

The pastor, often amazed at his perceptive daughter, replied, "God forgave you, and I believe we both now believe that Jon, as well as the other two men, realize that we have forgiven them. I really don't believe any of the three men will ever be nightriders again. I think that it is possible that all three men's lives will be changed — especially Jon's. I even think that he might actually come to church and even bring Weldon. I think Weldon will come if asked by such a prominent man of the community. Of course, none of this should ever get out. I'm okay. Thank God you are okay, and the men and their families are together. You know, Rosalie, as we say, the Lord works in amazing ways."

"He does indeed, but, I'm not even going to mention this to Willis," Rosalie said, looking at her father.

"But, gal, I thought for a while that you were going to shoot the two men who beat me up," her father said, looking off in the distance before turning back to his daughter. "I was praying that you wouldn't."

"Father, I couldn't kill that possum that got in the chicken house," she said, looking back at her father.

The reverend laughed out loud.

Chapter 18

Fayetteville

February 1862

THE EASTWARD MARCH TO Fayetteville took three more days. Not far from Fayetteville, a man and his family, in a wagon loaded with furniture and personal items, met the leading cavalry unit. Captain Hunt went over to the wagon to speak with the man.

"Sir, can you tell us why there is so much smoke up ahead?"

The man looked at the captain and then back at the trailing Reb army. "The town's been burned down. Lot'a folks with no home. We going to Lincoln to live with family."

"Federals burn the town?"

The man looked at the stationary Reb army and then turned his attention back to Hunt. "No, the Rebs burned the city, and McCulloch was watching. They not only burned our town — they completely ransacked the place. I own a store there and they came and took all the food in the store. Rebs were carrying off huge quantities of meat. What they couldn't carry off, they burned. I am a Southerner from Texas and my sympathies were with the South and the Confederacy. I'm not sure now."

"I'm sorry," the captain replied. "Our men were not involved. I guess McCulloch thought the Feds would confiscate the food and use it. I will assure you that our men will be disciplined."

"I hope so," the man said as he flipped the reins of his mule team. "Git up."

Later, Lyle told the story to his friends. The army arrived at their designated camping area about 3:15 p.m. on March 2. Cavalry and pioneers had set up a temporary camp on the pasture of a local farmer who owned ninety acres east of the town of Prairie Grove.

Like the last two days, it was now much colder. Willis thought it looked like snow. After each company had claimed their own camping territory, there was an order to search for wood. Fortunately, wind and weather had felled three or four old hickory trees. The early arrivals picked up the wood in a hurry. By dusk, campfires dotted the farmer's pastureland.

Due to Bartis's secret patrol the night before, the Gravelly men had fried chicken for supper. With beans and bread, the meal was delicious. Lyle came by briefly to pass the word that they would begin the march the next morning at 7:00 a.m. sharp. They would be marching north. And yes, scouts had sighted the Federal army not more than thirty miles away. The men were to check all weapons. There could be action tomorrow or the day after. Though few would admit it, most of the men did not sleep well that night.

The early morning was extremely cold and windy. The north wind was strong enough to blow the settled snow into deep drifts and onto the heavy loaded wagons. Even the birds found the chill too great to be moving. The snow had stopped after leaving a layer of six or eight inches, but due to the north wind, there were snowdrifts up to two feet deep. On the north side of the stationary wagons, snow was up to the wheel hubs. The loaded wagons looked even more loaded with the heavy layer of snow on top of the loaded boxes.

By now, soldiers had begun to move about the temporary encampment, looking for firewood in the snow. The more industrious men had collected enough firewood on the previous day. There were already fires in scattered areas of the camp—some made early, others kept burning through the night by men on sentry duty. Willis was sitting by a small fire, which was growing larger due to the newly placed logs on the fire. He moved closer to the fire to combat the icy chill. He glanced back to the sleeping men, most with snow on top of their blankets.

The mounds of the sleeping men looked much like the graves at Young Gravelly Cemetery. Heads could not be seen since the men had pulled the blankets over their heads to protect their ears. Willis then looked over at Bartis. He was the only one near the fire that had not moved. Lyle, who had slept here, was sitting up. Eslie had turned over and was gazing sleepily into the fire. Walter, the most recent addition to the company and another jokester, raised up from his bedroll.

"Wher's my slave, Bartis, the fat Negro that's supposed to dress me?"

Willis chuckled and glanced again over at Bartis to see if he had heard the comment. Bartis looked to be sound asleep.

"You sit up the whole night?" Eslie asked Willis.

"Just about," replied Willis, not looking away from the fire.

"I had second sentry duty last night," Eslie said. "I guess Bartis had third duty."

Willis again looked over at the unmoving Bartis, "No, he had second duty. I had duty with him."

"Fat slave, put wood on the fire so I can get up," Walter said, raising his voice again. This must have got Bartis's attention, because the big pile moved.

"The name's Turner—short for Nat Turner, and you gonna

get it before long," responded Bartis, referring again to the notorious slave that led the rebellion in Virginia in the early 1800s.

Willis wondered when he could talk to Bartis alone. He needed to bring up the situation that occurred during the night. It was nothing that anyone else needed to know—especially Lyle. Eslie had already put the old coffee pot full of soft snow on the fire. Eslie, the guy who ate the least, was always the first to begin preparing a meal, Willis thought.

Bartis threw back his covers, stood up, stretched, and mentioned that he had to take a leak. He started toward the open-earth latrine area. Willis quickly got up and started after Bartis, who was just finishing relieving himself when Willis walked up.

"Bartis, about last night," Willis began. "Do you know what trouble you would have been in if anyone else had relieved you and found you asleep? Man, you can be arrested and even shot."

"Come on, Willis, they's not a Yank clos'en fifty miles," said Bartis, who didn't like the topic being brought up again. "We's in no danger."

"That's beside the point, Bartis. That's serious training, sentry duty."

"You ainst gonna rat on me?" Bartis asked, now agitated.

"Bartis, you are one of my best friends," Willis said, looking back at the campsite. "I'm sure not going to tell anybody, but I don't want a good friend to get in serious trouble, and I sure don't want you to sleep on sentry duty when the enemy is close."

Bartis said nothing as the two approached the campfire again. After a brief breakfast of coffee and leftover bread, Lyle came up to inform them of revelry. He explained that they would receive instructions as to when they would leave the encampment. Willis reached into his pocket and pulled out the letter that he had got the day before from Rosalie. He had read it several times already, and before he began reading it again, he lifted the letter up to his nose. He thought he could smell Rosalie's perfume.

In the letter, she related that everything was going well at the farm. The reverend was in reasonably good health, and she said the church was doing well for the winter. Thirty people had attended church on the Sunday previous to the letter. Willis, knowing how slow the mail service was, figured that the letter was probably three weeks late. Willis was surprised when he read that Weldon, the colored blacksmith, attended church with his entire family. Bessie, his oldest daughter, was delighted that her entire family had come for the first time.

As Willis read the letter again, he was really surprised that a white family from Plainview had convinced the black family to come with them to the service. Willis thought about this, and he recalled Rosalie telling him about Weldon, the blacksmith at Rover. He knew that the reverend and Rosalie had really tried to convince Weldon to attend their church. And yet, a family from Plainview, a man and his wife and their two girls, had been able to convince the former slave family to attend the all-white church. The white man must be a good friend of the colored blacksmith, Willis thought. Yes, his world was changing.

Willis ignored the third page and moved on down to the last two paragraphs of page four. "Willis, please be careful," he read again. "We learned that you all might be fighting this next week. Don't try to be a hero. Stay behind trees. I pray every day for your safety, and I pray for Eslie and the other men. Don't take this wrong, Willis, but I really love you. I want to be with you for the rest of our lives."

Willis noted that Rosalie ended her letter with, "Your loving wife to be, Rosalie." Would he survive the expected battle? Would he be able to see his family and Rosalie again? Willis carefully folded the letter and put it back in his pocket as he heard the bugle blowing up near the front of the encampment.

Chapter 19

The General

March 1862

IT WAS ALWAYS COLD in Arkansas in February. Willis could remember in '57 or '58, it snowed more than a foot. He must have carried firewood in for the fireplace at least four or five times each day that month. Ahab, who usually slept under the open foundation near the fireplace, was allowed to come in at night. It was the only time that Willis could remember the mules, Murt and Kate, staying in the barn. One of the young calves froze to death. But it was at least that cold the last two days.

Bugles had sounded more than twenty minutes earlier. Everyone was lined up for the daily orders, most wearing as many extra clothes as they could wear. Willis had stuffed some old rags from worn-out socks in his old shoes. The shoes, a hole in the right one and a missing shoe heel on the other, were not going to last long. Captain Hunt said that they might be getting shoes from Little Rock sometime. Fortunately, Willis's shoes were better than some other men's shoes.

The metal barrel on Willis's musket was so cold; it almost hurt to touch it.

"Dress Right," the captain commanded as he moved in front of the company.

"None of us are dressed right," Willis heard Bartis mutter at the drill command.

Bartis usually had a comment and it was usually critical. "Men, we have a new general reporting today." The tall lieutenant went on to say, "He is a graduate of West Point and has already been fighting back in Virginne. General Van Dorn is a fighting man," Hunt continued after looking over the company.

Willis believed that all generals thought they were fighting men.

"We will probably be leaving the Fayetteville area in a few days to see if we can find some Yankees," the officer continued. Hunt usually talked longer than necessary. "Men, I want General Van Dorn to see some real Confederate soldiers. And men, the rumors are true. We now know the Federals are camped near the Arkansas line. They may even invade our state today. I need not tell you why we must stop them and run them back to St. Louis. Today will be a busy day. Eat well and then check your gear, especially shell and powder. Those of you who did not receive your bayonets yesterday, see that you get them today."

Willis actually hoped for some kind of activity that day or soon, anyway. He was tired of marching and drilling. He wondered what the Federal army was thinking now.

Captain Hunt was finishing up. "After breakfast, we will reform for a brief time. We want the new general to be impressed with Arkansas troops."

The men moved back to their camp area, where the morning fire continued to burn. The pinewood burning there smelled good. Crows were already flying about, as if looking for leftovers. There was little sun due to the heavy cloud cover.

"We better eat the last of the bacon, 'cause I'm sure we will be on hardtack for a while," Elsie said as he sat down.

Willis was stoking the fire. Bartis walked over and sat down on the ground by the fire. The chunky Bartis shouldn't be too hungry, thought Willis; he ought to be able to live off of his over-the-belt stomach. Bartis then got up, went back over to his bedroll, lay down, and pulled his blanket over his face. "Wake me when it's time to form up."

Eslie dropped the remainder of the bacon in the old, blackened skillet. Quickly, the smell of bacon replaced the smell of the pinewood and the burning fire. Even the sizzle sounded good. Several men walked by the fire and asked where they had got the pork. While Willis never mentioned it, he really hated that Bartis had stolen the pig. He felt even worse when he found that Bartis had stolen it from an old widow woman who had no family.

Eva had always taught the evil of sin. Nothing was more serious than stealing. Willis couldn't remember which one, but he knew that one of the Ten Commandments spoke of stealing. Willis would never forget the hard whipping Amos had given him for picking up the Jewish peddler's pocketknife and not returning it to him before the peddler left. That knife remained on the fireplace well over a month until peddler Openhiemer came to Young Gravelly again. When the peddler came by, Amos made Willis give the knife to him and apologize for picking it up.

Bartis smelled the bacon, sat up, and asked if it was done.

"Let's eat," said Eslie, removing the skillet from the fire and putting it on a nearby rock.

Bartis reached for a piece of the thick-cut slab and then quickly dropped the hot bacon back in the old skillet. He then reached for the old coffee pot and his old tin cup. "Makes me think of Ma's breakfast."

"Your ma cooked up a stolen hog?" Willis grinned.

"Doubt it, but she's eaten stolen watermelon, though she didn't know," Bartis replied.

Willis wondered if Bartis felt any guilt over swiping the pig.

"Man, I sure know how to pick a hog," exclaiming Bartis, after tasting the bacon.

"You're going to be so fat, you can't catch a Yankee," said Lyle, who had just walked up to the fire.

"We leaving today," Willis asked, looking at Lyle and motioned toward the frying pan.

"Depends," said Lyle, taking a piece of bacon and wadding into his mouth. "If Van Dorn gets here, we may move north of Fayetteville. Don't say anything, but we gonna move north to find some Yanks."

Eslie poured the bacon grease into the fire, causing it to leap higher. He looked over at Lyle and asked, "You think we's trained enough?"

"I think so," Lyle said, glancing into the fire and then back towards the road. "Like I said, we already know how to shoot, and we have learned how to march."

The lieutenant said that most of the Yanks still needed to learn how to shoot a gun. "Only thing the captain worries about is enough powder and balls."

"We all shoot straight," Bartis said, removing the tin coffee cup from his mouth. "And it only takes one bullet to kill a man."

Eslie had been listening while he cleaned out the old skillet with dirt. "Only problem is the Yanks can put more men on the field. They's likely to put more shells in the air."

"Supposed to be more Federal army officers joined up with the South than stayed with the North," replied Willis, who thought Eslie made more sense than Bartis and was better aware of the army's resources. "McCulloch and Van Dorn were good Federal soldiers. Van Dorn has been fighting with Lee back in Virginiee. We may be stronger in officers."

"Need you guys to help the teamsters load wagons," Lyle said as he finished his coffee and dropped the tin cup. "Want Van Dorn to see a neat camp."

The three privates started back toward the supply wagons with Lyle. While loading boxes of supplies on the wagons, the trio heard a commotion back towards the east side of the camp. Several cavalrymen were riding into camp in two neat lines. Included in the group was a medium-built, black-haired officer in a neat, gray uniform. Like many Confederate officers, Van Dorn had the characteristic goatee. His dark hair hung beneath his hat. The general appeared relaxed and confident as he rode by, glancing neither left or right. One might have even accused Van Dorn of displaying signs of arrogance. The horseman rode on toward the white house that now served as headquarters for the army.

Later, most of the troops learned that Van Dorn had left Pocahontas about two weeks earlier. In crossing a river, possibly the Little Red River, Van Dorn fell or was thrown from his horse into the frigid water. Due to the cold weather, he came down seriously ill. He had traveled most of the way to his waiting army in an ambulance. When the general neared the army, he finally decided to again mount a horse.

"Shoot, I would rather ride in an ambulance than on a horse," said Bartis, who had some doubts about the story's authenticity.

Lyle assured the Gravelly men that Van Dorn was still coughing a lot from the illness.

"Looked like a real general, didn't he?" Willis said as he watched the cavalry unit move toward headquarters.

"They all look like real generals," Eslie turned to Willis and said.

"Looks highfalutin to me," said Bartis, who had been sitting on the end of the wagon they were loading and was still looking toward the departing Van Dorn. "You can bet that he won't have to eat the grub that we eat."

"Hurry up, men," Lyle commanded as he moved over to the wagon and looked over the load. "It's starting to snow again."

Sure enough, the snow was drifting down in small flakes. Willis, observing the falling snowflakes, thought about the time back home when he had gone to look for Bossy's small calf. It had begun to snow by the time he had reached the northwest pasture. Moving along the north fence line, not more than 100 yards south of Rock Creek, he came across a section of fence that was on the ground. As he examined the fence, he knew a large animal must have damaged it. He knew that the Jersey bull he had named Goliath did not cause the damage because the bull was in the southeast pasture. The mules were also in the same pasture. Willis noticed some animal hair on some of the old barbed wire. He knew that whitetail deer could not have created that much damage.

Willis recalled that the snowflakes in the pasture had become quite large and that he had gone through the gap where the fence was damaged and began to walk up toward Rock Creek. The snow was getting heavier and it was sticking to the grass. Then Willis heard sounds. In the heavy, falling snow, Willis could see a large animal that was eating something. It was a black bear, and he had almost finished eating the young calf. Smelling the human scent, the bear turned, ready to defend his late dinner. Willis froze, and the bear took a couple of steps toward him. Willis turned and began moving back toward the fence, carefully watching the bear's actions. The bear decided to forget the intruder and finish his meal. Willis was sure that this was the bear that had gotten into the smokehouse and finished off most of the family's ham and bacon. Willis forgot about the bear incident.

As he lifted one of the last boxes up on the wagon, Willis noticed that the present snowflakes were much larger now here in the Fayetteville area. After loading the last box, Eslie turned to Willis and suggested that they gather extra firewood for the fire. It was near sundown and the temperature was lower than during the day. Suddenly, the bugles sounded again. Willis couldn't believe that the men would have to form this late in the evening. Surly they weren't going to march.

Lyle was yelling at other men in the company. Eslie had dropped an armload of firewood and Bartis was already complaining out loud about forming up. "That darn Mississippian is going to make us drill at dusk in the snow."

Company C had already moved into the open pastureland that had been used the past three days for camp. Other companies were in the midst of forming. Willis heard other men behind him complaining about the late formation. Others were complaining about their supper getting cold, while others complained that they needed daylight to collect wood for the fire.

After a call for attention, Colonel Ledbetter, with Company C, stepped forward to speak to his men. Since Company B was only about twenty yards away, most of those men could hear the speaker.

"Men, we have done quite well, for the most part, since leaving Van Buren. I know, we had the mishap crossing the flooding creek, but we have learned much about being part of an effective army. However, there is one important item that I must bring up. That is desertion—or leaving without permission. Men, we all love our relatives and families back home. We would do anything for our folks. And," the speaker paused, "it looks like Arkansas is in for a cold, late winter. This will be a hardship on many families. While we must always think of our families, yes, and even pray for them, we cannot jump up and leave for home without proper authorization. We have lost more than twenty men since we left Van Buren, not counting those we lost in the creek crossing. Your officers have talked to you about this problem. We caught two deserters only to have them escape again. General McCulloch has stated that we may have to take serious measures to stop desertion. We all know what that means."

Several men turned to look at their friends. Willis heard someone making light of the officer's comments. It sounded like Bartis. Ledbetter had concluded with most of his remarks and was leading up to an introduction of the new general. By then, Van Dorn had walked up behind the speaker. Ledbetter was saying something about President Davis assigning another Mississippian to Arkansas, because he knew that the state of Arkansas was high priority in terms of the war. He also mentioned that Van Dorn had fought bravely in the Mexican War prior to his recent experience in Virginia. He finally concluded with some comment about one of the best cavalry officers in the Confederacy, that being Earl Van Dorn.

The general stepped forward with a confident manner, quickly thanked the colonel, and began speaking in a self-assured tone. He gave no reference to himself or his past experience. Rather, Van Dorn reminded the men that the Army of the West was responsible for western Arkansas, which was in fact the western part of the Confederate States of America. He reminded the men of the importance of their mission. That mission: Stop the invasion of Arkansas by a foreign power. By invasion, Van Dorn explained, Yankees have crossed the Missouri state line into Arkansas. He assured the army that the invasion would be met with stubborn resistance. He concluded his remarks with a statement that the general officers would provide more information as to the movement and direction of the army. The general turned, saluted the colonel, and smartly walked back toward the headquarters at nearby Camp Stephens.

Orders were given to form regiments. Once the groups were organized, the regimental officers began to give information about breaking camp and the next day's activities. The most surprising information given out to the men was that Union cavalry patrols had been sighted only about twenty miles away, near the town of Bentonville. The Reb staff believed that most of the Federal army was thirty or so miles northeast, possibly, near a small Arkansas crossroads called Pea Ridge. The small hamlet was just west of a vine-covered mountain also called Pea Ridge Mountain.

The Federals had also slowed down and were moving with more caution. According to the officer's information, an experienced leader, General Samuel Curtis, was leading the Federals. It was stressed several times that the Federals were also well trained and well equipped. It would be a tough battle. All soldiers should carefully check all equipment and carry no extras in their haversacks.

As Willis glanced around in the twilight, every soldier's face was serious. All knew the fight was here. Many would be wounded and many would be killed. Within an hour, except for the sentries, almost everyone was in their bedroll. Sleep came difficult for most of the men. Willis again thought about Rosalie. Would he be alive to marry her or would she be the wife of someone else?

The thought of death was horrible. However, the thought of losing an arm or two legs was worse. Willis thought he would rather die than be maimed for life.

Lyle, the last to get into his bedroll, had similar thoughts. Are the men trained well enough? Will they fight under the terrible assault and gunfire by the Federals? Would any men run away or desert? Lyle knew that as a general officer, he would be out front. He knew that the lower ranking officers were often killed before a lot of the regular foot soldiers. Could he handle it?

Eslie, in his blankets, stared up at the cloudy skies. What would daylight bring? Would he die tomorrow? If so, who would take care of his pa? If he would only quit drinking. Eslie doubted that his pa would ever give up alcohol. He was hooked on it.

Bartis was afraid. He had given much thought to battle. It seemed, especially here in Arkansas, that a soldier could hide behind a tree or rock. He did not plan on being a hero. The smartest move, he thought, was to lag behind some and watch what developments took place in front. He would remember this.

Chapter 20

The Deserter

March 1862

MARCH 4 WAS MUCH warmer. The snow was melting. The Army of the West was asked to and delivered a sixteen-mile march—over Telegraph Road, which connected Fort Smith and Fayetteville. The road, the normal route of the Butterfield Stage, was not much of a road. Stage drivers often referred to the route as "the camel's hump" because of the hilly, rocky terrain. The road at lower levels was now nothing but mud. The supply trains and artillery batteries required constant help from the infantry to get through the muck north of the Boston Mountains.

Even though the army was delayed and detoured, at the end of the day they had covered the worst part of the march. Just as dusk was nearing, the army moved through the outskirts of Springdale and prepared for encampment. Through Lyle, Willis had heard that the Yanks were close by. He noticed that everyone was quieter today. Bartis really seemed concerned about an encounter with the Federals.

As the men of the 20th Regiment fell out to prepare their evening fires, a brief commotion occurred off to the east side of camp. A cavalry attachment came by with a trailing prisoner. Eslie had just put the coffeepot on the fire. He and Bartis glanced up to see the prisoner.

"You mean we already caught us a Yankee?"

"Looks like it," Eslie said. "Poor guy."

Willis noticed something familiar about the prisoner. Then he knew why. The prisoner was Frank.

"What's going on?" questioned Bartis, who now recognized Frank as well.

Lyle had walked over to the fire. He looked at the departing cavalry detachment and the trailing prisoner. "He deserted."

"Deserted? Frank wouldn't desert. He was marching with us all morning. I had lunch with him."

"Maybe so, but the colonel said he came up missing right after lunch," Lyle said, looking back at Bartis. "Cavalry picked him up about ten miles south — said he was running south. They think that he was going home."

"Well, what did he say?" asked a now excited Bartis.

"Said he was going home to his family."

Willis had been listening to Lyle and knew he probably had the right story. "Can you help him, Lyle?"

"Doubt it," Lyle said, looking into the fire. "McCulloch is tired of deserters, and they told us that more than thirty men had deserted since we left Van Buren."

"We won't have an army if we allow everyone to leave when they want to," said Eslie, who had never respected the nervous Frank. "Hey, we're still here."

"Lyle, will they shoot him?" asked Bartis, obviously worried about Frank.

"I'm afraid they might," Lyle said, looking back toward the detachment. "Van Dorn, McCulloch, and Price have all been threatening to punish deserters by making an example out of someone. And Frank is the first deserter that has been picked up."

Once he had made that statement, Lyle abruptly left to attend to more business. The men continued to prepare for possible battle.

Willis observed some soldiers who appeared to be writing notes with their names and towns on paper so that if they were killed, their relatives could be notified of the death. However, he did not see any of his friends prepare such a note. Shortly, the encampment was surprised to hear the firing of muskets. Was the enemy in sight? Was this the enemy? Several soldiers reached for their muskets. But, then, no more shots. However, there was more excitement. A man came running from the frontal position of the army.

"They shot the deserter! They shot him!" he shouted, running by the Yell County group.

"What—they shot Frank?" Bartis shouted as the man ran by them.

None of the other Gravelly men could open their mouths. They could not believe the man, but yet, they knew that it was probably true. Later, Lyle admitted that the story was true. On McCulloch's orders—and after thirty-one desertions—they selected Frank to be the example. No more desertions. From an administrative standpoint, the lesson proved to be an effective one. Desertions stopped; however McCulloch made no friendships among the Gravelly men.

After a delayed start on March 5, the army moved out for a confrontation with the Union Army of the Southwest, led by General Curtis. Van Dorn stopped the march several times as he attempted to analyze the position of the Federals. Such delays could be encouraging to the infantry or discouraging. Delays sometime caused the troops to feel that the officers were unsure of what to do. In Van Dorn's case, this was not true. He was seeking out Curtis and he intended to clean out

Arkansas and follow with an invasion of Missouri.

~~~

LYLE CAME UP TO the regiment to check on the men. He said they could rest and eat with the stipulation that they not light any fires. Since it was late in the evening, this had to mean that the men would see action soon.

Eslie asked if anyone knew the name of the community they had just marched through. Lyle, who was usually quiet, but even more so today, replied that it was Elm Springs.

Willis noticed that everyone was not taking a break. Three or four regiments had continued to march to the northwest. Even before the departing Rebs had gotten out of sight, several shots rang out somewhere to the north.

"Those are not hunters," Eslie said, looking over at Willis.

Willis looked down at his musket. It was finally here. They were going to battle with the enemy. They would be shot at and they would be trying to kill the Yankees. Willis thought, I may even be killed. He thought he could shoot at a man; however, hand-to-hand combat or use of the bayonet worried him. He wondered if he could take his musket, with attached bayonet, and stab someone. Then, he remembered that he might be the one being bayoneted. He wished that he had concentrated better in the drill session. Suppose the Yanks are better trained than us, he thought. His thoughts were interrupted as the men were told to reform for further movement north.

"I think we ought to establish a defense line here and have the Yanks come to us," proposed Bartis, who had also been very quiet.

No one answered as the regiment resumed marching out of the Elm Springs community. After another ten-minute march, they heard a considerable amount of firing to the northwest again. Suddenly the artillery units opened up. Unlike the drill time, the earth literally shook as the big cannons threw out shell after shell, only to receive a response from the Federal batteries. Once again the men were told to take a break.

As the men sat down, two cavalry units rolled by in a hurry to reach some destination north of the main army. Buglers blew their horns, horses ran, cannon sounded, teamsters drove ammunition wagons to designated points, and officers yelled. Willis thought, this is war. Yet, the regiment continued to sit, awaiting further orders to advance.

To the west, the sound of horses and men approaching created fear in the waiting army. Could the Yankees have used a flanking movement and gotten around behind them? Willis had read some about Napoleon. He knew that a poorly positioned army could be flanked.

Men began to jump up and look to the west, as if awaiting a Yankee charge. Willis focused his attention on the officers. Their actions should show whether the soldiers should be concerned about the approaching sound. Most of the officers seemed to be aware of the movement. Shortly, most of the men realized that the approaching group was friendly.

"Looks like we have been reinforced," Willis said to Bartis.

The new arrivals now came into sight. Willis noticed something strange about the newcomers. The first cavalry unit that arrived moved through the west side of the waiting army. By now, the faces of the soldiers could be seen.

"Indians! There're Territory Indians!" exclaimed a teamster standing nearby.

Their regimental flag, blue with the face of an Indian, had printed across the top "1st Cherokee Mounted Rifles." Following close behind was a contingent of the 3rd Texas

Cavalry. Over the next hour the Indian infantry slowly marched through the area and moved somewhere to the north side of the encampment.

"You know anything about them, Lyle?"

"The colonel said they are part of Albert Pike's Confederate army. Van Dorn believes they may have 500 to 600 men."

The territory infantry did not seem much different from other Southern units. For the most part, the Indians were dressed about like the other soldiers, in their everyday clothes. Most of the Indians carried shotguns, and most had knives on their belts. Lyle watched as the Indian reinforcements slowly moved past.

"We must have 10,000 soldiers here," he thought out loud, watched the marching Indians. "The Yanks can't have that many."

As Willis, Eslie, and Lyle moved back to their camping area, they could see two wagons arriving at the camp from the north. It looked like both wagons were in a hurry. The worried soldiers now directed their attention toward the hurriedly moving wagons. Men toward the front of the encampment moved up to assist the arriving wagons. Willis and others could not see what was holding the attention of the men crowding around the wagons.

"Let's see what's going on now," Bartis said, looking at Willis.

The shooting in the distance had slowed down over the past half hour. Hardee's Arkansas Battery fired only an occasional shot. As Willis and Bartis followed others in the direction of the new excitement, other artillery units rolled through camp, heading north. Bringing up the rear of the moving artillery unit was a huge cannon, obviously very old, pulled by two yoke of oxen.

"Look, they're bringing up Old Jackson!" someone yelled.

The old cannon, from the Little Rock Arsenal, was supposed to have been used in the War of 1812.

"At the rate it's moving, the battle will be over afore it gets there," Bartis said, noticing the huge cannon. "Why are they pulling it with oxen?"

"They say it's too heavy for horses or mules," answered Lyle, who had caught up with the twosome and overheard the question. "Got to use oxen."

By then, the Gravelly trio had gotten close to the arriving wagons. Even before then, men were overheard making comments about wounded and dead soldiers. Soldiers had already picked up some of the men from the wagons and moved them over to the hospital wagons. Willis stepped through a group of men that were watching the men being removed from the wagon. You could already hear the moans and cries of the wounded soldiers. One soldier, certainly not more than nineteen years of age, was screaming.

Bartis looked over another observer's shoulder at the sight. The screaming soldier had his right arm missing. He could see the blood through the makeshift bandage.

"Son, you're going to be all right," said one of the attending soldiers that accompanied the wounded. The boy never heard the last part of the comment, because he became unconscious once again.

An officer of some rank was being removed from the same wagon very carefully. He was obviously in great pain but doing everything possible to conceal it in front of the crowd.

"Wonder what happened to him?" asked Bartis.

"Gut shot," an observer answered. "Could see him holding his hand over the hole—big as a hickory nut. Never make it—those gut shots are usually the end."

"Forget it," said someone about a third man that was being lifted from the wagon. "He's dead."

The workers laid the man back on the wagon and began to assist a fourth wounded man. Willis never noticed the next soldier being removed. He was still looking at the man declared dead. Bartis was also in a trance. The only time that either had seen a dead person was at a wake or at a funeral. Willis had seen his Grandfather Elliott's body during the funeral wake, which lasted almost two days. People from all over Gravelly, Bluffton, and even as far away as Rover had come for the wake. Someone sat up with the corpse at night and during the day.

Willis was ten years old at the time and Amos had taken him to view the body. The thing that struck Willis was that his grandfather's mouth was slightly open. He hated to ask why. Grandpa, a healthy, old man, was never big, but he looked much smaller lying on the newly constructed table. Willis remembered that his grandpa was very pale. He had reached out to touch the old man's hand, and it was cold and stiff. Willis felt that he should hug and kiss his grandpa, but he could not do it. He remembered later that Eva said that her pa was in heaven all this time, maybe even watching. She explained that grandpa's body was just a shell and that God would give him a new body—one to be used in heaven.

Willis looked at the stiff body of the soldier, as if trying to learn something about the man. The soldier was dressed in old brown pants that were obviously too short; a tattered, faded blue shirt with only one button; and some worn boots. Even though he had a beard, Willis guessed him to be about thirty-five years of age. He probably had children and a family, Willis thought. He probably had a mother and father back home. Willis knew that the man would be buried nearby. He would not ever get to be buried at a place like Young Gravelly Cemetery.

Bartis had still not moved.

"Let's go," Lyle said, reaching out for his arm. The three men were silent as they moved back to their camp.

"Colonel said we are moving out," Lyle broke the silence. "Looks like more snow."

Still neither Willis nor Bartis spoke. Eslie had already heard of the command to move out, and he had begun to organize his possessions in preparation for the march. As Willis began to pick up his possessions, which included a knife, musket, canteen, and blanket roll with food provisions, a mounted officer rode up to speak to Lyle. The two conferred for three or four minutes, and then the officer rode on to speak with other officers. Lyle walked back over to the remaining threesome.

"Are we marching?" asked Willis.

"We move out at 6:00 a.m.," Lyle said, looking over at Bartis. "Van Dorn thinks that we've got Federal General Sigel cut off and that we can whip him before turning back on Curtis's main army. We hope to defeat Sigel near Bentonville. Get to sleep early tonight, 'cause we will be forming up about 5:00 a.m."

Lyle went on down to speak to other men in the regiment. Willis and the other two men sat back down and decided to eat something. Since fires were not permitted, the snack consisted of bread or hardtack.

"You reckon the generals are getting' long any better now?" Eslie said after a period of quiet. "Everyone says that McCulloch and Price hate each other. Don't know why, but they don't git along."

Willis had discussed the generals before with Lyle. Of course, Lyle's knowledge was mainly secondhand, and he would quickly say so. As Lyle had explained, the 20th Regiment was part of McCulloch's division. General Price commanded the other half of the army. Most of Price's troops were Missourians with a few Arkansans. The way that Lyle understood it, Price had been in command in Missouri and he decided to retreat back into Arkansas. Once back in Arkansas, Price, a veteran of the Mexican War, had requested that McCulloch, a former Texas Ranger and Indian fighter, combine forces and invade Missouri again. Again according to Lyle's sources, McCulloch refused to work with Price, believing that his mission was to provide internal security for the state of Arkansas. President Davis had been unable to get the two generals to work together, one reason being that both armies were heavily made up of state militia, Missouri militia under Price and Arkansas militia under McCulloch.

Finally, in exasperation, President Davis sent Van Dorn, the ex-West Pointer and Mexican War veteran, to command the newly formed Army of the West. Van Dorn now had the problem of getting the two antagonists to work together. According to Lyle, Van Dorn was doing it mainly by keeping the two generals separate and uninformed. However, since both Price and Van Dorn had fought in the Mexican War, it was assumed that Van Dorn might listen to Price more than McCulloch.

Eslie was cleaning his .58 caliber musket. As usual, he was making the best preparations. After some more talk about the wagons with the wounded and dead Reb soldiers, the men got into their bedrolls early. Snowflakes already drifted in the night air. The men had laid out their blankets near the loaded wagons. Unlike other evenings, they were relatively quiet after preparing for a short night's rest.

"You guys reckon we should have prayer before we go to sleep?" Willis finally broke the silence.

Bartis said nothing.

"Go rite ahead, Willis," Eslie replied.

Willis moved up on his right elbow, then bowed his head and began to speak." God, we thank you for being with us today. We ask you to take care of our families back home in Gravelly. Be with Reverend Gotham and heal him."

Willis stopped for a few seconds, as if trying to decide how to word his prayer. "God, be with the Generals sosen they know what to do tomorrow. We hope that you will protect us against the Yankees and help us shoot straight. Be with the wounded today and…" Willis again delayed, "be with the family of the dead man we saw while ago. We hope he's in heaven. Amen."

No one said anything else. It seemed to Willis that he had hardly turned over before Lyle was awakening him.

Chapter 21

Bentonville

March 1862

IT WAS ALMOST 7:00 a.m. when the Confederate army began marching in a northerly direction. The men had been informed that Bentonville was the general destination. From the instructions, though brief, Willis could tell that they would be meeting the enemy before long. He wondered if the Yankees were as worried as he was.

Willis also remembered that a few men in Yell County had joined the Federal army. He only knew one of the men that had decided to answer Lincoln's call. Arthur Sparks, a friend of Lyle's from Plainview, had decided to join the Federal army. His only explanation was that he was answering his country's call to arms. Arthur, the son of a shoe cobbler, and very likely to be one himself, had hoped that Lincoln would not invade Arkansas. He had also expressed hope that Arkansas would rejoin the Union before hostilities broke out. Willis knew that Arthur had been assigned to one of the Missouri units. Even Lyle had not heard from his friend. As the slow march continued toward Bentonville, Willis wondered what he would do if he had to personally fight Arthur.

Within an hour the army could see the outskirts of

Bentonville. By then, shots could be heard from the north side of town. Willis expected to form battle lines at any time. Bartis had again begun to openly second-guess the Rebel generals. He believed that the Rebs were moving too close to the Federal army.

Then the army received orders to delay. Several artillery batteries moved on past the now idle army. Cavalry units had moved across the front of the army several times. And then, once again, the overall activity in the army suddenly increased. The bugles sounded, officers began shouting orders, and men began moving into their respective regiments.

A Rebel officer rode into the middle of the stationary troops and began talking fast to another officer. McCulloch himself and two aides conferred with the officer before he quickly saluted and rode back to the north. In terms of minutes, the army was again on the march. More shots were heard in the distance. Several large cannon, Eslie thought six-pounders, suddenly began firing into the front ranks of the Reb army. The Yankees were ready to do battle.

Willis noticed McIntosh's Indians ride pass toward Bentonville. He looked to his right. What was it? A cannonball had hit Russell Lamb, an acquaintance from Belleville. The shot tore off about half of his face before it hit a teamster driving a supply wagon. Both men were killed. The driverless-wagon bolted forward as the scared mules reacted to the screams of the men. A second shell hit a huge pine tree not far from Lyle. The Yankees had found the range.

Officers began shouting orders for dispersal as frightened men bunched together. Willis noticed several men in front of him turn and run for the rear. One man, not more than eighteen years of age, had thrown away his gun and started running south. Before he got a hundred yards, a shell hit him in the middle of the back, killing him instantly. Officers screamed for the men to organize and form battle lines as the shelling continued. Even with all the action, Willis heard Old Jackson, the old twelve-pounder, fire. The huge pine trees seemed to shiver at the noise. For an instant, everyone was deaf as a result of the Rebel guns. The regiment was instructed to move to the right. Lyle tried to bring order to the disorganized unit. Suddenly, Willis heard what sounded like hail hitting near the unit.

"Grapeshot," said Eslie. "They're firing grapeshot." Several men started firing toward the sound of the Yankee guns.

"Hold the fire! Hold your fire!" shouted an officer that Willis had never seen. "You will hit our own men."

Battle lines were partially formed. No order had been given to advance. Willis expected to see Yankees coming out of the smoky area to the north. He checked his musket. He now knew that he would shoot at the enemy. The huge guns continued firing.

"What we gonna do?" shouted an obviously terrified Bartis.

"Stay where you're at," Lyle shouted back.

"Oh God, please help us," prayed Willis.

Suddenly, a huge explosion occurred to the rear. An enemy shell had hit a munitions wagon. Willis noticed a loose mule running through the lines, dragging a wagon tongue. The mule had blood on its hindquarters. Willis didn't know whether the blood was from the mule or from a soldier, but no one bothered to stop the runaway mule.

When Willis felt a sting in his left shoulder, he knew he had been shot. But when he quickly grabbed for his shoulder, he found that it was all right. It must have been a rock that was kicked up by a cannonball. Still no advance was called as more soldiers were forming to the rear behind the regiment.

187

Taking the chance to look around, Willis saw several men that had been hit. One man, a fellow from Louisiana that Willis had visited with earlier, was on the ground screaming. Willis quickly crawled over to the soldier.

"I'm dying! I'm dying!" screamed the man. "Oh, God, help me. I'm dying."

Willis noticed that the man's right arm was gone. Blood was everywhere. Before Willis could help the man, he suddenly leaped to his feet and began running to the rear—without his arm. Willis could not believe what the man was able to do.

In ten minutes, the shelling from the enemy slowed down. Bugles sounded in the distance. The Reb cavalry was on the move.

"Let's get out of here," Bartis pleaded, grabbing Willis by the arm.

"No," Willis said, jerking his arm back. "The fight's over."

Sure enough, the action died down. Colonel Harvell rode back to confer with the officers. Lyle had moved down to listen to the colonel. Willis was close enough to overhear the loud officers.

"Sigel's retreating. He's trying to move east and link up with Curtis. He's left several batteries to protect his retreat. Get ready to move." Bugles sounded and word was passed down to advance.

"Let's go men," yelled Lyle.

Willis, Bartis, and Eslie begin moving forward. An occasional shell hit near the advancing line. More bugles sounded near the front. Musket fire began to occur, all along the front line area.

Willis looked to the right to see men —Rebels—running. They were running from someone. Then Willis saw blue cavalry soldiers firing into the regiment to the right. He raised his musket and fired into the advancing cavalry. A huge horse carrying a cavalryman fell. Willis had hit the horse. He quickly began reloading his musket. Bartis had also fired and was reloading. Before either could shoot again, the Union cavalry began to withdraw. Slowly, McCulloch's army began to advance toward the retreating Federals.

After a couple of miles or so, Willis noticed that the area in which the skirmish occurred began to drop off into a small river valley. Lyle said McCulloch's staff referred to it as Little Sugar Creek Valley, a valley formed over the ages by Little Sugar Creek. As the gray battle line moved over the ridge and looked off into the valley, they could see Sigel's army retreating further northeast in an attempt to link up with General Curtis's Federal army.

The grays begin to fire everything down on the retreating army. With their backs to the north bank of the creek, the position was precarious for the invaders. Willis noticed that Rebel cavalry had made it to the top of a high-rising bluff on the west side of the valley. There, they had positioned a small cannon. The Federals could not contend with the fire from this strategic position.

Up and down the battle line Southern soldiers were encouraged to advance and catch the entrapped Sigel army. Willis and Bartis moved forward slowly, occasionally firing toward the Federals. Willis fired once at a man and saw him fall. He believed that he had injured or possibly killed him.

The advance across the valley seemed sure to produce a Southern victory. Within a quarter of a mile from the creek, Willis realized that the Federals had brought up other batteries on the north side of the creek. These cannon, supported by Federal infantry, began firing shells and shrapnel over the Federal army and into the rapidly advancing Southerners. The Southern advance slowed and then stopped, as Southerners began to move back out of the range from the Union guns. The Northern cannon had done the job.

Willis could see the last of the retreating blue-clads move on toward the safety of Curtis's lines across Little Sugar Creek. Meanwhile, the Federal shelling was now creating havoc for the Reb army, causing devastating effects on the Arkansans. Withdrawal was called in order to await artillery reinforcements.

By then, it was late in the afternoon. Most of the Southerners had not eaten since early morning. The army was directed to settle down for the evening in the line of trees bordering on the valley. Occasional pickets would be placed closer to the swollen creek in the distance. Eslie, Willis, and Bartis sat down on the sloping downhill.

"Wonder when the grub wagon will be here?" Bartis asked. All three men knew that there might not be any food.

"You gonna have to find us a pig," Eslie replied, looking over at Bartis. "We passed a couple of farms near that little settlement back there."

"I wouldn't go out away from the army," Willis said, glancing at Eslie to see if he was serious about his request. "We don't know where all of Curtis's army is and we know he wasn't far from Leetown. Besides, you might be arrested as a deserter."

Lyle walked up while Willis was speaking. He had been meeting with officers about battle plans.

"How many killed today?" asked Eslie.

"More than one hundred," answered Lyle. "We had almost that many to desert."

"Van Dorn got any food?" asked Bartis.

Chapter 22

Sentry Duty

WILLIS AWOKE TO LYLE's touch on his shoulder and wondered when Lyle ever slept anymore. Lyle and Eslie both sat up.

"Wake up Bartis and the rest of the group," ordered Lyle as he moved on to wake other members of the regiment.

Willis was hungry. They had only had cold, damp corn mash for supper and they had not had a good meal for at least three days. Willis thought of his home back up on the hill in Gravelly. Eva would be getting up before long to prepare breakfast for Amos and the kids. Ahab would be eating better than Van Dorn's army.

The story was that the Yankees were eating high on the hog. Ben Caveness, a cavalryman from Wing that Willis knew, said several Yankee supply wagons were captured east of Bentonville as Sigel was retreating. They were filled with salted meat, canned goods, and even whiskey. General McIntosh had confiscated the wagons for his Cherokee brigade.

"Man, I would love to have some biscuits and gravy," said Bartis as he got up, stretched, and began rolling up his blanket.

"Probably will after we lick the Yanks, cause theys got a lot of food," said Eslie.

"Let's get some ammo," Willis said. "Lyle said we are to get forty rounds."

"That's not enough ammo," whined Bartis. "We'll shoot that up before eight o'clock."

"I think they don't want us to carry too much till after we cross the creek," said Willis.

A sergeant was issuing the cartridges at a nearby supply wagon. Willis picked up his rations and moved back to the campsite to wrap everything up in his blanket roll. He did not see Bartis go through the ammo lines twice.

The early morning was still extremely cold. Since the men were not allowed to build fires, it was quite uncomfortable. Most of the men wondered why fires were not allowed since the enemy knew where they were.

Willis examined his old shoes. The sole on the left one was almost gone, though the heel remained. Willis had taken a piece of cowhide and wrapped it around his foot, creating a new sole. It was not too comfortable, but it helped keep his foot warmer. But it was not warm now, nor was his other foot. He would be glad to start marching.

By then the regiment was forming. Officers along the line were giving orders to prepare movement down the hillside into the Little Sugar Creek Valley.

"What time is it," asked Bartis.

"Almost six o'clock," Lyle replied.

"What we doing up at this hour," asked Bartis.

"Gonna surprise the Yanks and have their breakfast," repeated a nearby soldier.

The regiment was ready. The early morning cold seemed even worse now, partly due to the anxiety of the moment. Men standing in formation marched in place to create warmth in their feet and legs. They could hear noises back to the west and to the rear of the army. Supply wagons had begun to move forward. Batteries of artillery were also moving into place, preparing for advancement. Cavalry units had already passed the outlying sentry pickets and began descending the hillside.

The night was as dark as it was cold. Even after becoming accustomed to the dark, one could only see a short distance in front of him. Heavy clouds, possibly snow clouds, concealed the stars and new moon.

If Van Dorn was hoping for a surprise, it looked like he had chosen the right time. Slowly and silently, the huge army moved out of the pine trees and down the side of the valley. While the men had been told not to talk, Willis could hear a lot of whispering, most of which was criticism directed at the army staff.

"We not gonna surprise them, even at six o'clock on a frozen night," Willis heard Bartis say. "They got sentries too."

"Think we want to get as close as possible before they realize we're moving," Willis whispered back.

Others complained. One man complained about being hungry. Another complained about his feet. Willis knew that the feet of several men were partially frozen. He also knew that the men might lose toes or more before long, as the frozen areas would deteriorate. Several men were coughing, and some sounded very ill.

They were now about a quarter of a mile from Little Sugar Creek. The swollen creek was out of its banks in every low place in the lower part of the valley. Before long, men would be wading water six to eight inches deep. Willis noticed drifting snow flurries.

The men were soon told to halt. Some of them already wanted to sit down. But it was not possible to sit down in most places because an inch or two of water covered the soil. Almost everyone's feet were wet. Willis hoped that they would not delay long, because his feet were like ice.

One of the men was coughing so much that he was told to report to the rear. The officers wanted it as quiet as possible. After about fifteen minutes, a work detail including officers returned from the front of the moving army. The men could overhear the officers talking about temporary bridges to cross Sugar Creek. One of the officers began to select men to be a part of the work detail. The men selected would assist the pioneer corps in constructing the bridges. Eslie was selected to be part of the detail.

"Be careful," Willis whispered.

The detail disappeared in the dark. It was even colder now. His feet were wet, and Willis was shaking. He asked himself if he was afraid. He didn't think he was afraid to die, but he hated to think about never seeing Amos and Eva again. He wanted to see Rosalie again. If he had a choice, Willis preferred to die in warm weather rather than cold weather.

Sergeant Roland was posting the pickets for the east side of the creek. He looked at the five men selected.

"You have all been trained for sentry and picket duty. You know what to do. You are there to alert us if the Federals begin to advance. Stay alert. You will be on duty for three hours. Another picket will then replace you, unless we advance. Our code word is Dixie. If another soldier reports to relieve you, he will identify himself with the code word. Remember, if anyone approaches, they must use the code. Understand?"

"Yes, sir," replied Willis.

The sergeant placed the pickets in a line about fifty yards apart.

"Cross the creek and go forward, quietly, exactly fifty paces," he instructed the men. "Select a good place to watch from. Try not to cough or make noise. If you are threatened, use your gun and alert our army. Understand?"

"Yes, sir," Willis again answered for the men.

The men spread out and then looked back at the officer. When he waved a white handkerchief, the pickets began to step off the required distance of fifty paces.

A northern wind was now blowing. Still cloudy, there was little moonlight. While Willis thought that he was brave, he knew that he was also scared. It was so quiet out there all alone. How could one forget that the enemy was close by? But, they were also scared and armed to kill. Again, he thought about what Colonel Harvell had told them months ago at Dardanelle: "Be ready to use your weapon. The enemy will certainly kill you."

In the dark, Willis glanced down at his musket. Yes, he had put powder in the barrel. Yes, he had put the ball in the barrel, and yes, he had seated the ball with his ramrod. He reached down to his right hip. The hunting knife was there in the sheath.

Willis jumped when a large owl flew over near the tree that he nervously stood behind. How far away were the Federal pickets — maybe only thirty feet or so? Did he arrive at this point after a Federal picket had selected a post not far away, he wondered. Was a Federal picket watching him even now? He carefully scanned the trees in front. But then he realized, if a Union picket had seen him, the picket would have sounded an alarm or shot him.

Willis again moved forward near a small cedar tree. He remembered the sergeant's instructions to be alert for any movement of the enemy. It was colder now. His wet feet were so cold that they hurt. He had to cough, but he was able to suppress it. Willis noticed that he could definitely see better now. His eyes had adjusted somewhat to the early, dark morning.

As Willis carefully looked around and listened for any movement, he thought of his many coon-hunting experiences. He thought of all the nocturnal sounds that one heard while out on a coon hunt: the sounds of night birds, coyotes yelping, even an occasional mountain lion scream. And then it hit him. He heard none of those sounds here. It was so quiet. Had the animals all left with the arrival of the two armies? A sound—was it the enemy? No. A hanging, broken limb bumping the trunk of the tree had caused the sound. The noise could be heard only when there was a light gust of wind.

I can't be so jumpy, he thought. And then he thought about what he might do if the enemy suddenly showed. What if four or five Yanks stepped out of the trees in front of him? He reached down to make sure his knife was in the scabbard. A commotion back near the creek suddenly interrupted his thoughts. He heard loud calls, orders, and instructions. He wondered why the officers were permitting so much noise, since they had emphasized a noiseless crossing. Soon it was quiet again.

Willis suddenly heard footsteps. He readied his musket. He knew he would use it. This was going to be it. He would have to kill to protect his army.

"Dixie. Dixie. Willis. Willis," whispered a familiar voice.

"Here," whispered Willis, recognizing that it was Lyle. "We need to move?"

"No. Willis, something terrible has happened."

"What?" Willis asked. Lyle hesitated before answering.

"It's Bartis. An officer was checking with the pickets—"

"Did Bartis desert?" Willis interrupted.

"No, Willis. He went to sleep on duty."

"Oh, no," Willis again interrupted. "I warned him about that when we were on sentry duty earlier."

"Willis, Bartis was asleep and a Federal picket bayoneted him."

"Oh, no. Is he dead?"

"Yes, he is gone," Lyle said in a shaky voice, lowering his head. "I wanted you to know. I also wanted to make sure that you are alert. I'm sorry; we'll talk more later."

"Thanks, Lyle," was all Willis could manage to say.

Tears rolled down his face. He couldn't believe Bartis was gone. He would never live again. They would never again hear his jokes or his humorous, critical comments. Bartis was a great friend, Willis thought. And then he had a different thought. If the Feds were that close to Bartis, they were probably still close by.

Willis prayed silently. He prayed for Bartis's parents and friends. He knew that Eva and Amos would be shocked. He wondered if Lyle had been able to tell Eslie about Bartis's death. Again, Willis thought of the times that he and Bartis had spent hunting and fishing. Bartis would never sit around the campfire on a coon hunt. First, Red, the old redbone hound, was killed, and now his master.

Willis was now silently crying. A shot rang out, echoing through the hills. Lyle turned and walked back to Willis. Either the Yankees knew they were advancing or they soon would know they were crossing Little Sugar Creek. No further shots occurred.

"One of our advance pickets probably fired," Lyle said.

He patted Willis on the shoulder and then retreated back toward the creek and the continued crossing. By then, Willis could hear many footsteps as the Southerners reached the east bank and began to reform into ranks. Soon the pioneers would be constructing permanent bridges for the wagons to use. The artillery would follow later, once positions were made secure.

Willis again heard low voices. But he could not understand what was being said. Then he knew why. The language was foreign. He relaxed—it was Cherokee. Some of Pike's army, mostly Cherokee and Choctaw Indians, were moving up.

Willis reasoned that he must be on the right flank, possibly touching one of McIntosh's corps. Everything was soon relatively quiet again, except for muffled sounds of the army that had now made it across Little Sugar Creek. An officer soon came by each picket and ordered them to move forward approximately 100 yards and standby for further orders. Slowly and cautiously, the pickets began moving forward. Willis, using his best deer-stalking skills, moved forward without a sound.

He had walked almost 100 yards when he heard a horse whinny. The horse was definitely in the direction of the Federal lines. He crept forward, making every effort to avoid making any sound. Then he saw the horse. There was no rider. He waited at least a minute. Then he heard other sounds. It sounded as if a man was either wounded or hurt badly. By then his eyes were picking up almost everything in the fading darkness. The Federal is on his knees, thought Willis. Maybe his horse threw him. The sounds were both grunting and moaning.

Willis carefully scanned the small clearing where the soldier was. He saw no one else around. By then, he could see much better. The man, obviously a cavalryman, was taking a dump. Willis could even smell the feces. He tightened his grip on his .58 caliber musket and quickly stepped into the clearing. The soldier heard the movement, dropped some dried leaves that he was preparing to use, and reached for his pistol, lying about three feet away.

"Don't do that," said Willis, unable to think of anything else to say.

The soldier froze, straightened up, and raised his arms slightly.

"Sorry, but I have to capture you, sir." Willis still didn't know what to say. After all, he had never pointed a loaded gun at the enemy at such close quarters. Willis moved closer, his rifle held chest high in ready position.

"Look, Reb, I'm sick. I've had the scours all day."

"You all through?" asked Willis.

"For now, I hope," said the bluecoat. The man had gone ahead and buttoned his pants and straightened his shirt.

"You can put your coat on, if you want. Just don't make me shoot you," Willis said, going over to where the man had been squatting. Sure enough, the cavalryman's pistol and holster were lying there.

"What's your name?" Willis asked, picking up the pistol.

"Name's Tom Welch, from Illinois," the man replied.

"How far is your army from here?"

"Sorry, Reb. We's told not to give any information out," the man said as he looked at Willis. That's probably what I would say if I was captured, Willis thought.

"Gonna have to take you to the colonel, Tom. He'll know what to do." Willis walked over and took the bridle of the horse, pointed his gun back toward his own line, and said, "Down that way." The two men started back down the hill and toward the area of Sugar Creek, with Tom leading the way.

"Halt! Halt or I will shoot!" said a firm voice.

"Dixie! Dixie! Don't shoot! I'm Willis Lofland, a picket in the 20th Regiment. I have a prisoner."

Four men moved from behind trees and started toward Willis and his prisoner, their guns ready.

"Somebody get an officer," ordered Willis.

"I'll get one of the officers," said a short, pudgy Southerner.

"Mind if I sit down?" the prisoner asked.

The men looked at Willis, expecting him to make the decision.

"Reckon so. Far's that goes, we all might as well rest."

The men squatted down, still looking cautiously at the prisoner. No one said anything for a short time. Funny thing, thought Willis, everyone of us are curious to see a Yankee, yet, we would never know the difference in this man and a Southerner on a Saturday at Bluffton.

"You Yanks got any food?" asked one of the Southerners, a tall slender man with a beard at least five inches long.

"Had taters and cornbread last night," the prisoner answered. "Had pork the day before."

You'ens got enough food?" asked the Illinoisan.

"We doing just fine," replied the second soldier, "'cept maybe for shoes and blankets." The prisoner noticed that the man was eyeing his shoes.

"You guys ever wonder why we're fightin'," asked the cavalryman.

"Yank, do you know which state you are in," a third Southerner quickly replied in a critical manner. "It's Arkansas, not Illinois."

"We didn't march into Illinois," the Reb continued. "Ya'll marched into Arkansas. We just protecting what is our'n. You go back to Illinois and won't be no war."

"If'n I'm correct, you guys were up in Missouri 'fore we run ya back into these hills," replied the cavalryman, in defense of his army. "Ya'll protecting what's your'n in Missouri?"

"Tom, reckon ya'll weren't told that the Missouri Legislature voted an act of secession and joined up with the Confederation," Willis spoke up. "Believe that we were helping them protect our new government."

"Don't make no difference," said the prisoner. "We all probably gonna be killed tomorrow anyhow. We got more than ten thousand men under arms and you'ns got about the same number. When those cannon start and we charge each 'uns lines, lot'a folks going to be dead."

The Southerners listened to the cavalryman, some believing him, others doubting what he said.

"Where's the prisoner?" asked a staff officer that had just arrived.

"He's right here, sir," Willis spoke up. "Name's Tom Welch from Illinois. Also got his horse."

The officer stopped in front of the prisoner. The cavalryman slowly stood up in front of the officer.

"I'm Private Thomas Welch. Your man captured me while I was taking a crap." The other Southerners laughed.

"What cavalry unit you with?" asked the officer, looking first at Welch, and then toward the horse.

Willis was surprised to hear the man reply Company A, 36th Illinois Cavalry.

"You get lost?" the officer asked, studying the prisoner.

"We's on patrol when I got the scours," the prisoner complied. "Had'em all day. I stopped to take a crap and your man caught me."

"How far is your cavalry unit camped?" the officer asked, offering a chew of tobacco to the soldier from Illinois. The prisoner took the chew and bit off a decent amount.

"Bout two mile, I reckon."

"Take the prisoner back to headquarters," said the Confederate officer, looking toward the bearded Rebel. "It's back near the creek on the far side."

The bearded soldier motioned toward the prisoner, who obediently moved in the indicated direction. The two men started back toward the Little Sugar Creek crossing with the Confederate leading the cavalryman's horse. The officer turned to go, then stopped and looked over at Willis.

"Good job, young man. You'd better move back to your picket station."

Willis turned without a word and began to move back in the direction of the capture. He had walked a short distance when he heard shouts and then a gunshot. Then he heard a horse moving back toward the enemy line. He realized that the prisoner had escaped. More importantly, Curtis's army would now be aware of the movement of Van Dorn's army.

There was little activity during the rest of the early morning, as both Generals Van Dorn and Curtis waited for the other to make a move. By midmorning, both armies expected a serious attack.

After Lyle had handled the burial detail for Bartis, a courier from Colonel Harvell met him. He stated that Lyle was to report to Colonel Harvell's tent. Lyle flagged a teamster who gave him a ride to division headquarters at Camp Stephens. When he entered the colonel's tent, he found Harvell packing items in a bag. The colonel turned, saluted, and asked Lyle to take a chair.

"Lyle, first of all, I want to thank you for the great job you have done for our army. You are officer material. I only wish that you could also attend the academy."

"Thank you, sir," Lyle responded when Harvell had finished talking.

"But I didn't call you down here just to compliment you. I have some instructions to give you," Harvell continued. "As you know, we have had a serious bout of influenza in our army. Three of my officers are sick—one may not make it. General Van Dorn has requested a staff officer meeting—actually three meetings—to inform officers of our battle preparation. Lyle, I've put a lot on your shoulders, really since our Dardanelle days. In some cases, I've kept you informed better than a couple of my officers. But, with the officers' illness, I want you to attend one of Van Dorn's meetings to represent Regiment 20. You may not know anyone there, outside of me, but you need to understand Van Dorn's plan of attack. By understanding the plan, you can really help us out front when the attack gets underway. Later, I will elevate your rank. Can you do this?"

Lyle had listened carefully. "Sir, I would be honored to help represent Regiment 20."

"Thank you, Lyle. I will see you there."

Lyle saluted, turned, and exited the officer's tent.

Chapter 23

The Detour

March 1862

LYLE WAS STILL SURPRISED that, with his rank, he would be invited to an important meeting involving staff officers. He arrived early and took a seat near the back of the meeting room. Within ten minutes, most of the officers were seated. An aide opened the door and in came General Sterling Price. The hatless gray-haired general, dressed smartly in a well-fitting gray uniform, moved across the room to take a front-row seat. General McCulloch, dressed as usual in his black velvet suit and tie, entered shortly after that and took a seat nearer the door and a considerable distance from "Old Pap," as his men called Price.

Again the door opened, and in came three more generals, none of which Lyle had seen before. Later, Lyle learned that the very large, heavily bearded man was Albert Pike. The general with a darker complexion was McIntosh and the smaller general was Louis Hebert. All took seats on the front row between McCulloch and Price. The seated aide jumped to his feet as the door opened again. General Van Dorn, dressed in his blue uniform, entered. As usual, the general was very serious. His dark eyes scanned the room in seconds.

"Be seated, men. Obviously, we are close to serious battle. And you are the third group of officers that I have met with, so we won't be long. I believe that you, as general officers, must understand what has taken place since the Wilson's Creek victory, and what our intentions are at this time. Without going into great detail—"the general coughed a couple of times, prompting the aide to quickly leave the room to get some water. After coughing again, the speaker continued.

"After the Wilson's Creek victory, General McCulloch moved his Arkansas militia back into Arkansas. After bringing his division back across the state line, General McCulloch set up our present camp, Camp Stephens. His division has been here since the Wilson's Creek victory." Again, the general coughed and cleared his throat.

"Now, for our other division. General Price's division remained near Springfield after the battle at Wilson's Creek. Once a sizable Federal army began to descend on Springfield, General Price made the right decision to move back down Telegraph Road toward Arkansas. He brought his division to a point near Mudtown, where they are presently camped. These two divisions, led by great generals, have defeated the Federals earlier at Wilson's. But, as you know, we have received additional troops from Indian Territory and from Van Buren."

The aide had returned with a cup of water for the general and Van Dorn paused to take a drink. Lyle wondered if the general had fully recovered from his previous illness. The general wiped his mouth and continued.

"Men, our force is greater now than at Wilson's. You as general officers have done a good job in preparing your men. My staff has not been idle. We have studied the situation and discussed it thoroughly. We have developed what we believe is a sound plan of attack. I will briefly refer to the plan. However, this information is not to leave this room. Remember that."

The general paused again and looked over the group of officers. He picked up a pointer and turned toward a large map that had been placed on a rough, supporting standard.

"We are here," he pointed at an exact spot on the map. "And, Curtis, the Federal general, has established a preliminary battle line on the north side of Little Sugar Creek. His right wing was originally extended west to the town of Bentonville—here. We attempted to destroy his right wing and General Sigel, with the idea of then turning on the main army." Van Dorn pointed to a location east of Bentonville on the map. After another cough and another drink of water, he continued.

"Unfortunately, we were unable to prevent the Federal right wing under Sigel from joining the main Federal force under Curtis here," he said, again using his pointer. "Now, for our plan. Approximately five miles north of us is a mountain that the locals refer to as Pea Ridge Mountain. Telegraph Road, which both of our divisions used in returning to Arkansas from Missouri after the battle of Wilson Creek, comes out of Missouri, crosses Pea Ridge Mountain, and runs on to Fayetteville. Many of you, especially our Van Buren reinforcements, used the southern part of Telegraph Road in getting to our present camp. On the top of Pea Ridge Mountain is a stagecoach stop on Telegraph Road near an old tavern called Elkhorn Tavern. It is now a private residence. That tavern is our bull's-eye. Now, if you look over here on the left side of the map, you will notice a road going north and in a clockwise fashion around the big mountain. That detour road intersects with that part of Telegraph Road that crosses the state line and enters the state."

The general put his hand over his mouth, coughed again, and then pointed to the intersection of Telegraph Road and the detour road. "Now, General Price's division will move north on the detour road and proceed around the mountain and behind Curtis's forces here." He again pointed to the Federal lines. "Price will one, cut off Curtis's supply line from Missouri at Telegraph Road, and two, move south up the mountain, toward the tavern. Back south and north of here, General McCulloch and General McIntosh will push east toward Curtis's present line near Little Sugar Creek.

"With this two-pronged, pincher movement, Curtis will be in serious trouble from both the north and the west. His supply line and escape route back into Missouri to his base at Rolla will be closed. Victory is in our reach, and then on to St. Louis. But a caution—we are again seeing a considerable amount of desertion. Deserters sometimes desert to the enemy. If you leave this meeting and relate our plan to your soldiers, an informed soldier could desert to the enemy and relate our plan. Keep your mouth closed."

The general glanced at General McCulloch and then at General Price. "Gentlemen, we will meet in my office in ten minutes."

Van Dorn turned and walked over to the aide standing by the door. The aide held a long, rolled-up item, either cloth or paper, in his hands. As the general approached, the aide reached out to give Van Dorn the item. After taking it, the general walked back to the podium where he had been speaking.

"Gentlemen, a close friend of mine from Louisiana, General Pierre Beauregard, recently had a flag designed for our Southern army. We already have our new, national flag, but Pierre had this flag designed for us as a battle flag. You men will be the first Southern force to carry this new flag."

Van Dorn released the flag and allowed it to extend down to full length. Lyle leaned forward to look at the new flag, which was square rather than rectangle. It was solid red with two wide stripes of blue, one extending from the upper left corner down to the lower right corner, and the other extending from the upper right hand corner and extending down to the lower left hand corner. The two crossed blue stripes made a huge X across the red banner. The blue stripes had a thin, white border. Placed across the blue X were thirteen white stars.

After the officers had several seconds to observe the flag, strong applause broke out in the room. All of the men were soon on their feet applauding, and many whistled and cheered. Van Dorn was obviously pleased. As the applause died down, the general spoke.

"That's the way I felt on seeing the flag for the first time. Incidentally, the stars stand for the thirteen states that have aligned themselves with the Confederacy. And one of those stars represents the state of Arkansas, and one star represents the state of Missouri, the state that has seceded but is not being allowed to follow its desires—mainly as the result of the army we are now facing. Gentlemen, General Price, seated in front of me, was at one time the governor of Missouri. We know how badly he wants the defeat of the Federal army in front of us."

Price was vigorously shaking his head in approval. Van Dorn raised the new battle flag and shouted, "For the Confederacy." Everyone was quickly up and applauding heavily. The general rolled up the flag, quickly walked to the door, and left.

With no recognition, General McCulloch moved up in front of the officer group. "Officers, it is your responsibility to have your men ready to go—do your duty." He then moved toward the door, closely followed by General Price and the other three generals. The staff officers filed out of the room, followed by the general officers.

Lyle watched as General McCulloch and General Price walked toward Van Dorn's office. McCulloch was in front and Price followed. Neither said a word to the other. Will they work together in battle, Lyle thought. Of course, the two generals would be in completely different locations. Mac would be in charge in this area, and "Old Pap" would be with Van Dorn on the north side of Pea Ridge Mountain.

Lyle thought about Van Dorn's plan. Was it smart to split the army? Yet, the idea of getting behind Curtis and cutting off his supply line and avenue of retreat seemed to make sense. Will we be successful or will we lose, he wondered as he walked back to his regiment.

Glancing back toward Van Dorn's headquarters, Lyle noticed a rider moving toward him. He recognized Colonel Harvell.

"Lyle, the 19th and 20th Regiments will be transferred to Price's division," the colonel said as he pulled the horse's reins and stopped near him. "Gather the men together. I will be there in about an hour to address them. We need to be ready to move out as soon as possible. I will explain more to you when I get a chance."

The colonel saluted, wheeled his horse, and rode back toward Van Dorn's headquarters. As Lyle continued walking back to Regiment 20, he noticed that the teamsters were already loading and moving wagons in preparation for battle. He also noted much activity on the east side of the camp where the cavalry was stationed. No doubt, they had not yet experienced serious warfare, but it was here now. In less than an hour, Regiment 20 had moved west through the encampment to the new location of Price's division.

Chapter 24

Pea Ridge Mountain

March 1862

SHORTLY AFTER SUNRISE, THE Confederate ranks were formed and ready to move. Colonel Harvell moved up to address the 20th Regiment. The colonel's excellent speaking voice was now quite low and rather hoarse, probably due to a head cold.

"Men, battle plans are complete. However, as you realize, some minor changes were necessary before we could proceed this morning. General Van Dorn has decided to transfer four of our regiments from General McCulloch's division to General Price's division. All officers will continue to lead their respective commands. Regiments 19, 20, 42, and 23 will now fall under the command of General Price. These transfers will only strengthen the northwestern part of our army. We believe that the western portion of the army under General McCulloch will not be hampered in the least. Regardless, we fight to protect our heritage and homeland."

The colonel, followed by a young aide that almost looked black, turned quickly and moved to his nearby horse. Captain Hunt quickly took the colonel's place in front of the Reb troops.

"We will continue marching on a northern course until we come to another road leading east. Your officers will direct you on the march. Be ready at all times."

The captain left as quickly as Colonel Harvell had. Within another forty minutes, Price's force, now four regiments stronger, reached a narrow road that appeared to go in a northeast direction. Lyle recognized the road from the general's map as "the detour." The march in the new direction continued for about an hour before the division was given an order to halt. After considerable delay, word filtered back to Regiment 20 that the Federals had cut trees down to block the detour. The use of the detour was not a surprise to Curtis's army.

Willis wondered if Thomas Welch's escape had anything to do with the blocked road. The army was delayed for more than an hour while felled trees were cut and removed from the detour road. After moving past the roadblock, Willis heard gunshots ring out up ahead. Pickets from the opposing armies were making contact. Looking up toward the direction of the gunshots, he could see in the distance a high, rocky, tree-covered ridge that ran west to east. He reasoned that part of the Union army must be on or near this long mountain that was referred to as Pea Ridge.

After another half-hour march, felled trees across the road delayed the army again. By now, there was enough light and Willis and Eslie could clearly see the high, hilly ridge. On the south side of the ridge, Willis could see huge rocks and boulders, good places for soldiers to hide. While awaiting the movement at the second roadblock, Willis, Eslie, and Lyle talked about the approaching battle. Lyle explained that Curtis had come south out of Missouri, across the Arkansas line, and this was his general encampment.

Lyle informed his friends that Van Dorn was trying to move around behind Pea Ridge and cut off Curtis's supply line to Missouri and defeat the Federals with a pincher movement, with General Price on the north and General McCulloch on the west. Before they resumed the march, a great deal of shooting and then artillery fire began to occur back to the south from the general direction that the division had come. McCulloch was already making his presence felt. Once again, orders were given to resume the march. The men had certainly gone no longer than twenty minutes when they were again stopped, pending further orders.

The Southerners were growing anxious. A few men were talking bravely about beating the Yanks. Most were quiet. Willis was again thinking of death. He thought about Bartis and how Bartis had said that one Southerner could defeat three Northerners. Willis wondered if Bartis knew he was going to die after being bayoneted by a Yankee. Willis thought back to the day before when they had been given permission to bury his friend. He, Eslie, and Lyle had dug the grave. They had wrapped Bartis in his blanket and then placed another blanket on top.

Lyle asked Willis if he would read a passage from the Bible and say a prayer. Willis had been to several funerals at Gravelly and he again thought of his grandfather's wake and funeral. He did not know what to read from the Bible, so he just opened it and began to read. The Scripture was from Luke and it was about Jesus' birth in Bethlehem. Willis realized that what he read from the Bible was probably not appropriate for a funeral. Later, he realized that if he had not been so upset over the loss of his friend, he could have selected a more appropriate Scripture. After Willis had finished with the Scripture reading, Lyle spoke briefly about Bartis. He related that Bartis had been a good friend.

"He was someone that kept us laughing a lot," Lyle said. "He helped us have a lot of good times. Gravelly will not be the same without Bartis. At the same time, he was a good soldier. The enemy killed Bartis; therefore, he died for his country. Willis, will you offer a prayer for Bartis?"

Willis and Eslie noticed the emotional break in Lyle's voice as he said, "for Bartis." Willis prayed for Bartis's parents and friends. He thanked God for the friendship that the four boys had. He also asked for the safety of the remaining three men. The first few shovels of dirt on Bartis's body were difficult. But soon a small amount of fresh soil covered the grave. Lyle provided a rough cross to place at the head of the grave. All three of the friends were hesitant to walk away from their buried friend.

By now officers were breaking down the ranks by company and placing men in position to advance on the Union army. As to exactly where the Federals were, Willis did not know. Captain Hunt began to explain the military procedures that the regiment would undergo.

"Men, there's a couple of hollows up ahead that lead up the northern side of that high ridge in front of us. We will first move east and cut any supply line that Curtis has established out of Missouri. Be ready for action at all times. It's possible that Union cavalry will be trying to keep Telegraph Road open up to the Missouri line. Once we cross Telegraph Road, we will move east and then again south up the hollow to the top of the ridge they call Pea Ridge. We can expect plenty of activity near the top of the ridge.

"Regiment 23 will be to our left and Company A, Regiment 42, will be on our right. Stay in contact with these groups. Don't shoot our own men. When we get to the top of Pea Ridge, we will come out on a road that runs back east to Huntsville. We will move west toward Elkhorn Tavern. Stay up, keep your gun ready, and use it. Remember, they will kill you, so be ready to kill them. Any questions?" Seeing that there were none, he addressed Lyle. "Lead out toward the hollow."

The local farmers called the first hollow in question Tanyard Hollow. It was named for a small, private leather works that had been located approximately a mile north of Elkhorn Tavern. Lyle led Company B east, staying in sight of Company A's flag still further east. Captain Hunt had also told Lyle that an advance cavalry unit under Lieutenant Colonel James Claremont, Missouri cavalry, would lead his forces to a point on the western rim of Pea Ridge.

In less than an hour, Price's army was in position north of the imposing but rough mountain with the pea vines growing around it in various places. On a signal, Regiment 20 and the other parts of Price's army began the ascent up Tanyard Hollow. Willis soon heard shooting off to the right, toward the western end of Pea Ridge. Later, the activity shifted to the left of the infantry. Claremont was using several approaches to attack the Union position on the western mountain rim.

The shooting intensified the closer the infantry units advanced up the mountainside. Before long, Willis realized that the Federals were not only shooting at the advance cavalry, but they were also shooting at the advancing Southern foot soldiers. They could hear bullets overhead and voices near the rim of the mountain. The enemy sounded like anyone else from Arkansas.

Black smoke began to build up in the area near the top of the ridge. Willis could smell the sulfur of exploding gunpowder. He heard a scream as a soldier down the line yelled that his brother had been hit. A heavy blanket of clouds now shielded the sun. It seemed to Willis that the time must be near sundown, but he knew differently. It would be several hours and many deaths later before the sun would decline in the west.

A bullet hit a huge pine tree near Willis and tore off a chunk of bark. Sounds were louder, bullets were closer, and smoke was heavier. He was still moving forward with the line of Southerners. Then Willis could see bluecoats—behind trees, behind rocks, some even in the open. Most were firing down the hill at the advancing lines. Someone began yelling. At first, Willis thought they were hurt. Then he realized that they were screaming about the Yankees. Others picked up on the half scream-half cheer.

Before long, the entire Reb line was yelling. With the hair on his neck rising, Willis too began to be a part of the soon-to-be-famous Rebel yell that would motivate Southern arms all over the southland. Willis was braver now. He was more aggressive. He suddenly remembered that people of foreign origin were invading his home state. These weren't people from Yell County, Scott County, or Montgomery County—they were here to kill and destroy Southerner homes and property. They were here to kill the Lofland family and destroy their home and farm.

For the first time, Willis became angry with the Federals. Once anger took over, caution was pushed to the side. Willis stepped from behind a tree as other Rebels were doing and began moving up the hillside in open view of the Federals. The screaming bullets passing near Willis did not bother him. It was if none of them were marked for him.

Lyle was off to the left and slightly in front of the company, encouraging the men to continue their assault. Willis had never seen Lyle so talkative and so aggressive. He heard more screams near Company B as men were hit. For some strange reason, Willis suddenly remembered Bartis saying, "Yankees can't shoot guns." Willis thought, someone up there knows how to shoot.

He suddenly felt very thirsty. He had not had a drink of water since the last roadblock delay. His mouth was so dry. He reached for the canteen as he ducked behind a huge pine tree. The canteen felt light. Then he knew why. A bullet had hit the side of his canteen as it hung along his side, and the bullet had gone completely through it.

A slight breeze from the south pushed much of the heavy, black powder smoke down toward the Rebels. Willis saw Lyle step out, dash back toward the company, and motion them forward. Suddenly, Lyle stopped, staggered, and fell. Willis quickly scrambled toward his fallen friend. Lyle did not move. His throat was a mass of bubbling blood. Willis put his hand behind Lyle's head, slightly lifting it. With his right hand, Willis tried to reach clothing in his haversack. He quickly placed an old shirt on Lyle's bloody throat. He heard a gurgling sound as Lyle swallowed and choked on his own blood.

"Oh, God, save him! Lyle, I'll take care of you. Lyle!"

Lyle's brown eyes rolled back in his head. He was already gone. Willis could not move. Other soldiers moved past him. Tears came into his eyes. I hate those Yankees, thought Willis. Carefully, Willis lowered the dead man's head to the rocky soil.

"I'll be back to bury you, Lyle," whispered Willis as he started up the hill. Then he screamed, "Let's kill the murderers," so loud it was heard over most of the area.

Willis was now running. Other Southerners also got up and followed their inflamed comrade. He saw a Union soldier step out from behind a tree and raise his gun quickly to stop the crazed Rebel leading several other soldiers. But the Union private missed.

His gun was still loaded, and Willis jerked the musket back and then thrust it forward quickly as the Union soldier started to back away. The dirty, somewhat rusty bayonet penetrated the soldier's rib cage, slipped around the fourth rib, and passed easily into the lungs near the heart. The soldier's blue cap fell off as he desperately reached for Willis's musket in an effort to deflect the blow. The soldier's left hand caught the barrel of Willis's rifle, but not with enough force to deflect the bayonet. Willis could see the soldier's face, the freckles that covered it, and his red hair. He looked to be about eighteen years old.

"You have kilt me," the Federal blurted out in surprise.

Without hesitating, Willis jerked the musket backward, removed the bayonet, and quickly pulled the gun to his shoulder. He fired at a Yankee that was quickly running back up the hill to safety. The soldier went down, made an effort to rise again, and then crumpled to the ground. Willis went to his knees, jerking out the ramrod to reload. Within thirty seconds, he had reloaded and was on his feet.

Willis heard a loud explosion off to his right, and then another to his left. He heard thousands of particles flying through the trees. Grapeshot! Then Willis could see the cannon off to his right. It was aimed to his right. Willis saw one of the artillerymen place the ball in the six-pounder. He fired at the man and the soldier grabbed for his right shoulder.

Other Rebs were also over the rim of the hill. Several Southerners rushed the Union battery before they could fire the cannon again. When they saw the advancing Southerners, two of the battery mates turned and began to run south. One of them screamed and fell. Someone had shot him. Four or five Federals had dropped their guns and raised their arms to surrender. Willis fired at one of the men and saw him fall.

Southerners poured over the top of the ridge and on to Huntsville Road. Willis looked back to the west where Confederate cavalry were fighting hand to hand with defending

Union soldiers. Then he saw the tavern up on the hill. It was two stories with fireplaces on both ends. The front of the home faced the east and Huntsville Road. Union soldiers were moving in and out of the residence, which seemed to now be a Union field hospital.

By then, the Rebels had captured three cannon along with several Union artillerymen. Willis looked off to the south. A long line of bluecoats was advancing in the direction of Elkhorn Tavern. Curtis was trying to rally his troops with a counterattack. A heavy volley of cannon fire from the revived Union line sent the Southerners scrambling for cover.

To Willis it seemed that the Yankees did not have to reload. He thought the Federals must have moved even more cannon in position. Willis noticed a fellow soldier near him. Then he realized that the soldier was Eslie.

"You okay?"

"So far so good. Willis, you got any cartridges?"

Willis reached in his pocket and handed Eslie five or six cartridges. "Aim low," stated Willis. "You know about Lyle?"

Eslie had reloaded and was gazing into the distance. "Yeah, we're the only Gravelly boys left now. Captain Hunt was also wounded a while back. Looked bad to me."

Willis remembered what the captured Yankee cavalryman had said about everyone getting killed. He looked at his bayonet. It still had the dried blood of the dead, red-haired, Federal soldier on it.

"The Federals are taking it heavy too. It depends on who can stand their ground. I believe we will. You got any water, Eslie?"

Eslie reached for his canteen and handed it to his friend. Willis could not remember water tasting so good. As he lowered the canteen and handed it back to Eslie, he noticed that the cannon had quit firing. This could be bad.

"Forward," a nearby Southern officer yelled. "Let's take Elkhorn Tavern."

The Rebel yell rang out over the hillside as the Southerners jumped up and began to move forward. Willis could see the regimental flag off to the right. It was the first time he had seen it in more than an hour. Shots poured through the trees in the direction of the Arkansans. As Willis and Eslie advanced, Willis could see several gray-clad soldiers go down, either wounded or killed.

"Close up! Close up!" came the oft-occurring command as officers attempted to keep the line uniform. The two opposing armies were now within 100 yards of each other. They continued to move toward each other with a minimum of firing. Willis noticed a Reb artillery battery dragging up a James rifle. The battery unit quickly positioned the big gun in place. Hurry, thought Willis, get that thing ready. The shooting intensified on both sides. Both Willis and Eslie, still side by side, were almost out of ammo. Willis could see the faces of the enemy.

"Forward," came the cry from the Confederate officers. Willis fired his musket, hit a near bluecoat, and realized that he had no time to reload just as a Yankee came at him with his bayonet ready. Willis swung his musket like an ax, striking the oncoming musket/bayonet and knocking it to the side. Willis's gun butt snapped into two pieces, leaving him holding the barrel of the musket. He quickly swung the heavy musket barrel, hitting the soldier across the side of the head. The man went to the ground, struggled up, turned, and ran toward the rear of the Northern army.

Willis looked back from checking on Eslie just in time to see a sword slash toward him. The blade caught him just below the right shoulder on his upper right arm. The Union officer with the sword recoiled for a second strike. Willis threw his left shoulder into the man's waist, sending him down. Willis landed on the man's chest. The Federal officer was screaming and cursing as he threw his right fist at Willis.

Willis brought his left forearm down across the throat of the officer and threw his entire weight forward. "Kill them because they will kill you," Captain Hunt's words echoed through his head. As the man struggled and coughed, Willis continued to apply pressure to his throat. He struggling finally seized and his breathing stopped.

Willis was suddenly knocked forward off the dead man. A Southern artillery battery was arriving. In quickly turning to place the gun, one of the mules had hit Willis in the back of the head.

"Watch that man," Willis heard one of the battery mates say.

Willis rose back up to look for Eslie. He was nowhere in sight. The huge explosion of the near gun almost deafened Willis. He began to crawl off to a safe distance from the six-pounder and then suddenly remembered his shoulder. He sat up and turned to examine the wound. His old, worn shirt was cut and drenched with blood. Willis lowered his shirt over his right shoulder, exposing the wound. He reached his left hand over to touch and examine the cut. Rubbing blood away, he could see a huge cut, probably to the bone, extending down his arm about five inches.

He reached for his haversack and some kind of covering for the wound, before remembering that he had used his other shirt to help Lyle. He looked around and saw a dead Union soldier lying a few feet away. He crawled over to the dead man, turned him on his stomach, and began to unfasten his haversack. He reached into the haversack and found that it was full. He found a shirt, underwear, a pipe, two or three letters, and food.

Willis took the shirt, tore it in two pieces, and began to wrap half of it around the cut. After wrapping the arm, he decided to eat some of the Yankee's food. He found salt pork, some dried fruit, bread, and apple butter. Within three minutes, he had eaten much of the food. He put the rest of it back into the Federal haversack, along with some coffee and sugar he found in another of the soldier's pockets.

Willis grabbed the haversack, the soldier's ammunition, and his musket. He stood up and began walking in the direction of the battle. He determined that the Southerners must have won, because there were no Yankees around, except those lying dead on the ground. He also saw several dead fellow Southerner soldiers. He could see at least five horses that were dead or at least seriously wounded. He continued to hear shouting in the distance and reasoned that the Southerners had forced the Feds to retreat. An officer rode by Willis and looked at him briefly.

"Let's get with the army, soldier," he commanded Willis.

Willis said nothing but continued to move south. The slope of the land now began to move slightly downhill toward the south. Willis looked back to the west, where he could again see Elkhorn Tavern. The new flag, the Stars and Bars, were flying over the old tavern, which would now serve as a Rebel hospital. Injured soldiers were being moved into the building.

Willis began to move in that direction, realizing for the first time that it was late afternoon.

Chapter 25

Victory

March 6

IN THE DISTANCE, WILLIS could hear bugles and other battle sounds. It looked like the Federals were going to try to regain the mountaintop before dark. Many exhausted Rebs were sitting on the ground. Others appeared to be in near shock because of what they had just seen and experienced over the last eight hours. Hearing the new sounds, some reached for their weapons. Several Rebs, like Willis, had now picked up discarded Federal muskets and cartridges. Many, like Willis, were angry.

On his feet, Willis angrily stared south toward the enemy. You murdering Yankees have already caused the deaths of some of my best friends," he thought again. Lyle, Bartis, even Frank—and probably Eslie. He knew other acquaintances had died here.

"Why did you come here?" he suddenly screamed. Other Reb soldiers, many with similar thoughts, stood up quickly and looked over at the screaming, angry Reb soldier.

"Yeah, let's get em!" they shouted.

The long line of Reb soldiers began running—south toward the hated Yankee invaders. Even when an occasional Reb would fall as the result of a Yankee shell, the line continued south. The Federals could not believe what they saw. Even worse was what they heard. The bloodcurdling, Rebel yell was in itself terrifying. And then, Willis, the angry leader, stopped, quickly knelt down on one knee, and fired at the startled Union army. The charging Rebs again emulated their leader. The moving Reb army proved to be a lot more difficult target than the stationary Union line.

It seemed that almost every fired Reb gun brought down a Yankee. The Reb officers were as surprised as the Union lines. Officers, catching the fever, began to run forward, chasing their inspired men. Southern artillery batteries then opened up. The Reb foot soldiers would take aim at a bluecoat only to see a Reb artillery shell get there a second earlier and several Federal men would no longer be a part of the line. The Federal officers were quickly trying to restore order and prevent retreat. The officers yelled at their men and even threatened to shoot them if they retreated.

By then the Rebs had reached the stationary Union line. Both lines had empty muskets. It was now hand-to-hand combat. Much later, Willis could not remember how many Federals he wounded or killed. He did recall reaching a Union artillery battery. He used the Yankee gun that he picked up as a club. He was sure that he killed two members of the battery before he wrestled a Federal officer to the ground over his sword. He remembered killing a fourth man with the sword.

The Federals had retreated all the way back to the base of Pea Ridge Mountain. Exhausted, Willis fell to the ground, only to look back toward the Union lines, and then another Rebel yell, from the eastern part of the Rebel line.

"Here they come — must be hundreds of them."

Willis raised his musket and fired at the nearest Union soldier. The soldier, maybe twenty years old, dropped his gun and reached for his stomach, where the shell had entered his body. As he fell forward a second Union soldier, who had also fired his musket, quickly moved it into position to use the bayonet on Willis. Willis sidestepped, only to lose his balance. In extending his arm to cushion his fall, Willis lost his own gun.

On the ground, Willis moved quickly to avoid the oncoming Union bayonet. It sank into the earth at least six inches. Surprised at missing his target, the Union soldier quickly jerked the musket bayonet back from the soil, pulled it further back, and prepared to hit the targeted Rebel this time. As the Union soldier shifted his weight and began a new downward thrust, a body quickly moved in between him and the Rebel on the ground. The third soldier, a Reb, thrust his knife up under the rib cage and into the lower chest of the Union soldier. The surprised soldier never saw who killed him. He only felt the knife enter his lungs. Although he screamed, no one heard it due to the normal battle sounds. Willis, also surprised, saw the entire incident. But now he noticed something different about his savior. He was black—yet he was a Reb.

"Thanks. You saved my life," Willis said to his benefactor.

The black Reb looked at Willis without saying anything. Then Willis noticed something familiar about the man. He had seen him some place before. Then he remembered.

"I met you on the road to Rover," Willis recalled. "You are a slave—but I don't remember your name."

"George," the Reb finally said. "I's George, Massa Harvell's nigger. Yo remembers me from giving me a ride on yo wagon. I's going back home after runnin'."

A lull in the battle occurred, giving the men a chance to talk.

"Massa Harvell 'lowed me to join up with him," the slave continued. "I just came 'long to help him."

"But why?" said an amazed Willis. "Why don't you leave Sherwood, with the war going on?"

"Sur, I's free," said the black man, glancing back down the hill. "Massa freed me. I 'least can help him. That time I left, when I gets back with yo note to him, Massa listen to me and he shaked my hand. Never done that afore. He took me back to my ma and I believes we all three cried up a storm. Massa is a good Christian man. I likes him lot. Reckon that's why I's here."

By then, the battle activity had increased again.

"Come on, George," Willis said, looking at his friend. "Let's win this battle."

The two loaded their muskets and got up to move toward the frontal action. The Rebs again appeared to be winning, since they were moving south toward the Union lines. Both men had fired their muskets several times and reloaded as they advanced with the pressing gray line. Both had noticed that the big Union cannon had begun to fire more regularly. Was the Union artillery trying to slow the Union retreat?

Willis realized that one shell had been very close. He turned to see George on the ground. From what he could tell, he had been hit below the waist. George had both hands on his face, and he was obviously in great pain. Willis quickly went to the ground near George. What should he do? Then Willis remembered. He took off his belt and made a tourniquet just above George's left knee. The blood spurted out of the damaged leg. By then, George had lost consciousness.

"Hold on, George. I will get you to the hospital."

Willis lifted the freed slave up and put his arm around his back. He began to move back toward the field hospital. Willis partially carried and partially drug George as he moved in that direction. Shells were still hitting near Willis as he struggled to save George, who regained consciousness only to begin screaming.

"George, we'll make it. Hang on!"

Another Reb moved quickly to assist Willis. Someone opened the tavern door. Due to the numerous wounded men who were shouting and screaming, it was louder inside than on the outside. Attendants moved hurriedly, trying to meet the needs of the wounded and dying. Two men came past Willis carrying a dead soldier. Willis and his unknown helper stopped to ask a man with a big apron where to take George.

"Put him on the last table," the man said, motioning toward the northeast corner of the room. "The man on the table has died."

They carried George over to the table and gently moved the dead man over. A man appeared at the table.

"Are you the doctor?"

"Let's look at him," the man replied without looking at the questioner.

The bloody trouser leg prompted the medic to examine the left leg first. Using a knife, he cut what was left of the trousers. The leg below the knee was a bloody mess, and the leg looked smaller than it should have looked. Willis had to look away.

"You men carry the dead man outside," the medic looked at Willis and said. "Put him on the north side of the building."

Willis and his new friend picked up the limp body and carried it toward the front door. They moved down the porch and around to the north side of the tavern. Willis could not believe what he saw. At least twenty dead men had already been placed here. He also saw several dead Union soldiers. He also saw several discarded arms and legs of wounded soldiers near the tavern's outside north wall. Boots were still on some of the feet.

Willis considered looking for Lyle's body but he thought again of George and his agony.

"Thanks."

"You're welcome," the stranger replied. "Hope he makes it."

Willis hurried back inside the tavern. The moaning and screaming was even louder. He pushed past several men and moved back to George's table where George was now conscious and pleading for help. The medic completed his evaluation, glanced up at Willis, and then looked back at the trembling George.

"We gotta take off that leg at the knee joint."

"No, I needs my leg," George screamed again. "I's a field slave. Lord, I needs my leg."

The chloroform acted quickly. The attendant had already begun placing his equipment on the table near George. He repositioned Willis's tourniquet, and after a quick washing of the wounded area, picked up his knife and began cutting the flesh away from the bone. Willis could not believe how quick the medic worked. After placing some absorbent cloth on the area of the leg where the flesh had been cut away, the doc reached for his saw.

"Young man, you can go now. Nothing else you can do except pray for —" he paused. "What is his name?"

"George," replied Willis, slightly sick to his stomach. "That's all I know. He belongs to Colonel Harvell."

Willis slowly moved back to the door while looking at some of the wounded men. He silently prayed to God for George and all the wounded men, including the wounded Union soldiers.

It was quieter now outside. The shooting had almost stopped. Willis looked out over the area in front of the tavern and saw many wounded and dead. The healthy were helping those in need. He saw several dead horses and noticed many weapons of both armies on the ground. He also spotted what looked like a twelve-pounder cannon with one wheel gone and the other wheel destroyed. Enemy cannon fire had hit it.

Not far away was a teamster wagon. Both mules, still in harness, were dead. Ironically, the driver was still in the wagon seat, still holding the reins, but he was lying to one side of the wagon seat, also dead. Several trees were down. Others had the treetops removed. As Willis surveyed the scene, he thought, this is war. This is what we trained for. Kill or be killed. Why? Why did it have to happen?

Willis slowly sat down on the porch of the tavern, but out of the way of the still heavy traffic going both directions. Bartis, Lyle, and probably Eslie will never go hunting again. They will never go to Gravelly and visit on Saturdays. They will never marry or have children. God help us.

Chapter 26

Defeat

March 7

WITH THE SUN DECLINING in the west, the day's battle was over. Pea Ridge was secure. The field hospital at Elkhorn Tavern was now very busy treating Reb soldiers. As the shooting completely stopped, the tired Rebs began to move back north up to the top of Pea Ridge Mountain.

"We won!" a Reb shouted. "We turned them back!"

Willis, his shoulder now very sore, thought, yes, we won, but at what cost? His lifetime friends, Lyle and Bartis — along with Captain Hunt and Frank — were dead. What about Eslie? Was he dead too?

As he walked back up the hill, Willis suddenly realized he had been walking around bodies — human bodies, both Reb and Federal soldiers. Hundreds of men that would never go home — never see their families again.

"Lord, I thank you for saving me today — so much," he prayed as he slowly moved up the hill. "But please comfort the families of all the dead men — especially the families of Bartis, Lyle, and Frank. And please take care of Eslie if he is alive. And, Lord, please be with George the slave. He saved my life."

Willis reached a point where he could see, off to the south, into the valley south of Pea Ridge. It looked like the entire Union army was formed in line. Artillery batteries were further back. There was definitely a lot of activity in the valley.

"Help me, help me," came a plea off to Willis's left.

Willis moved around a small grove of persimmon trees, some of which had the tops completely shot off. At least half the bark on the trees was gone. There he found the wounded soldier, lying on his back. Both of his arms were extended down his left thigh. He was grasping the leg with both hands. The left leg from mid-thigh was gone. Blood was everywhere.

"Oh, God, let me die," muttered the Federal between his teeth.

Willis stopped and knelt down beside him. Cannon fire had hit him, and his lower leg was nowhere in sight. Willis reached for the man's canteen, only a few feet away. He started to raise it to the groaning man's mouth and then heard a strange scream behind him. He quickly turned to see an injured horse. A huge shell, probably a six-pounder, had hit it just below the saddle. The horse was in serious pain. The wild eyes of the beautiful, black animal showed signs of death.

Willis turned back to the soldier, who was now motionless. The man's eyes, still open, stared off into the heavens. Willis knew he was dead. Then he realized what had happened. The soldier was cavalry. He had been on the horse when it was hit.

Willis took a drink from the Union canteen and then tossed it aside. A slight breeze was pushing the heavy clouds of black smoke back to the east. The smell was still exploding powder and sulfur. An ambulance went by on the road, moving toward the tavern. Men continued to come from the north, as the latter part of Van Dorn's army moved up. Willis heard several commands as regimental officers tried to recognize units and account for men. The advance had stopped, and he could see regimental flags.

Both armies paused to catch their breath. Both had waited for the delay that night would bring. An artillery battery moved behind Willis, preparing for the next morning's activities. Willis approached one of the unit's soldiers, a gangly, tall, dark-headed boy with a couple of front teeth missing. Powder and powder smoke covered the soldier. He had only one shoe but didn't seem to notice.

"You wouldn't know which direction Regiment 20 is, would you?"

"Only thing I know is that direction is Curtis's army," replied the boy, looking at him in a slightly crazed manner.

"Should be east, 'bout a quarter or so," said an officer with the unit, overhearing the conversation.

Other wagons continued to roll in with supplies and ambulances moved in both directions. Officers and aides moved quickly in the direction of their units. Foot soldiers were sitting everywhere now. The dead had not been touched. As Willis began to walk east down toward Telegraph Road, he noticed a mess unit preparing to build a fire and ready for nightfall. He met two Rebel soldiers who had captured four Yankees and were taking them back to wherever headquarters was. The Federals looked as dirty and tired as their guards. Gunfire of all kinds had ceased.

Willis came up on another soldier who seemed to be carefully checking the identity of a fallen comrade.

"You think it be okay to take his boots?" he stammered, looking up in surprise at Willis.

"Reckon," Willis muttered and continued on.

The regimental flag was up ahead and off to the north of the road. Willis stumbled down into the location, hopeful that he would see Eslie. He spoke to several men that he recognized. Some were talking in low tones. Others sat and stared. One or two were crying. Willis recognized one familiar face. It was

Raymond Pierce, a man from Rover who had a large family, including four children.

"Well boys, we whupped em," Pierce was saying. "We drove 'em off the ridge. They probably goin' to cut out tonight."

Willis approached the three men in Pierce's group.

"Good to see you Lofland," Pierce said when he recognized Willis. "Did the Gravelly boys make it all right?"

Willis dropped to the ground near a fire that had just been started. An old coffee pot was already on it.

"Hadn't been a good day," he responded. "Lyle Parker was killed. I believe it was early this morning. Got shot in the throat. I haven't seen Eslie Southard. You seen him, by chance?"

"I bet he was captured this morning," Pierce said, tapping his tin cup against his knee. "They got about six of our boys. Eslie might be in that group."

Willis looked into the fire. He hoped that it was capture and not a serious wound or death. A man across the fire—Willis thought his name was Cooper—had reached for the coffee pot and began to pour the coffee in a bent, rusty, tin cup.

"Got a cup?" he asked Willis, looking up.

Willis took off the Union haversack, reached inside, and pulled out a cup.

"You lost a letter," Pierce said, glancing at Willis.

Willis glanced back to the ground and saw the letter lying there. He quickly picked it up and put it back in the dead Yankee's haversack. The coffee was weak, but good.

"Got anything to eat?" asked Pierce, again looking at Willis.

Willis suddenly remembered they had not eaten for a while. Then he remembered the food left over in the Federal soldier's haversack. He pulled out the salt pork, cut it into four pieces, and passed a piece of meat to each man seated near the fire. He poured a little of the sugar in the coffee and passed the small pouch around to the others. A little hardtack was also passed around. Willis noticed how hungry the three men were.

"You smell that meat cooking?" said Pierce, "That's A Company. They's eating one of the horses killed today. Wouldn't mind having some of that myself."

Willis's mind was again on Eslie. Surely the Lord was not going to permit Bartis, Lyle, and Eslie all to be taken in the war. Then he remembered—he should write Lyle's parents about his death. He still had trouble believing that Lyle was dead. Lyle, as everyone knew, was always a reserved, quiet, and humble leader. He was not a loud, cheerleader type of officer. Instead, he was a dedicated leader who led by example. Willis thought that he respected Lyle more than any officer in Van Dorn's army. Why did such a hard-working, dedicated officer have to die, when so many officers were lacking? Willis thought if Lyle had survived he would have become a high-ranking officer, maybe even a general. He was glad to have known such an individual. Willis looked across the fire at the other men. He knew that they had also fought well.

After finishing the salt pork, and while the others were talking, Willis slowly took out the envelope containing the Yankee's letter, opened it, and drew out the two-page letter. To his surprise, the letter written by the dead soldier was to be mailed to his family in Indiana. He slowly unfolded the pages and noticed that the letter had been printed. It was very neat writing. The boy addressed the letter to his sister, Claris.

Dear Claris:

I can't believe our mom died. I know she has been sick for years, but she would never complain. Even when Dad died, Mom just worked even harder for us five kids. And now I'm here and you are the oldest left there. I've been thinking about just leaving and coming home to help you. When this battle is over, I will be home. Tell little Kim, Leon, and Sara that I love them. Don't worry about me.

Love, Billy

After he'd finishing reading Billy's letter, Willis had to turn his head away from the men so that they could not see the tears running down his cheeks. Willis thought, Billy didn't want to come to Arkansas and we didn't want him to come. Grandpa was right—old men make war, but young men must fight the war. Lincoln didn't have to send troops to kill Southerners. Why didn't they just leave us alone? There would have been no war.

Willis bowed his head, as tears came into his eyes. He prayed for the parents and friends of Bartis, Lyle, and Eslie. He thanked God for protecting him, and he also asked God to forgive him for killing the Feds today. He thought of his family back home. Amos, his pa, was the hardest-working man he had ever known, yet he was a very religious man and a dedicated father. He thought of his ma, Eva—gosh, he loved her. He wished Eslie could have had a mother like Eva. He missed Hayes and was sorry about being cross at him for wanting to go everywhere with him.

And Georgia Ann—he knew that she idolized him. How was Rosalie? Was she safe? He thought, oh to be back in Chula with Rosalie tonight. But then, Willis felt guilty. He was alive. Two, and maybe three, of his friends were gone. The conversation of the group sitting around the fire interrupted his thoughts.

"Tomorrow will tell the story," said Pierce. "We finished

strong today. The Yankees retreated and we took Elkhorn Tavern. But it's not over. We got low on ammo and powder today. We also lost a lot of good men."

"Man, those Yankees fight lot harder than I've been told," Cooper said, taking over the conversation. "Word's going around that they may have licked McCulloch and McIntosh's boys near Leetown."

Pierce pulled out an old pipe and filled it with tobacco. After a couple of puffs, the group could smell the pleasing aroma of the tobacco. Cooper stirred the fire with a broken stick.

"Boy, where'd you come up with that salt pork?" asked Cooper of Willis.

"Guy gave it to me," Willis said, not wanting to tell about it. Lyle was on his mind again. He could still see those dark brown eyes, the blood, and he could still hear the gurgling sound as Lyle choked on his own blood. Willis wondered if Eslie had suffered the same fate. The conversation had changed now to General Van Dorn. The original three men were discussing the general's strategy today, especially splitting his army. Willis removed the tattered, old blanket and oilskin from the Union haversack.

The temperature had dropped to what felt like freezing temperature. Willis spread one of the blankets out near the fire, pulled the second blanket over him, and turned away from the fire. The third man in the group, older than the other two men, had pulled out a Jew's harp and began to play.

Willis did not know the song, but he knew it was sad. Willis thought, I could be dead and Lyle could be sitting here. Why? He tucked his chin down and began to silently pray to God.

By 6:00 a.m., the army was up and moving around. Artillery batteries were moving into position. Couriers moved about in the dark. Orders and commands were issued. Men examined their guns and checked their ammo and powder. They would have no breakfast, because no food was available. Mess wagons had not shown up. Ammunition supply wagons had yet to arrive. Officers were organizing the regiments into a battle line.

The last picket duty change had occurred more than an hour ago. Willis and his new friends had assumed positions in the forming battle line. The low morning temperature and the anticipation of battle caused many soldiers to shake with chills. Even the battle-scarred veteran soldiers were anxious and worried.

Captain Blair, Regiment B's new captain and replacement for Captain Hunt, was moving down the line of the regiment talking with lower-ranking officers. The information was passed on to the soldiers. Company B would be held in reserve when the battle began on Saturday. Most of the remaining company members knew the reason for the action. Company B had been hit the hardest on Friday. The company moved out of line and back north behind the artillery batteries.

Not surprisingly, the men of Company B began to complain about their withdrawal. Willis, also disappointed, overheard one man in the company say, "If they want a fighting company, they need us up at the front."

Company B, along with four other companies, moved back near Telegraph Road, stacked arms, removed haversacks and other equipment, and sat down in small groups. In the distance, the Rebel army began to move south to prepare a battle line to meet Curtis's army. The opening blasts of the opposing army's artillery batteries soon drowned out the mixed sounds of the moving army. The ground near Elkhorn Tavern again shook as the twelve-pounders leached their artillery salvos.

It seemed that the opposing batteries delivered their terrible greetings for more than an hour. The clear, cool morning slowly began the transformation to another dark, smoke-filled, dreary day. Willis and the men of Company B could now no longer see what was happening at the front.

"There're over there," shouted a voice.

Seated on the ground reading his last letter from Rosalie, Willis looked back toward the voice. A familiar figure came limping toward the company.

"Eslie!" Willis jumped up to greet his friend, in old trousers and looking sound, except for the tears in his eyes. "Where you been?"

"You not going to believe it," Eslie replied as he slumped down. "Got anything to eat?"

Several men in the company reached for their haversacks, only to remember there was no food for Eslie. They did offer him a canteen though.

"Boy that tastes good," Eslie muttered after drinking the water.

An officer rode by on a big, black horse. "Where's the supply wagons," he yelled to someone south. "We need ammo."

They turned their attention back to Eslie, waiting to see where he had been.

"I got captured yesterday after I had fired my musket," he explained.

The men watched as Eslie again took a long drink of water and patiently waited for Eslie's story about his capture.

"Yesterday, we were pushing Yankees back toward Elkhorn. As ya'll know, it was a terrible fight. I don't know how many were killed."

"I heard over 200," someone interrupted. Eslie nodded his head and went on with the story.

"I had raised my musket and fired it when a Yankee stepped from behind a big pine tree with his gun pointed at me. Then two more Yankees appeared through the smoke. One of our men behind us shot one of the Feds. The first Yankee, a big, husky man said, 'Reb, you are my prisoner.' What could I do? We started back to the southwest, moving down the mountain. It took us close to an hour. We wound up at the rear of that part of the Yankee army. I joined four other Reb prisoners there. We sat there with only one guard, a German fellar who we could hardly understand.

He recalled that things began to happen then.

"Our forces began advancing toward that area. More Yankee troops were sent to this area and soon the battle was on. It was worse than what I saw earlier up on the mountain. For a while the Yankees were winning and then our men began to push the Yankees back to the east. Wasn't long before more Rebs arrived. They were Indians—part of Pike's troops. The Yanks finally turned tail and ran—'least what was left. Must have been thirty or more killed or wounded.

"Us prisoners were hiding behind a big rock—except for one fellar. Stray shell hit him, I guess. We were glad to see those Indians, but they were crazy. Some of 'em climbed on a captured cannon and began riding it like a horse, yelling and screaming. That wasn't the worst part, though; some of the Indians pulled out their knives and went around scalping the dead Yankees. They even scalped one live, wounded Yankee. Man, I felt sorry for him. I bet ya'll could have heard him screaming. Those Cherokees are crazy. I was a little worried that they would think we were Yankees."

"Did you just leave?" interrupted Willis.

"No, we did get some food from McIntosh's troops; I think it was horse meat. The Indians thought the war was over—even had a dance. Within an hour, the Federal artillery opened up full blast. Me and the other two prisoners took off running for the rear of McIntosh's lines. Those crazy Cherokees were terrified of the big Yankee cannon. We were running, but they passed us. It took quite a while to get the Cherokees to settle down. McIntosh himself had to lead them back to battle. I picked up a gun and shell and started back with the once again advancing Indians. McCulloch had some Texas cavalry there as well. Men, you had it bad yesterday, but it was much worse down there. The Yankees struck back first with the cavalry and then with infantry. At one time, I got down on the ground because of the terrible shelling between the two armies. There had to be more than twenty horses killed and huge numbers of men."

He recalled that the tide of battle then turned in favor of the Yankees.

"The Rebs sounded retreat, and somehow I managed to survive. McIntosh and McCulloch were both killed. General Albert Pike was in command by nightfall. We were beaten there. Later, I began walking north in hope of finding our company. Dead men were all over the place. As long as I live, I will never forget the moonlight reflecting off the faces of the dead. I really wondered if all of our regiment had been killed. Our cavalry was looking for deserters, and they stopped me twice. But they believed me when I told them I was looking for my regiment. So, here I am."

"That's bad about McCulloch and McIntosh," Pierce said. "They were two of our best generals."

"It could have been worse if the 20th Regiment had not been transferred to Price's division," Willis said. "Well, except for Lyle."

"You never know what can happen in war," Pierce replied.

"We winning or losing?" Cooper again spoke.

"Who knows," replied a soldier with an unfamiliar face.

"We'll sure find out in a few hours though."

It sounded like the enemy shelling was beginning to increase. It even seemed closer now. An officer rode by the group. It was Van Dorn, angrily questioning an aide about the ammunition. They overhead the aide saying something about the supply wagons being sent to the wrong place.

"We're out of ammunition," Van Dorn screamed.

Orders soon came down the line for the reserve units to begin advancing. They were to form a battle line approximately a quarter of a mile south. Company B and the other reserve units were to begin moving forward.

While the enemy was nowhere in sight, the shelling from the Federal artillery was getting closer. Willis and Eslie were now moving forward together. Eslie had picked up a new Federal, Sharp's rifle and ammunition from a dead Yankee. The advancing reserves units soon began to see the backs of their own soldiers. The Rebs were retreating.

"Why we retreating, Eslie?" Willis asked. "We took this mountain. We can hold it. What's going on?"

"Don't know," Eslie said, shaking his head.

"Fall back! Fall back!" came the orders up in front, and Captain Blair came down the newly formed line.

"Men, we're going to protect our army. Fight like the devil!"

"We're fighting rear guard," Willis said to Eslie. "We're leaving the field to the Feds. We're leaving after winning. Why?"

The retreating Rebel line began to reform where the reserve units had set up. The shelling became fiercer. Several large trees were on the ground and several huge holes had formed in the ground where cannon shells landed. Dislodged rocks flew through the air. Cries for more ammo went unanswered, since there was no evidence of supply wagons. Once dominate, Van

Dorn's artillery was now slow to answer the loud blasts from the Yankee cannon.

In the rear, wagons, horses, and the wounded were leaving the field hospital at the tavern, moving east toward Huntsville Road. It was becoming evident that the entire Rebel army was trying to move east on Huntsville Road, as if Van Dorn was trying to save his army for another day. Curtis could smell victory, as the Yankees continued their advance up the south side of Pea Ridge Mountain. Southerners continued their retreat mostly to the east.

Several men had thrown down their guns. Some were helping the wounded. However, most of the Rebs seemed to be angry at the idea of giving ground to the invaders. The grays complained as they retreated.

"Why did we fight like heck to take this place just to give it back?" screamed one Rebel soldier.

"Why did Lyle have to die in a losing effort?" wondered Willis, still in line. "Why did Bartis have to die?"

Rumors were flying now that Van Dorn had been killed, that Price was captured and Pike was in charge. No one knew what to think. The movement east on Huntsville Road was now more organized. Only three regiments would remain to fight a rear guard action to protect their fleeing countrymen. Company B would be part of that force.

The Federals, not yet sure that Van Dorn's army was staging a retreat, came on slowly. Willis could soon see the first bluecoats, cautiously moving up the hillside. Much of the remaining Rebel ammunition had been left for the new battle line protecting the eastward retreat. Before long, Willis could make out Yankee regimental battle flags. A bugle suddenly sounded, followed by another, and then the men could hear a distant cheer.

243

Out of the trees and from behind boulders came the line of Union soldiers. Officers urged the men forward, swords glistening in the poor light.

"Wait for them, men," yelled a Southern officer. "Conserve your ammunition."

On came the blue-clad soldiers.

"Fire!" the Reb command came at about fifty yards.

A huge hole quickly appeared in the Yankee line as twenty-five to thirty men went down immediately. The Yankee line slowed, stopped, and then began to fall back. The Rebel cry that would occur many times throughout the war went up from the defenders.

"Check the wounded," cried an officer.

Willis looked around. No one near him and Elsie had been hit. Soldiers had been hit down the line. Willis could see men helping the wounded back northeast toward Huntsville Road. If not seriously wounded, these Rebs would make it to safety before nightfall.

"Reload. Get ready again. Check bayonets," came the command.

Company B, unhurt by the charge, received instructions to move to the west to fill up a gap created where several gray-clads were either killed or wounded.

"Wish I had something to eat," mentioned a soldier. "Nothing to eat for two days."

Willis was glad he had taken the food from the Union soldier. He was hungry too. Maybe that evening they would have the supply wagons ready. Another Union charge may be it, Willis thought. They may take us. Lord, protect us; keep us.

"Here they come again," screamed an officer. "Shoot straight."

The blue line had reformed intact. They advanced forward as if nothing had happened earlier. Willis knew that the defenders were just about out of ammunition. Could they hold out?

"Fire!" came the command after the Union line had moved within forty yards. Once again, the men in blue paid a heavy price for their courage.

"Charge!" This time it was a Union command.

Willis could barely make out where the enemy was due to the clouds of smoke and burned powder. He could only see moving figures. After firing, Willis and Eslie were hurriedly reloading when they heard Yankee cries and curses right in front of them. Willis looked up to see a Union officer leap toward him with his sword in a ready position. Willis threw his musket up in a circular manner, hoping to ward off the moving sword. His bayonet caught the officer near his left ear. The continued motion of the moving musket caused the bayonet to rip across the officer's throat, penetrating three to four inches deep. The man made a frightened sound, dropped his sword, and reached up to his throat. He fell forward, blood streaming over several Rebel soldiers.

A second soldier who had not fired his musket replaced him. He brought his musket up and fired at Willis. Willis waited for the pain. It wasn't until later that he realized that the mini ball had gone under his armpit, striking part of his Union haversack.

Meanwhile, Eslie had drawn back his musket and thrown it forward, bayonet exposed. The dull bayonet caught another surprised Fed soldier in the groin, causing him to scream in pain. The heavy smoke from the cannon and other firearms was so thick that one could hardly tell friend from foe. Where was Eslie? Was he dead?

Willis turned to look for his friend. Eslie was quickly reloading his musket when a Yank appeared in front of him.

"You're dead, Reb," the Yankee said pointing his gun at Eslie.

Willis fired before the Yank. The dead Union man hit the

earth at Eslie's feet.

"Thanks, Willis. He would have killed me."

"Forget it," Willis said, quickly reloading his musket.

Several Yankee cannonballs flew overhead and struck Reb soldiers behind Willis and Eslie. If the Yankee artillery was on target, it would go over the charging Yankee infantry and the Rebs upfront should be safe from the enemy shelling. Willis looked over to check again on Eslie. A Yankee soldier had run right up in front of him. He was aiming at Willis, who was attempting to load his musket. Willis waited and then "click"— the Yank's musket failed to fire.

Willis quickly threw up his musket, with the ramrod still in the barrel, and fired. The ramrod projectile went straight through the stomach of the surprised Yankee. Willis glanced back to see his friend in a life-and-death struggle with an enemy soldier. A scream caused Willis to look around as a Yankee thrust his bayonet toward him. Willis threw up his left hand, grabbed the bayonet, and pushed it further left. He swung his empty musket with his right hand and struck the man's head near the left ear. The blow brought the soldier to an unconscious state.

Willis quickly looked back to his friend. Eslie had picked up a cantaloupe-sized rock. He brought the rock down hard on the Yankee's nose — once, twice, three times. The man fell off to one side, badly hurt. Willis looked back to his friend and then looked back to see three Union men, rifles pointing at Eslie and him.

"Better give up, men," said a craggy looking Union soldier. Willis looked at Eslie. They both knew it was over. The two, along with three others, slowly got out of the gun pit. Much of the shelling had stopped, except back to the east. Willis hoped that most of Van Dorn's army had gotten away.

Chapter 27

Prisoners

March 7, 1862

THE UNION FIRES WERE as cozy as the Rebel fires. Surprisingly, the Union soldiers were quite friendly. It was already apparent that there was admiration on both sides. The captors began to break open rations, and Willis realized that the Yankees had plenty of food. They had salt pork, biscuits, dried fruit, and coffee. Several Union soldiers even had tobacco.

The atmosphere around the fire was much like that around the Rebel fires. There was some laughter and some storytelling, some humor and much sadness. Some of the conversation was accented. Willis knew that many of the Yankees were immigrants that had been here for only a few years. The Federal conversation switched to the day's battle. A blue-coated sergeant, probably near forty years of age, was describing the previous day's activity.

"Everything was all right, when suddenly, the Rebs started moving toward us. They overwhelmed us and we's forced to give ground. That's when those crazy Cherokees rode in screaming and hollering. They scalped half a dozen, I'd reckon. I know they got Hoss, cause he'd already been shot in the knee."

"I bet Hoss fought to the last," said a young, fuzzy-cheeked private, probably not more than eighteen years of age. "That's one strong man."

Willis looked at Eslie. He could tell that Eslie was thinking the same thing.

"Where's this Hoss from?" Willis asked when the younger soldier had finished talking.

"He's an Arky," the older soldier answered. "Had a brother called Mule. Reckon old Mule killed a dozen of you Rebs after he learned of Hoss's scalping."

Willis sat looking down at the ground. Tears once again came to his eyes. Hoss and Mule must have joined the Federal army. Poor Hoss. He remembered Hoss saying that he wasn't fighting just 'cause Lincoln called for troops. How many more would die, thought Willis. Why don't the Yankees go home and leave us be?

Willis and Eslie slept until a Union sergeant awakened them. That morning was warmer. They ate the food their captors provided.

"All right, Rebs," the sergeant said. "The party is over. It's time you get ready to spend some time in a prison camp. Get your belongings and be ready to move out in half an hour."

The smell of the salt pork cooking made Willis think of his ma and his home in Gravelly.

"Wonder where they will take us?" Eslie asked, interrupting his thoughts.

Activity in the area indicated that Curtis's army was preparing to catch up with the retreating Van Dorn. A cavalry unit rode by traveling east on Huntsville Road. Several Federal units had already made formation in preparation to move. The ever-moving teamsters were already rolling wagons with supplies and the wounded.

Willis couldn't help noticing the similarity of the two

armies. Except for the blue uniforms, the men might have been Southerners. The sergeant soon returned to remind Willis and Eslie to move north of Elkhorn Tavern near the spring. Willis noticed several other prisoners, possibly as many as thirty around the spring. As the two men reached the larger group of prisoners, they begin to look around for men from Regiment 20. They saw several familiar faces, but no one from their company.

A second cavalry unit came by. After passing the prisoners, the unit stopped a short distance from the prisoner group. A colonel dismounted and began walking back toward the guards. The fast steps, the neat uniform, and the quick glance made Willis think that the tall, bearded colonel was to be in charge of the prisoner detail. After talking briefly with the sergeant, the officer turned, quickly looked on the group, and began speaking in a strong, clear voice. It was the kind of voice that probably usually got results.

"Men, I'm Colonel Pickens, 6th Federal Cavalry, Missouri. I will be in charge of the prisoner detail. We will move out shortly, and I'll expect you as prisoners of war to follow all instructions. Assuming you do so, you will be given adequate food, water, and an occasional rest stop. I will not tolerate straggling, and we will shoot escaping prisoners in the field."

Willis believed that the officer would do as he stated. The officer paused and stroked his black beard for a few seconds before continuing.

"You will be going to Springfield, where many of you will stay for a while. It is likely that most of you will eventually go on to St. Louis and maybe even Chicago. If you have a friend that is injured or wounded, you will be expected to help them out. Forget about getting sick and riding a wagon—I will not tolerate illness. If you Rebs are as tough as your newspapers report, you will beat us to the prison camp." He did not smile, but continued to look around at the mostly gray-clad group.

"One last thing. Forget about your army; Van Dorn is headed back south again, probably to Fort Smith. He took his licking and went home. You can't count on him to rescue you."

The Yankee officer glanced briefly over the group of prisoners, turned, and quickly walked back to where a young private was attending to his horse. He grabbed the reins, mounted quickly, and moved north on Telegraph Road. Three other cavalrymen followed.

"Fall in." It wasn't hard to hear the sergeant. "Remember, Johnnies, what the colonel said about straggling. We'll travel in double lines — that's two abreast. Rebs, let's move it."

Being toward the rear, Willis and Eslie had to wait about five minutes until the soldiers in front had formed and moved on ahead. Willis noticed that six mounted Yankees were going to follow the group. Four wagons and another ten to twelve cavalrymen would follow them.

Willis took one last look at the tavern. Remarkably, it was in good shape. One corner of the chimney on the north end of the house had been hit, probably by cannon fire. Except for several splintered holes, the old hotel was in good shape. As Willis surveyed the tavern area, he wondered, what happened to the wounded Reb soldiers? What happened to George? Was he moved after his leg was removed? Did someone bury Lyle? Willis thought, if only they had won the battle on the second day. Then Willis noticed a man and a woman come out of the tavern and begin to examine the home for damages. They had survived the last two days inside the tavern.

The first mile or so, the long line moved down Pea Ridge Mountain. Then they moved over to Telegraph Road, past the first spring where both armies had taken water during the past two days. Willis noticed a couple of bodies near the floor of the valley. They had to be Rebels, killed two days earlier. Again he thought about Lyle. He hoped that someone had buried his friend. He also wondered how long it would be until Lyle's parents were contacted. Eslie, walking with his head down, suddenly looked up at Willis.

"How did we lose? We slipped around behind the mountain and surprised Curtis and then ran him off the heights."

Willis, looking at the rocky ground, was also thinking much about the events of the past two days.

"Eslie, we lost some generals, McIntosh and McCulloch, anyway," he said, looking over at his friend. "But you know, I wonder about Van Dorn. He sure pulled out and left. Eslie, I believe we had as many men as they did. But one of the officers said something about being low on ammunition. Maybe that was it, but we should have whipped the Yankees."

Neither man spoke for some time. Then a command was given to halt. No one knew why until one of the Yankee officers rode back from the front of the line and told the prisoners that they had reached a creek. He said everyone should fill his canteen.

It was at least ten minutes before Eslie and Willis reached the stream. The stream was muddy where all the men in front had been crossing. Willis, Eslie, and others moved upstream about twenty yards to reach clear water. Eslie lowered his canteen down into the cold water. Willis stopped near a small cedar tree that was growing at the edge of the creek.

"Eslie, move over this way."

Without looking up, Eslie slowly moved toward Willis, who was now behind the small but heavily branched cedar.

"Eslie, don't move. They may not see us."

After filling their canteens, other prisoners slowly began moving back toward the long line of Reb prisoners. Willis had been watching the nearest guard, a heavily whiskered man on a beautiful, grey horse. The guard had not seen him and Eslie move behind the tree.

"Let's move," called out the whiskered guard. He looked upstream, to his rear, and then toward the front of the line. By then everyone seemed to be in place.

"Move it," came the command after a couple more minutes.

Neither Willis nor Eslie breathed as they saw the guard glance back in their direction. The line moved off, only to be replaced by the Yankees cavalry unit and supply wagons behind the prisoners. They also made a brief stop before moving on.

"I'm 'bout to pee my pants," Eslie whispered as the last soldier disappeared up rocky Telegraph Road. The two waited another ten minutes before turning and moving back up the creek.

"Eslie, you know what will happen if they catch us," Willis finally spoke after walking about a half of a mile. "They will shoot us."

"I know," replied Eslie, who had been thinking about that possibility.

Neither men spoke as they got out of the creek and moved in an easterly direction. The trees, vines, and thickets were heavier now as the two men hurried on, tearing their clothing on occasional blackberry vines.

Willis looked back in the direction from which they had come. Sunset was approaching. They should be safe in another hour. Willis stopped, reached in his haversack, and pulled out some Union hardtack. As he started to hand it to Eslie, he heard a shout and then another. Horses were moving in their direction. They were both hidden behind a large gum tree. Willis silently prayed that the men would be wearing gray. The voices were closer now.

"Probably Rebel deserters," Willis overheard a soldier say. "Once we got the upper hand, Rebs probably started clearing out."

"Well," Willis heard the voice behind him. "What have we here?" It was the whiskered sergeant. He was staring at the men with what Willis thought were the bluest eyes he had ever seen.

"We surrender, sir," said Willis, quickly standing up and raising his hands over his head. "We left our regiment on Huntsville Road. We are tired of the killing."

Eslie had turned to look at his friend. What was he saying? Then it hit him. Willis was trying to save them by convincing the officer that they had never been captured. The officer had not spoken again. By then two other mounted soldiers had joined the party.

"Well boys, you are now prisoners on your way to Springfield."

"Sir, have you got any food? Eslie spoke for the first time. "We haven't eaten nothing for two days since we left our regiment."

It was now Willis's turn to look at his friend.

"Corporal, take them back to the group and see that they are fed," the colonel said, looking at one of the mounted soldiers.

"Sure thing. Let's go, Rebs," replied the corporal as he ushered the men back in the direction of the prisoner detail.

Please, God, don't let any of the other prisoners recognize us, Willis prayed as they walked. They rejoined the prison detail, and both men were relieved when no one recognized them as escaped prisoners.

"Thank God," Willis quietly said.

Within an hour of the men being placed back into the Yankee prison patrol, the whiskered sergeant called for camp. It was near 6:00 p.m. The men started fires and prepared food.

Once again, the Gravelly boys ate well.

"Eat as much as they offer," Willis whispered to Eslie while he ate an old but delicious piece of salt pork. "We are leaving tonight."

"What?" Eslie said, quickly looked toward Willis.

"We are still near the Arkansas border," Willis said. "We are still halfway familiar with the area. We can't get too far up in Missouri, if we plan on escaping. Be ready tonight."

The night was not made for escape. There was a full moon with few clouds. And it was cold. About an hour after everyone had settled down for the night, Willis nudged Eslie.

"Wait about half an hour," he quietly whispered. "They have only two guards posted near us and they are a long way apart. I will watch them for a while, and when they are far enough apart, we will try to run between them. They can't get more than one or two shots at us in the dark. Watch and follow me."

"Okay," Eslie said. " I'm on your heels."

It was probably forty-five minutes before Willis saw one of the posted guards, about thirty yards away, light up his pipe. He knew that the other guard was about thirty-five yards away in the opposite direction. Willis thought, if we run east, we will run between the guards. Hope the Yankees can't shoot those Sharps muskets.

Willis touched Eslie and then quietly removed his old blanket. Eslie followed his lead. In his mind, Willis had picked out an approximate direction earlier. Willis still saw no one moving as he slowly got up. He eased up and then broke out in a hard run in the direction between the two guards. He heard Eslie hot on his heels.

"Escape!" they heard someone shout, and then other cries. "Rebs are escaping."

Then came the dreaded gunshots. Willis heard one shot go by his head.

"Eslie, are you okay?" he whispered.

"Keep on running," breathed his friend. "I'm here."

Then several shots as the sleeping soldiers were aroused. Willis knew that if they could get as far as a hundred yards, or about like the hog barn, they would be safe. He knew that few of the soldiers could be freed up to look for them since they had to guard the other prisoners. Willis also hoped that the cavalry unit would have to saddle the horses before pursuing them.

"You still okay?" Willis stopped and reached back to catch his trailing friend, after running for about ten minutes.

"Man, we made it," Eslie said, still breathing heavy.

"We won't make as much noise while walking, but keep an eye out for torches," Willis replied. They walked for another ten minutes or so and then turned sharply right.

"We will turn south in the direction of the Yankee army," Willis said. "They won't expect that."

Eslie soon grabbed his friend's arm to stop him. Back to their left, maybe fifty yards away, he saw lit torches and horses. The cavalry unit had made good progress. The escapees bent down low to the ground, hardly breathing. The searchers proceeded on in an easterly direction.

"We'll make it," Willis said, putting his hand on Eslie's shoulder after the troopers were out of sight. "Don't worry."

They walked south toward Pea Ridge Mountain for another ten minutes or so.

"Now, we go back east again, but we must get a long way before daylight," Willis said, turning to Eslie.

"Suits me," said his partner.

Suddenly there was a shot and then two more shots. Willis

felt a terrible pain just above his knee and knew he had been hit.

"Willis, you all right?" Eslie asked as Willis slowed down.

"I caught a stray ball in the leg, but we got to keep moving for a while," Willis panted. He continued to walk slowly, dragging his right leg.

"Let's look at it," Eslie said, stopping and turning back to address his ailing partner.

Willis slowly and painfully pulled up his tattered trousers. He could feel a lot of blood. Eslie tore off part of his shirt and wrapped it tightly around the wound. Is this the end, Willis thought as he anxiously looked back in the direction of the shots.

"We got him," he heard a voice say. " Here he is, plumb dead."

"The other one got away," someone else said. Then other voices. "Forget him. We may run into Rebs this far east." Willis and Eslie listened carefully, hardly breathing at all.

"Willis, what happened?" Eslie spoke first. "They must have been shooting at us, 'cause they hit you."

Willis had also been thinking the Yankees were shooting at them. Did others also escape, or did the Yankees come across a dead Reb and think it was either Willis or Eslie that they had shot? How could they be so lucky—or was it luck? Had God intervened to save them? Willis reached down and felt the wet bandage before answering his friend.

"Eslie, the Almighty just may have allowed us to escape. That cavalry unit either shot someone else or more likely found a dead soldier and thought it was me." Eslie didn't speak for a half-minute or so.

"You know, Willis, you might be right," he finally spoke. "Maybe God helped us."

The sunrise brought a clear but cool day. Their progress

had slowed considerably since Willis had been wounded. The bleeding had stopped, but his leg hurt badly. A small pine sapling now served as a makeshift crutch. Somehow, Willis kept moving. The two friends stopped briefly for the last of the food that the Yankees have given them.

"Best food I've eaten since one of your mom's breakfasts. How do you feel, Willis? We didn't sleep more than four hours?"

"My leg hurts bad. But, Eslie, we have to go on. Just remember, I will have to go more slowly."

Willis was hoping to walk toward the sunrise and then veer south in hopes of reaching part of Van Dorn's army retreating toward Huntsville. But Willis also knew they could run across a Union cavalry patrol following Van Dorn's retreating army. Willis was very weak by the second day. He knew that he had lost a lot of blood. Continuing to move didn't help the situation.

"Eslie, I can't go on. I am beat," said the exhausted Willis.

Eslie helped his friend sit down against the base of a large oak tree. Then he gave Willis a drink from the canteen. Willis leaned back against the tree and closed his eyes.

"Eslie, go on," he said. "I can't go on. If we are captured, we may be shot. You can still escape."

"No, we will rest for the rest of the day and through the night," Eslie quickly replied in a firm voice. "Maybe you will feel better in the morning."

Two squirrels playing tag were the only activity in the heavily timbered area. Eslie would have liked to have shot one of the squirrels. What a meal. But even if he had a gun, it would have been too great a risk to take. Willis was now asleep. Eslie wondered if it was possible to find an isolated home nearby. He decided to climb the hill to the south and look around. He might even run across a Reb patrol. It was worth a look.

Eslie took the empty haversack that Willis had pulled off as he sat down and hung it on a low, hanging limb as a marker. He took a careful look around at the ridges to the south and east. The ridges were running mainly east and west. Deer hunting had taught Eslie much about knowing where he was in the forested hills around Gravelly. Fortunately, the day was almost clear and he could use the sun to help maintain direction. After one last look at his friend, he started south toward the ridge, probably no more than a mile or so.

Without Willis, Eslie now moved at a brisk pace. A doe and fawn scampered across a small clearing in front of him. As he walked, he carefully scanned the area in the direction in which he was walking. Three buzzards were circling in the distance. Probably a dead animal, he thought. But then he remembered Willis. Would the buzzards locate his friend? What about a black bear? Should he leave Willis?

After slowing his pace while second-guessing himself, Eslie decided that he must go on and check the other side of the southern ridge. The ridge ahead was covered with large boulders and stunted pine trees. Eslie came across what appeared to be a deer run or possibly a hog trail. The trail was easier to follow than fighting the boulders, vines, and stunted pine trees up the ridge. He had followed the trail for a while when he heard noise. It sounded like men walking through leaves. He stopped and waited. The leaf movement continued.

A deer would never create so much noise. Straining his eyes to see in the direction of the sound, Eslie saw something moving. It was a huge sow hog. And then Eslie noticed several small pigs. It looked like the pigs were eating acorns underneath a stand of oak trees. He turned and began walking in the direction of the hogs. Sniffing the mountain air, the old sow quickly picked up the human scent. She began to round up her brood and usher them on down into the valley. There must be ten or twelve young ones, Eslie thought. When he got to the clearing where the hogs were, he still heard noises nearby, yet the pigs had disappeared into the valley below. He decided to investigate.

He soon discovered the noisemaker. A small pig had caught its leg in a forked limb of a smaller bush. While trying to free itself, the pig had caused a second branch to tighten on the leg. It was desperately trying to get free of the trap.

Eslie looked up toward the top of the ridge. He knew why the buzzards were interested in the area. He scanned the ground for a good-sized rock and found one about the size of a large shoe. He took the rock over to the squirming pig.

"Sorry, but we need you." Eslie brought the rock down twice on the pig's head. The pig quit moving. Using his feet and hands, Eslie was able to break the forked limb and the second limb and remove the dead pig from his trap. He picked it up by a hind leg and again began climbing the hill. He finally reached the top of the ridge, hoping to see a farm in the valley below. All he saw were pine trees and still more pine trees.

After carefully looking in all directions, Eslie turned to go back down the hill. The buzzards had given up on a pork-chop dinner. It was late afternoon and Eslie knew that he had to get back to Willis before dark. He took a good look back north and then chose a direction that he thought was correct. In less than an hour, he spotted the blue haversack hanging in the huge oak tree. He could now see his friend.

Willis had managed to lie down on the leaves at the base of the tree and was fast asleep. Eslie moved over to a place about a hundred yards from his friend. He found a sharp stick and used it to puncture the carcass of the pig. After creating a hole in the carcass cavity, he was able to use his thumbs to rip open the pig's underbelly. He pulled out the pig's stomach and intestines and then washed the carcass in the nearby stream.

After returning to the oak tree and Willis, Eslie took the haversack, put the pig's carcass in it, and hung the haversack back on the tree limb. He took the canteen over to the stream, washed his hands, and filled the canteen. He walked back to the resting Willis and felt his face with his hand. It was warm. Willis stirred when he felt Eslie's hand on his face.

"What time is it?" he asked, opening his eyes.

"Late afternoon," Eslie said. "Maybe 5:00 p.m."

"Wish we had food," said Willis.

"Hey, we gonna have pork for dinner. I'm sure we can light a fire when it gets dark and we'll cook it."

"Where did you get hog out here?" Willis quietly asked.

"Willis, you 'member you said God had helped us when we escaped?"

"Yeah."

"Well, he's gone and done it agin. I found this pig hung up in a tree branch 'bout a mile away. Already got it ready for the fire. Thought it best to wait till dark afore we start a fire. I still have flint stone—only thing the Yankees didn't take."

Eslie collected dried grass and twigs for the fire and then arranged them in a small compact pile.

"Before we start the fire, let's clean the wound."

While Willis remained on his back, Eslie raised his trouser leg and removed the old shirt bandage. He used water from the canteen to wash the red, swollen, injured leg.

"How's it feel?"

"I don't think its any worse," Willis answered, looking down at the wound. "But it still hurts."

"Hey, that pig meat and another night's rest will help a lot," said Eslie.

Eslie helped Willis sit up against the base of the tree. Then he took the flint and knelt down by the dried twigs and grass. After several strikes, a small glow occurred in the dried grass. Eslie began to blow softly on the grass until a small flame leaped up. He quickly placed the dried twigs in the flame. Soon a good fire was going and Eslie placed larger dried logs on the fire.

"Just like coon hunting behind your house," he smiled, looking at Willis.

After the fire was burning well, Eslie found a larger limb about two inches around. He found two large rocks and placed them on both sides of the fire. He pushed the large limb completely through the carcass of the pig and placed the ends of the large limb on each rock, causing the pig to be suspended over the fire. The men could soon smell the pork cooking.

"See what we learned from coon hunting?" Willis said, watching Eslie. "Hope the wild animals here can't smell that pork. Boy, it smells good."

The pork was delicious. Willis ate a good helping. After eating all they could eat, Eslie took the leftover pork and put it in the haversack.

"We can eat on that for couple more days."

Eslie moved away from the fire to find more firewood to use during the night. After bringing two arms full of wood up near the fire, he helped Willis get into a comfortable position to sleep. Several pine tree branches provided some cushion for the hard ground.

"I will keep the fire going," Eslie said, sitting down and relaxing against the base of the large tree.

The night was uneventful except for a brief time when coyotes had a scuffle over the remains of the pig that Eslie had thrown away. Willis slept through most of the night. Eslie was up around sunrise to feed the fire and warm up some of the leftover pork.

"How you feeling, Willis?"

"Leg hurts and I'm sure sore all over. Probably from walking with the crutch."

After some more pork, the men decided to put out the fire and continue on. Eslie helped Willis to his feet and gave him the crutch.

"Eslie, go on," Willis said after taking about five steps. "I'm going to be so slow. Maybe you will find help."

"Not going to happen." Eslie took his friend's right arm and put it over his head and right shoulder. "I will help support you as you walk."

He put his left arm around Willis's back. Now a human crutch, Eslie carried the limb crutch in his right hand. He also put the haversack with the extra pork on his own back. Progress was slow as Eslie carefully selected the best surface for walking. Rather than go south over the ridge where the pigs were, Eslie moved east where the terrain was not as steep. With frequent rest stops, the men walked all day in a southeasterly direction, finally coming to Huntsville Road. Willis again reminded Eslie that it would be dangerous to follow the road east due to possible pursuing Union cavalry.

"Let's cross Huntsville Road and continue on moving in the same general direction. We could run into the Reb army, which is probably retreating south toward Van Buren. At the same time, we are moving in the general direction of Gravelly."

They walked for a while before Eslie said, "Won't home be great?"

Willis thought, my home will be great—don't know about yours, or Lyle's, or Bartis's home though.

Chapter 28

The Farm

March 1862

ON THE FOURTH DAY, the men came across an isolated farm. They saw cows, chickens, hogs—and people. Willis advised caution.

"Could be Yankee sympathizers up here and they might report us." The smell of frying bacon convinced the escaped prisoners that they should at least check out the possibilities.

"Let me go up alone and see who lives there," Eslie suggested. "If it's all right, I will signal you to come on in."

"Okay, but be careful," Willis agreed after considering Eslie's suggestion. He watched as his friend left the wooded area and started across the pasture toward the lone farmhouse. *Lord, keep him safe,* Willis prayed. *We have made good progress.*

Willis watched Eslie as he went to the back door of the house and knocked. Immediately, an older man walked out of the barn and up behind Eslie. Stooped and walking with a limp, he looked to be in his seventies.

"What do you want?" he asked suspiciously. This wasn't the first deserter that had showed up here.

"Sir, I'm Eslie Southard from the Danville/Gravelly area," said the startled Eslie, turning to see the thin, old man. "I was a prisoner of the Federal army until I escaped. Been walking for about four days. I am hungry, but I don't have any money."

As Willis watched his good friend, he could only imagine how truthful Eslie's story would be. How could Eslie—raised by a lazy, drunken man—turn out to be such a good person?

"Yo not a durn Yank, are ya?" the farmer asked after studying the young man.

"You ever hear of Danville?" Eslie quickly replied. The older man said he had. "A Yankee wouldn't have heard of Danville, would he?"

The farmer studied Eslie for a minute and finally said, "Shor you're not a blame Reb deserter?"

"Van Dorn's army is probably moving south to avoid the Federals," Eslie said, frowning. "Would I be moving in the same direction if I was a deserter? No, I'd be going north or west."

"Guess yo right," the old man smiled and introduced himself as Ben Freeny. "Come on in and have some grub."

"Wait, sir. I have a friend up in that timber," Eslie pointed back toward Willis's location. "He has been shot and is on a crutch. Could he join us?"

"Shor, 'specially if he'un is hurt," the man agreed, looking in the direction toward which Eslie pointed.

Eslie waved his extended right arm back and forth to get his friend's attention. Willis, who had been watching anxiously, saw the wave. He came out of the trees and began to slowly limp toward the farmhouse, using the makeshift crutch.

"Should we go get him with the wagon?" the farmer asked, seeing Willis's condition.

"No, he can do it," Eslie said, watching his friend moving with the crutch. "He's one tough man, believe me."

Eslie did go out and help Willis after he had gotten closer

to the house. Mrs. Freeny, a petite lady, was almost deaf, but that didn't prevent her from being a great cook and a very compassionate woman. She quickly asked Willis if she could examine his injured leg. Willis was only too glad to allow the old lady to look at the wound.

After a struggle to get his trousers up above his knee, Willis removed Eslie's crude bandage that covered his leg. This was only the second time that Willis had looked at the wound. It looked clean enough, but it was very red and inflamed around the hole that the musket ball had made. The ball had gone into his leg just above the knee, scraped a bone, and exited through the back of the leg.

Mrs. Freeny put water in a pan to warm on the old wood stove. After the water was hot, she got an old towel and gently but thoroughly cleaned the front and back of his leg. Willis winched several times as she attempted to clean the damaged tissue around the wound. After another examination, she produced some bacon grease and thoroughly covered the wound with it. Then she began to apply a bandage over the wound with another towel.

While this was going on, Mr. Freeny had gone back to the barn. He soon returned to the house with a couple of makeshift crutches.

"He makes better crutches than you do," Willis teased Eslie, after trying them out.

Eslie laughed. Mrs. Freeny was also obviously proud of her nursing ability.

"You'uns can sleep in the other bedroom," she instructed Willis. "That was our son's bedroom. He was killed at Wilson's Creek several months ago."

"Oh, I'm real sorry, ma'am," Eslie quickly responded.

She explained that he was an adopted son they had taken in

six years earlier when his pa and ma died from dysentery.

"We never could have young'uns but we shor loved Tim," she said.

For some time, the old man looked down at the floor, not speaking.

"Gonna be lot more boys kilt before the wars through," he finally said. "And based on what ya'll say about this last fight, we may get whumped."

Willis had begun to talk earlier but hated to interfere while the elderly folks talked. Now he decided to join the conversation.

"We probably need to go on today," he said. "Yankee patrols are out and moving; 'sides, ya'll could get in trouble, allowing us to stay here. They might even burn your house."

"Phooey, ya'll are spending the night," Mrs. Freeny said, studying Willis. "Need to let your limb rest 'while."

"She's right, Willis," Eslie agreed, knowing how painful it was for Willis to walk. "You need to stay off the leg."

Once that was settled, the foursome enjoyed the day visiting. Willis described his family and even mentioned Rosalie. Eslie only reported that his mother had died in childbirth and that he lived with his pa. Willis felt bad when they asked Eslie what his pa did for a living.

"I guess you would say farming," Eslie replied.

By nightfall, even Mr. Freeny was talking. He and his first wife, now deceased, came to Arkansas from Tennessee in a wagon pulled by oxen. The story proved to be quite interesting, and before they knew it, it was nine o'clock in the evening.

Mrs. Freeny produced a Bible and announced that they would have a devotion. She opened the old family Bible and began to read from I Samuel. She read about David, the young shepherd boy who was being chased by the jealous King Saul. Both Eslie and Willis thought the story was very appropriate, since they too were on the run. Mr. Freeny prayed a short prayer in which he asked the Lord to protect the boys until they got home to their families. With the "amen," Willis thanked Freeny for the prayer. The lady took the boys into the vacant bedroom and pulled back the heavy covers.

"Hope you'uns don't mind a featherbed?"

"Not at all, specially after sleeping on the ground for six months," Willis said.

The two men noticed that Mrs. Freeny went to both windows and closed the heavy curtains. Not long after the men had gotten into the big bed, they heard the sound of horse hooves.

"Do you think they will turn us in?" Eslie whispered.

"Hope not."

Eslie quietly moved over to the window and very slightly pulled back the bottom of the curtain.

"It's a patrol," he said, turning quickly to Willis. "Too dark to tell which army."

They heard a soft knock on the bedroom door and the old lady pushed the bedroom door open about two inches.

"Be very quiet, its soldiers," she warned.

The two men heard a heavier knock on the front door. Freeny, with a lit candle, made his way to the front door. He unbolted the heavy latch and opened the door.

"Yes."

"You seen any sign of Reb soldiers?" a Federal cavalry officer quickly spoke.

"No, but a Reb patrol was by here about three days ago," Freeny said, lowering the candle.

"Did you see which way they rode off?" the officer asked.

"I believe south," Freeny replied, looking past the officer to the other mounted riders.

"Seen any deserters or prisoners?" the officer spoke again.

"No, but wish one would come by. I need a lot of help here on the farm," Freeny said boldly, moving the candle up closer to the officer's face.

"You a secesh?" the officer asked Freeny.

"Oh, I'm neutral," replied the old man.

"Mind if we search your barn?" asked the officer.

"Oh, no, go rite ahead—but don't go up in the hayloft. I have a couple of setting hens there."

"Sergeant, make a thorough search of the barn," the officer said, turning to another soldier. "Particularly the hayloft."

Freeny withdrew and closed the door. Willis and Eslie had heard every word of the conversation from the bedroom.

"What's Freeny hiding in the hayloft?" Eslie whispered to Willis.

"Don't know," replied Willis.

The Federals made a complete search of the barn, the hayloft, and all outbuildings. The search took almost two hours. When it was concluded, the patrol left with no further word with Freeny.

The next morning, Eslie helped the farmer with his chores. After completing them, Freeny and Eslie came back to the house to find breakfast on the table and Willis sitting there, ready to eat.

"Mr. Freeny, we thank you for hiding us from the patrol last night," Willis said as the biscuits were passed around. "And we thank Mrs. Freeny for bandaging my leg. Could I ask you a question?"

"Shor can," replied Freeny.

"Why did you act as if you were hiding something in the hayloft?" Willis looked at Mrs. Freeny, who was smiling, and then back to the farmer.

"Well, you see, I knowd them Yankees were dead tired when they rode in last night. I figured I would cost them another two hours of sleep by making them search the barn loft. It was the officer that made them do it. Sure hope they didn't bother those two red hens setting on eggs." Everyone broke out in loud laughter, including Freeny. "I knowd you boys would be leaving early this morning, and might as well have the Yankees getting some much needed sleep when you did."

Again, there was more laughter. Within one hour, the two men, with two days of food and Willis's improved crutches, boarded Freeny's wagon. The farmer volunteered to take the men about ten miles south before the road turned back west. There was no road over the mountains here so the men would be on their own again. After shaking hands with the old man and offering much thanks, the two soldiers got off the wagon.

"Tell Mrs. Freeny thanks for all she did for us," said Eslie.

"Thank ya'll. You both reminded us of Tim. It was like having him 'round agin. We will be praying for you both. If you ever get up here's agin, stop by." As he turned the wagon around, Freeny waved at the two men.

"Let's go toward that cut in the mountain," Eslie suggested, after a brief look south. "How does the leg feel?"

"Still very sore," Willis said, placing the new crutches under his arms. "But it may be better."

Willis could not move very fast with the crutches, but Eslie figured that they made six or seven miles on the first day. Mrs. Freeny's packaged food made the day bearable. The first night was very cold, but Eslie's excellent fire allowed the men to sleep quite well. On the second day, they sighted a Union cavalry patrol. Willis felt that they needed to delay awhile, even though he was sure that the patrol was probably fishing for Van Dorn's forces.

"I don't think that they are a threat, but we can never be too careful."

"Another day's rest would also be good for your leg."

By then, Willis's main concern was for his leg, which remained swollen. Three more days passed. Water was plentiful, but they had eaten the last of the food so hunger was a problem. They were fortunate that the weather had continued to improve.

While the men had to frequently stop for Willis, they were able to walk for seven hours or so each day. On the sixth day, a Sunday, the men caught a ride with a farmer and his family on their wagon. Willis asked the farmer the name of the next town. The farmer, an immigrant that could hardly speak English, was finally able to convey to Willis that the town was Clarksville. The family was on their way to Clarksville for church.

After the soldiers had arrived in Clarksville, some of the farmer's friends that lived there gave Willis and Eslie food. They also attended church with their new acquaintances in Clarksville. After church, Pastor Neal invited Willis and Eslie to his home for lunch. There they learned that the pastor's wife was an excellent cook and that the pastor, originally from Iowa, was a Union sympathizer. However, the preacher assured Willis and Eslie that he would not tell anyone about them.

After their meal, Willis and Eslie again set out on foot.

Chapter 29

Harpersfield

April 1862

Willis and Eslie had hoped they might be able to get a ride on a wagon going south. They were disappointed when the first two farmers they asked said no to the soldiers.

The third person that the men asked for a ride was a young black man, probably sixteen or seventeen years old, who was a trusted slave. A large plantation owner who lived north of the Arkansas River, Mister Brower, owned the man. The plantation was Harpersfield, one of the largest in the valley. The young man, driving a beautiful team of white horses, identified himself as Rufus. Willis quickly found that Rufus was a friendly, sociable slave. Eslie asked why Rufus was there, so far from home.

"Come fer feed," Rufus replied. "Horse feed. Massa Brower feeds horses good meal." The black man reached in his pocket and pulled out his slave papers.

"It's all right. We believe you, but could you give us a ride south toward Dutch?"

"Sur, git in," Rufus said after sizing up the men.

An hour later, after the wagon was loaded, the three men were on the way to Harpersfield. Rufus said little as Eslie and

Willis discussed the war.

"Willis, you think we are defeated? I mean, will the Yankees take over Arkansas?" Willis looked down the country road form some time before speaking.

"Well, Eslie, lot of Southern territory yet," he said. "They may beat us, but not before a long fight."

"What kind of farming does this Mister Brower do?" asked Willis, who had said little since they started south toward Harpersfield.

The young slave, still not sure about his riders, looked off to the east and then back at the beautiful team of horses. "We raises cotton, hay for the cattle, and the cattle. We's got a lot of pastur for the animals too. Massa must have over a hunared acres altogether. He gots lots of niggers too."

After a brief time of little conversation, Willis was surprised when Rufus spoke again.

"Ya'll heared about the bushwhackers?"

"Guess not. Who are they?" Eslie asked, turning to toward Rufus.

"Some of them like the Yankees and some like the Southerds," Rufus replied, continuing to look down the road. "They rides horses at night and robs people and kills some. Some kills both white folks and black folks. They's killed number of folks whar we live. Some hang the niggers. One reason I let you'uns ride the wagon."

Late in the afternoon, the threesome reached Harpersfield. The beautiful plantation was on the north bank of the Arkansas River. Even in the early spring the fields looked impressive. As Rufus pulled the wagon around to the big house, Mr. Brower came out to check on the feed. Brower was a big, heavy man with white hair growing long down his neck. He quickly moved to the wagon to meet the two strangers.

"Howdy. Name's Brower. Welcome to Harpersfield. Mother was a Harper," he said, explaining the plantation name. "Get down while the boy unloads the feed."

"I'm Willis Lofland and this is Eslie Southard," Willis said as he stepped down and extended his hand. "We're from Gravelly—also escaped Reb prisoners from Pea Ridge."

"Yeah, I heard about our defeat," Brower said. "That Van Dorn feller wasn't much of a general. If Price had been in charge, we'd have licked 'em good."

"You may be right," Willis said. "Some said our ammo was over at Bentonville and we run clean out."

"Come up on the porch and sit down a spell," Brower offered as a middle-aged woman came out on the big porch. "Mary Belle, bring us some lemonade," Rufus said to his wife.

She left, returned shortly with a pitcher of lemonade, and welcomed the men.

"Mr. Brower, what's this about bushwhackers?" Willis asked, after answering a couple of other questions about the recent battle.

"Who mentioned them?" Brower asked, looking quickly at Willis.

"Well, Rufus mentioned them on the road down."

"Willis, this is a divided state," Brower said, looking down toward the river and then returning his attention to the soldier. "Most favor the Constitution and smaller government. But some—maybe a third—favor the Lincoln government. Without getting too deep, the former group believes that states must retain the power extended to them in the Constitution. The latter group would turn their head and allow the federal government to extend its federal power over all parts of our society. The supporters of this view are in favor of excessive tariffs—tariffs that hurt the Southern agrarian society.

273

They favor a large number of big government ideas such as government-financed canals, roads, seaports, and even railroads and a transcontinental railroad. They favor financial advantage to manufacturing and shipping. These same people forget that cotton allows these business enterprises to excel. Sure, slavery is a by–product of the South. It will disappear if given a chance. But, at this time slavery is constitutional."

Brower chuckled and then went on. "You asked about the bushwhackers and you got a discourse about our Constitution and government. But remember, I said the state, like the country, is divided. Anytime there is an important issue and people take sides on an issue, there are always those who take the extreme view — from both sides of the issue. The bushwhackers are the extremists, from both sides. It is literally a war within a war. Those bushwhackers, who support the state — or the states' "rights view," are willing to do what is necessary in order to establish their view. Conversely, the other or opposite extreme has their bushwhacker element. They must establish their view regardless of what they must do. Both groups disguise themselves as nightriders and prey on those opposed to their view — even the next-door neighbor."

"Do you see them around here?" Willis interrupted.

"Yes," said Brower, again looking away. "Mostly the Northern sympathetic group. They have hit several neighbors — neighbors that show Southern sympathies. No, I haven't been hit, probably because we have a good number of men on our spread. We employ several white men along with our ninety-four slaves, but I do worry about the bushwhacker element.

"You men have been gone a while," he continued. "Some things have changed. You may even find that some people in your neighborhoods may oppose you. Believe me, this is a statewide problem."

"Willis, we better ask around about this in Yell County," said Eslie, who had been carefully listening. "At the same time, we probably need to go. It's getting late."

"Men, you have been fighting for our state," Brower spoke up again. "The least I can do for you is help you get home. I will have Rufus take you down to the ferry and send you on across the river. Ferrell Robinson lives down from the ferry landing. He will help you further if I send a note."

The owner called Rufus and told him to take the visitors on down to the ferry. They said their goodbyes and the two soldiers boarded the wagon again. Soon they were going south toward the river. Arriving at Brower's ferry, Rufus told the ferry serviceman to carry the two visitors across the river without any charge. Both Eslie and Willis shook hands with Rufus and thanked him for the day's ride.

Within twenty minutes, the ferry dropped the men at a dock on the south side of the Arkansas River. When Ferrell Robinson saw the approaching ferry, he met the men and accepted Brower's note. Robinson was especially friendly when he found that the men were Southern soldiers. Willis brought up the bushwhackers that evening as they sat talking after supper.

"Men, it is a serious problem," said Robinson. "We see mainly the Northern bushwhacker element around here, but the Southern bushwhackers are active down in the Hot Springs area, and they are just as bad. I had a cousin down there by the name of Blocker. The Southern bushwhackers murdered him one evening."

The soldiers spent the night in one of Robinson's bedrooms. The next morning, he had a hired hand transport the men to a small town about twenty miles south. As they neared the town of Paris, they sighted a Yankee patrol moving toward the small town. Willis convinced the hired hand to drop them off early so they could go around Paris and avoid the Yankees.

They would spend four more nights around a campfire before reaching the small town of Dutch Creek. Within half an hour, the whole town of forty people turned out to welcome the new heroes. After everyone had greeted them, including the children, the townspeople began asking questions.

"Did you'uns kill any Yankees?" one small boy asked.

"I don't think you ever know if you kill someone," Willis replied, noticing that everyone was listening. "You just fire your musket. I'm sure I probably hit some. But, I hate to think about ending someone's life."

"How far away are the Federals?" a teenager asked.

"Probably hundred or so miles, but they may be back in Missouri by now," Eslie said, looking over the small crowd. When he had a chance, he whispered to his buddy, "Never heard of the losers being welcomed as heroes."

"Know what you mean. I think we are heroes because no one else in Dutch Creek has been as far away as Bentonville or Pea Ridge Mountain."

The heroes spent two hours in the small crossroads community, including sharing a meal with one of Eslie's cousins, Wayne Southard. After the meal, Wayne, in a serious tone, called Eslie and Willis over to the side.

"Eslie, I have some very bad news. I hate to tell you this so bad." Wayne certainly had the attention of the two soldiers. "Eslie, something terrible has happened to your pa. He had an accident a couple weeks ago. I guess Ralph went out late one evening to draw water. He must have fell and hit his head on the side of the rock-encased well."

Willis quietly glanced at Eslie. A big tear was moving down his face. Feeling the tears in his own eyes, Willis quickly looked away. Wayne said that the temperature was freezing and Ralph lay there all night. The Reverend Gotham went to visit Ralph two days later and found him. The preacher had come by to tell Ralph that the militia had lost the battle near Bentonville. He held services for Ralph the next day and he was buried in the Young Gravelly Cemetery. Eslie was shocked.

"I wanted to see Pa so bad," he said, looking over at Willis, with more tears coming down his face. "I prayed every night that the Lord would help him overcome the drinking problem, I'm afraid he wasn't a Christian."

"We don't know if he was or not," Willis said, reaching over and put his arm around his best friend. But I know you were always a good example to your pa."

Wayne also was teary eyed as he observed his cousin's agony.

"Reckon we could go by the graveyard on the way home?" Eslie asked, wiping away the tears on his cheek.

"Sure we will," said his friend. "And you are going to move in with us. You have always been like another son to Ma and Pa, so that's settled."

"Well, I guess we had better go," Eslie said.

Again, they said their goodbyes and Eslie asked Wayne to come visit.

"We'll get down in a week or so," Wayne promised, giving Eslie a quick hug. "And you let us know if we can be of help."

With a ride offered by a local farmer who knew Wayne, the men hoped to be in Gravelly the next day. Neither man said much as they moved closer to home. Finally, Eslie brought up the bushwhackers. Both Willis and Eslie were surprised that men would create such organizations — groups to ride around and create violence for their neighbors who believed differently than they believed.

"Brower explained it pretty good," Willis said, glad to see

his friend talking. "The bushwhacker men are fighting a war within a war."

Eslie agreed. "If they feel so strong about it, why don't they join an army instead of fighting their neighbors?"

"That's right. They are really cowards except when facing unarmed men or women," Willis added.

Chapter 30

Gravelly

April 1862

WHEN THEY HAD AT last reached Gravelly, Willis suggested that they first go by Parkers Feed Store and see if Homer and Ilene had heard about Lyle's death. Then, Willis felt that they should visit with Bartis's parents.

"Sure hate to tell Cryril and Esther about Bartis," Eslie said. "Wouldn't be near so bad to say he was killed like Lyle in defending Arkansas."

"I feel the same way," Willis said. "Eslie, Bartis died fighting for his country. That's all we need to say."

People recognized the two Rebs and they quickly drew a crowd—or at least a crowd for Gravelly. At least eight or nine men came out to greet the soldiers and to get the latest information on the war. The militia had reported the deaths of both Lyle and Bartis. The report indicated that both had been buried not far from the battle site. Willis thought, I hope my friends are buried close to each other.

Over the next hour, Willis and Eslie told of their experience in the militia, including the escape and the journey home. They answered several questions about Lyle and Bartis and their deaths.

"What about Dorn?" asked Howie Ballard, owner of the pool hall and without a doubt the most aggressive man in town in support of slavery. "We heared you'uns ran out of ammo."

"Van Dorn," corrected Willis, "and yes, the story was that our ammo wagons were sent by mistake to Bentonville. We were out of powder and ball early the second day. Even the cannon couldn't be used due to lack of gunpowder. I don't know who was at fault."

"Well, things are going better back east," Ballard said. "We whumped the Yankees at a place called Manassee, somewhar in Virginee. Almost captured Washington and the tall man in the White House."

"Did you see Hoss or Mule?" someone asked. "They a'fighin' on the Yankees side."

"No, we never saw them," Willis said, although he recalled the story of the Cherokees scalping and killing Hoss. "Course, there were more than 20,000 men in arms."

Pastor Gotham had walked up to where they were gathered and was listening.

"Willis, won't you all have to go back to the militia?" he asked when he got a chance.

"Oh—hello, Reverend. Probably, unless my leg is too bad. I'm sure Eslie will have to in time." He paused and then asked if Rosalie was okay.

"She's fine," the minister smiled. "And she's going to wish she had come to town."

"Well, tell her I will get over as soon as I can."

Reverend Gotham turned to Eslie and told him he was sorry he had to come home to bad news about his pa. He told the soldier he would tell him about the circumstances later, when they had more time to talk. Eslie thanked him.

"We'd better go," Willis said. "My folks don't even know we

are here, and we need to go see Homer."

Homer was not one of the welcoming committee. Either he was busy in the store or he knew he would have difficulty talking to his deceased son's good friends. As Willis and Eslie entered the feed store, Homer looked up from his desk. He quickly got to his feet and moved toward the two men.

"Boys, it's so good to see you," he said, putting his arms around both of the men and hugging them.

As Willis looked into Homer's face, he noticed tears in his eyes. He also looked a lot older.

"Willis, you are limping," Homer asked. "You all right?"

"I'm fine, Mr. Parker; I took a shot in my leg when we escaped, but it's much better now."

"How 'bout you, Eslie?" Homer asked.

"I'm fine too, Mr. Parker."

"Mr. Parker, you know how much we thought of Lyle," Willis said after the other two had finished talking. "You also know how much Regiment 20 thought of Lyle, because they elected him lieutenant. Mr. Parker, if the regiment could have voted on the day before Lyle was killed, every single man would have selected him to be one of the best officers in Van Dorn's entire army. You probably didn't know, but Colonel Harvell asked Lyle to attend a staff officer meeting—the highest-ranking officers, including the generals, were there. Colonel Harvell told me after Lyle's death that Lyle would have become captain if he had survived the battle. Lyle was not only a good officer; he died a hero's death in leading our company up a hill against the terrible Federal gunfire. He was out in front of the entire regiment."

"We all had so much confidence and respect for Lyle," Eslie then spoke up. "We will sure miss him."

"He was a good boy," Homer replied, with tears in his eyes,. "We really miss Lyle. But, men, don't quit coming by the store."

"Oh, we won't, Mr. Parker," replied Willis. "But we better go on to see my folks."

The two men left the feed store and walked three blocks south to Bartis's parent's home. As they entered the yard, Eslie looked over toward the dog pen where Bartis's redbone coonhound had stayed. The pen had been empty since Red's death by the raccoon. Then the men saw Esther, Bartis's ma, hanging out washed clothes on the clothesline. When she saw the two young men, Esther draped a towel over the line and quickly came toward them. She was already crying when she hugged Willis and Eslie.

"Eslie, I'm so sorry about your pa," she said before the men could say anything. "It was such a tragedy."

Both boys struggled to keep from crying.

"Mrs. Edwards, we're so sorry about Bartis," Eslie finally said in a broken voice said. "He was such a good friend."

"He was almost a brother, like Lyle," said Willis, after Eslie had finished speaking. "We will miss him so much."

"I know it's hard on you'uns too," Esther said, wiping away tears. "He spent as much time with ya'll as he did at home. Cryril —oh, he's down in the bottoms, cutting wood—and me have visited several times with the Parkers. I guess that we grieve together. But thank the Lord ya'll are safely home."

"We'll get by to see you when we can," Willis said, looking over at the empty dog pen. "We're on the way to Young Gravelly; tell Mr. Edwards we came by."

"Come back soon," Esther said, hugging both boys again.

The men started back up to Main Street. They caught a ride with Pastor Gotham for most of the way to Young Gravelly. The preacher was glad he would get the chance to tell Eslie the details about his father's passing. Eslie listened while looking off in the distance.

"I don't guess Pa ever became a Christian," Eslie said, without looking at the pastor.

"We'll never know, but I did share the news with Ralph more than once," he said, looking at Eslie and then putting his hand on his shoulder. "So, who knows?"

Willis turned to his best friend and saw him looking down at the wagon floor, a big tear moving down his cheek. Willis hurt for him. They were just short of Young Gravelly Cemetery and Rock Creek Baptist Church, where Eslie and Willis attended church.

"Brother Gotham, would you let me off here?" Eslie asked. "I want to visit Pa's grave." The reverend had already planned on turning the wagon team up the drive to the small church.

"Eslie, I will take you to the grave site," he said. When they had stopped, the three men got down from the wagon and walked over to the cemetery gate.

"Eslie, your pa's grave is over past that large Ogden family stone near the fence," the pastor said as they went through the gate. "We put a big rock there for a headstone."

To give Eslie time alone to think and pray at his father's grave, the pastor asked Willis to walk with him over to where his brother had been buried. Willis's grandparents' grave sites were nearby and he stopped there to pull some weeds after that. Eslie joined them after paying respects to his pa.

"I'm ready to go, if ya'll are ready," he said. His eyes were red, but he had composed himself.

Willis reached his arm over, put it around his best friend, and hugged him. The men walked back to the church where the wagon and mule team waited.

"Brother Gotham, I thank you for preaching at pa's funeral and seeing he got a decent burial," Eslie said as they traveled east toward Willis's home. "And thanks for stopping today and 'lowing me to see his grave."

"Eslie, I was glad to do it. Rosalie was the one who asked your pastor to let me preach the service. I guess most folks never knew that I had known Ralph for forty years." Reverend Gotham decided it was a good time to share some things with Eslie that he probably didn't know.

"I knew Ralph before he married Lillie, your mom. Ralph went to church then, with your mom. They were crazy about each other. Ralph never touched alcohol back then. Your parents made all kinds of plans for the future. Back then, your pa worked for the Hunnicutts at the cotton gin at Bluffton. They were so excited about your expected birth and Lillie made a lot of clothes for you.

"As you probably know, Lillie had very serious problems at delivery time. Doc Melburn—he's dead now—arrived early enough. Your mom was in great pain. You were turned the wrong way in her womb. Doc said he had encountered this before. Once, he had been able to save the baby at the expense of the mother. He related this to your parents. Ralph said, 'No, save my wife.' Lillie, who Ralph dearly loved, said, 'No, Ralph. God gave us this baby to live. Doc, if there is a choice, save my child.'" The doc glanced at Ralph, who was crying. "He said, 'Do as my wife asks.'"

Reverend Gotham paused when he noticed that both Eslie and Willis were silently crying. "Your mom couldn't make it, but you survived. Eslie, the death of your mom almost killed Ralph. He loved you, but I think that he also blamed you for Lillie's death. Not long after your mom's funeral and burial at Bluffton, your father hit the bottle. I think he wanted to put your mom's death behind him with the alcohol. As you know, Ralph's most prized possession was that beautiful picture of Lillie. Over the years, Ralph and I talked about those days several times."

He paused again. "Eslie, there is one other thing I would like to tell you. You and your father were alike in so many ways. He, like you, was so easy going and also like you, he was also rather shy. Much of that changed with Lillie's death. Regardless, I can assure you that he loved you very much. He realized that you took care of him. He realized that, like him in his younger years, you are a hard worker. And you know, not long after you men left for Van Buren, I came by to see Ralph. Your father told me that he was really proud to have such a son and that he was proud you served our country in war. So, there are some good thoughts and memories of your father."

"Thanks so much for telling me those things," Eslie said, looking at the pastor with tears in his eyes. "I know one thing. I really loved my pa."

They had arrived at the lane running up to Eslie's old house on Carroll Mountain. "I need to get out," he said.

"Eslie, come on to the house with me," Willis pleaded. "Ma will have supper by now."

"Willis, I'll be over tomorrow," he said to his friend. "Let me see what I need to do around the house." To the reverend, he said, "Thanks, Pastor Gotham, for the ride and for telling me what you did."

The other two men continued on the wagon in the direction of Willis's home. The pastor talked about Eslie and his family for most of the journey. "You know, Willis, that's the best young man that I have ever seen for his background. No doubt, the Lord has been with Eslie Southard. By the way, son, Rosalie has not seen anyone since you left. She has really missed you and she has always prayed for all of you."

They had now arrived at the lane running up to Willis's home. Pastor Gotham said he would drive Willis up the hill to his house.

"That's all right, Pastor," Willis said. "You've been gone a long time. Rosalie will be worried about you. It's only quarter-mile or so. Besides, I want to surprise Ma."

"I understand," the reverend replied. "Hope to see you sometime soon."

"Tell Rosalie I'm home," Willis grinned.

He had enjoyed visiting with the pastor, but as he walked away, he realized how much his leg still bothered him. He was still limping, but his crutches helped as he moved up the hill. No one was in sight. That was most likely because of the cold weather.

"Ma, anybody home?" Willis questioned as he stepped up on the old porch and reached for the doorknob. Eva was sewing in the kitchen when she heard her son.

"Willis," she yelled, throwing down the new shirt she was preparing for Hayes. "Are you all right?" she cried out, running to her son.

Willis didn't immediately answer. He just tightly hugged his ma.

"I'm fine," he finally said, taking a long look at her. He was concerned that she appeared much older than when he had left.

"Where's everybody?" he inquired.

"Can you believe they went to Bluffton, as cold as it is?" Eva replied, still surveying her handsome son. "Should be back at anytime. What about Eslie?"

"He went home first. I think he will be over here tomorrow," Willis replied. "He's fine, except for being alone now. We stopped in Gravelly for a while this morning and saw most everyone. Reverend Gotham brought us home. We stopped at the cemetery for Eslie to see his pa's grave. It was really hard on him. I really felt bad for him."

"Willis, we have just got to get Eslie to move in with us," Eva said, after listening carefully as he talked. "He has no one. What's he going to do?"

"I know what he will do, Ma," Willis replied. "Since he is still in the army, he will go back. I will do the same, but they might not take me with this bad leg. Ma, Eslie has to go back or he is a deserter. I must talk to the army soon or I will be classified as a deserter."

As he again hugged his ma, Willis thought, I was not sure I would ever see my parents and this beautiful place. Things have changed though. Lyle and Bartis are gone. Ralph is gone. Hundreds of men have already gone on due to the war. Although those thoughts saddened him, he smiled when he thought of one person he hadn't seen since being back. I have got to go see Rosalie, he thought.

Chapter 31

Homecoming

May 1862

EVA HAD SET THE table for eight people. Amos had brought in a couple of pine board planks and made another table by placing them over a couple of carpenter sawhorses. The makeshift table could accommodate six more people. That was enough for those invited to the homecoming.

Outside of Willis's family of five, there were eight more guests: Pastor Gotham and Rosalie; Eslie; Bill Hansen and his beautiful wife, Susan; and the neighbors down the road, John and Joice Hunnicutt and their sixteen-year-old daughter, Leah. Amos had invited the Hunnicutts for a couple of reasons. First, John played a great banjo, and secondly, he invited Leah, a rather plain, modest girl, with Eslie in mind.

Eva and Georgia Ann had prepared a delicious meal of pork chops, mashed potatoes and gravy, canned green beans, corn, and homemade rolls. Of course, Eva had not forgotten Willis's favorite dessert, pecan pie.

Before the meal, the men gathered in the living area. Before long the conversation changed to a discussion of the war. According to Hansen, the Federals and the Confederates had fought a series of battles near Richmond, Virginia. The newspapers referred to it as the Peninsular Campaign. Union General McClellan had been defeated and forced to withdraw back to Washington. As in the earlier battle at Manassas, the Rebs were again threatening Washington. General Robert E. Lee, the great Confederate general, was now in charge of the Confederate forces.

"The war is not over yet," Hansen said. "And who knows what would have happened if the ammo wagons had reported to Van Dorn at Pea Ridge as they were supposed to? I believe that we would have won the battle. If that had happened, we might be invading Missouri right now."

"Men will fight awfully hard to defend their families, homes, and possessions," Willis quickly added. "Much harder than the invaders. I know. I thought a lot about our family and our home here on the hill while I was fighting."

"The North is trying to turn this war into a slavery conflict," said Hansen, who had been eagerly waiting for a chance to speak again. "No doubt, later generations will be taught that this war was fought over slavery if we lose the war. Lincoln has taken advantage of the conflict to issue his presidential executive order to free the slaves. But, the war in the South is one of defending our states."

"While slavery occurred in Bible times—Paul even encouraged a runaway slave to return home to his master in the New Testament book of Philemon—mankind was created to be free," Pastor Gotham said. "I believe we must defend our state and our homes, but I also believe that the Negroes should be freed, even if sent back to Africa. God can't continue to bless this country until all are free and equal, as in the sight of the Lord. Now, since I have finished my sermon, I will ask Amos to pass the offering plate."

Everyone laughed at his sense of humor.

"I agree with Brother Gotham—not about the offering plate, but about slavery," Willis said, and everyone laughed again.

Only Hansen was willing to take an aggressive Southern view.

"The South is at a tremendous disadvantage, both in terms of numbers of soldiers and manufacturing," said John Hunnicutt, voicing a point to which most agreed. "I'm afraid we will lose an entire generation of young men in the war effort and still lose. The odds are against us."

"I think we can win, if it's the Lord's will," Willis finally spoke. "Guess we will find out."

Eva interrupted the discussion when she called the men to the table. With the pleasing aroma of the food coming from the kitchen, the men needed no more urging. After Pastor Gotham said grace, the food was passed around the table. Eva instantly drew accolades from the guests.

Willis looked over at Rosalie. Her light brown hair hung down past her shoulders. She wore a beautiful, green dress that was a perfect match to her green eyes. Willis thought, she sure knows how to use makeup—just the right amount of red lipstick. How beautiful she is.

Noticing his attention, Rosalie smiled and looked down to put her knife and fork on a crisp pork chop. There was mainly small talk between people sitting together at the table. Someone asked Hunnicutt what he was going to play on his banjo.

"Whatever you want, but we start with Dixie," the musician replied. Everyone applauded.

"Remember, pecan pie for all except Willis," teased Eva, who had barely sat down. All laughed, knowing how much Willis loved pecan pie.

Then, above the talking and laughter, they heard the sound of several horse hooves.

"Who could that be at this time of the evening?" asked Amos, who was seated furthest from the front door. He moved his chair back from the table, preparing to get up and go to the door.

"I will welcome them, Mr. Lofland," offered Eslie, closest to the front door. He got up from the homemade bench and walked toward the front door. As he opened it and stepped out on the porch into the twilight, he could see seven or eight riders. He recognized a big, husky rider with broad shoulders. It was Mule, Hoss's brother.

"Thought you might be here, you cowardly Reb," he said, pointing a revolver at Eslie and then pulling the trigger twice.

Eslie felt the burning pain in his chest as he saw the riders whirl their horses and start back down the long lane to the road. Hearing what sounded like a gunshot, everyone at the table had stopped eating.

"Eslie!" shouted Willis as the menfolk stood up, uncertain what to do.

Willis hobbled out the door and onto the porch. He saw horses disappearing down the lane. Then he saw Eslie lying on the porch.

"Eslie! Eslie, what happened?" he cried out, quickly kneeling down and putting his hand under Eslie's head to raise it. In the evening twilight, Willis could see his friend's eyes close for the last time.

"Oh, God, please save him," Willis openly prayed for yet another friend. "Don't let him die."

By then, all the other men had gathered around Eslie. Amos quickly left to get a mule to fetch Doc Rhodes. Reverend Gotham had Eslie's hand and was praying.

"Tell Amos to stop," the pastor said. "Eslie is in heaven now."

"Bushwhackers," said Hansen, looking at Eslie. "I have an idea who they may be."

Chapter 32

A Divided State

1863

ESLIE'S MURDERERS WERE NEVER found, since Yell County soon fell under the jurisdiction of the new Union government in Little Rock. After the loss of Little Rock, the Arkansas Confederate government moved to the southern Arkansas town of Washington. There, the Confederate governor and legislature would govern the southern half of the state until the end of the war.

Willis, slightly crippled, was excused from further military service. However, Amos and Willis continued to closely follow the war's progress. Union General Steel, the Federal commander at Little Rock, attempted to destroy the Arkansas Confederate government in a campaign that the newspapers referred to as the Red River Campaign. The campaign consisted of the huge loop down into southern Arkansas.

The Rebs held their capital at Washington. After a brief victory at Camden, the Federals were routed and Steel barely made it back to Pine Bluff and then the safety of Little Rock. Earlier, Lincoln had issued his Emancipation Proclamation, an executive proclamation that all slaves within the eleven states of the Confederacy were to be freed. This proclamation created a lot of controversy in Gravelly, as in other parts of the South.

The Loflands and other families went to Gravelly in May. It was planting season again. The men needed seeds and the women needed sugar and flour. Willis noticed that the friendly atmosphere in Gravelly had changed. With the war, families had chosen sides. Some people even refused to visit with those who had different views from their own.

Amos, Willis, and Hayes went over to Parkers Feed Store. Willis could only think of the happy times that he, Lyle, Eslie, and Bartis had spent visiting together in the store. Willis had not been coon hunting or bear hunting since his friend's deaths. As he told his Pa, "It's not the same anymore." But Willis had taken Hayes deer hunting a couple of times.

As in the past Saturdays, the major topic of conversation was still the war. Bill Hansen, the lawyer, continued to be the group's moderator. He had certainly not modified his views on the Lincoln government. The lawyer was talking when the Loflands entered the feed store.

"And now Lincoln has freed the slaves. Let me remind you men of a couple of things. One, the only slaves that he said could go free are those in the Confederate states. None of the slaves in the border states, or even in the Northern slave states like Maryland and Delaware, were freed. Big deal; does he think that just because he decreed such, the Southern plantation owners will just let the Negroes leave?"

He paused to let them think about his question. "No slaves are free. We have heard the Northern abolitionists talk about doing away with slavery for fifty years. And believe me, some evil things come with slavery. Destroying the Negro family is only one of the evils. Slavery is and has always been questionable. But friends, our Constitution, the law of the land, permits slavery. Most of our founding fathers owned slaves. Do you realize that the U.S. Supreme Court, in the famous Dred Scott case in Missouri, determined that the slave, Scott, was, in fact, property? The court further found that since Scott was a slave, and a non-citizen, he had no right to sue in a federal court. Therefore, this court decision affirmed that slavery is legal. Until the Congress passes an amendment to change the Constitution making slavery illegal, slavery is here to stay."

The lawyer paused to wipe his brow with a handkerchief. "Read the U.S. Constitution. Where does it give the president the right to "decree" a change in our sacred document? Such executive proclamations are not legal. What will happen when a president decrees that Arkansas is to be a part of Texas? We may lose this war, but do we also lose the founder's Constitution?"

Again he paused, looking around at those gathered. "Secondly, Lincoln promised before he became president, and after he became president, that he would not interfere with slavery. Later, he even said that if he could save the Union with slavery he would do so. He said if he could save the Union by doing away with slavery he would do so. Mister Lincoln is your average politician. He will lie when it advances his agenda. The only legal way to free the Negro is by amending the U.S. Constitution, and that has not happened."

As the lawyer talked, Willis knew that most of what he said was correct. Yet, he was not sure about the slavery issue. But he did not believe that an invasion of the state was necessary. And, the invasion had cost him several of his best friends and left him with a deformed leg. Willis knew that six or seven men from Yell County had died at Pea Ridge, and many other Arkansans had died in other battles.

"Ben, let's look at the worst," Amos said when the lawyer stopped talking to take a drink of water. "Say we lose the war;

what happens to the seceded states like Arkansas?"

The lawyer spit another stream of tobacco juice at the brass spittoon. This time he hit it.

"No one knows, but we will probably have a military government headed up by a Union general. Be our luck to have someone like Beast Butler of New Orleans fame. It is also possible Lincoln will confiscate much of the land and then give it to the Negroes. That's what the abolitionists want to do."

Chapter 33

Back to Chula

1865

TWO MORE YEARS PASSED. The war was not going well for the Confederacy. Lee's Army of Northern Virginia was slowly being pushed south toward their capital at Richmond. The Northern newspapers were also quite critical of Lincoln's new general, U.S Grant, mainly for the heavy losses of men being sustained in battle. While Lee was making Grant's Federal forces pay a heavy price, the Rebs were also giving up much Southern territory.

Arkansas was still a divided state. The Union government continued to control Little Rock and the northern half of the state. Isaac Murphy headed up the recognized Unionist government in Arkansas. Murphy had cast the lone dissenting vote against secession in the second secession convention of 1861. The Confederate affiliated government still controlled the southern half of the state at Washington, Arkansas.

Willis, partially crippled, had been married to Rosalie for over a year and a half. The happy couple had faced a period of sadness just prior to their marriage when Rosalie's father came down ill again. Doc Rhodes visited several times to try to help the reverend. In the end, the dedicated preacher passed away with a bout of serious pneumonia.

Willis and Rosalie had set up house in Chula in the deceased pastor's home. Willis, with much help from Hayes, had made numerous improvements to the home and on the forty acres.

It wasn't long before a baby was on its way. When it was time, they had called Doc Rhodes, now seventy-two years old. The doctor arrived and parked his buckboard in front of the home, came to the front door, and knocked.

"Hello, Doc," Willis said after opening the door and reaching out his hand. "Sure glad you could come."

"Why wouldn't I?" the aging doctor replied. "I delivered you about twenty-five years ago. Willis, who was the black feller that you sent to fetch me? Had a wooden peg leg, I believe."

"You're talking about George. He lost that leg at Pea Ridge fighting for us. He's a good man. When we get time, I will tell you about George. He's a good worker and a great person."

The birth was not too troublesome for Rosalie.

"He is so healthy and beautiful," she said, after viewing her new son. "He is so quiet. I love his green eyes and sandy colored hair. I hope they stay that color." Rosalie handed the baby to Willis. "The Lord has really blessed us, Willis. He has brought you home safe, and he has given us a healthy baby boy."

"I know, babe," Willis replied, admiring the infant. "Let me thank God for our son." He handed the baby back to Rosalie and then began his prayer.

"Lord, the war goes on. Our South is not doing well at all. Maybe it is your will. But God, you have still blessed us so much with our farm, our resources, and most of all, our healthy, precious son. Regardless of how the war ends, we plan to do your will. We ask you to bless our new son, Eslie Lee Lofland."

As he finished the prayer, Willis heard Rosalie softly say, "Amen."

The End

www.ingramcontent.com/pod-product-compliance
Lightning Source LLC
Chambersburg PA
CBHW021314250626
47155CB00002B/524